ORIGINAL

ORIGINAL

THE HORN: BOOK TWO

J. KATHLEEN CHENEY

EQP Books

AUTHOR'S FOREWORD

THE THREE BOOKS of THE HORN *(Oathbreaker, Original,* and *Overseer)* are set in the same world as my earlier novel, *Dreaming Death.* The events in this book take place earlier than those in Dreaming Death by several months, and happen in a different province of Larossa.

Horn Province is little heeded by the rest of the country of Larossa. It's farther north, relatively poor, and sparsely populated due to its mountainous nature. It's also home to the largest glacier in the country (Horn Glacier), which once covered much of Lee Province as well. The glacier is a royal preserve, and none are allowed to trespass there.

When the Anvarrid invaded the country of Larossa, they had difficulty getting any Anvarrid House ruler to take over that province. The Senate finally sent representatives of the House of Evaryen to the province to take over running it. The Evaryen intermarried regularly with the Horn Family, and eventually decided to officially change their name to the House of Horn, making it the only Anvarrid House with a Family name.

CONTENTS

ORIGINAL

CHAPTER 1

AMAL FELT SHE'D BEEN waiting for Dalyan to wake forever. He'd lain unconscious in his infirmary bed for two days now. His dark hair was wild and half hidden by bandages. Freja had assured her that he was healing, but Amal couldn't dismiss the moment of horror she'd felt when the Fortress struck him down.

The infirmarians had planned to remove an illicit device from his head, a creation of metal that lay atop his skull behind his ear. Not implanted—he'd been created with the device already there, under his skin. Unfortunately, before the infirmarians had their chance to attempt removal, the Fortress hit Dalyan with a bolt of electricity, literally burning the device into slag that the engineers wouldn't be able to study. They might never know what that device was.

They did know, however, what it was attempting to do, why the Fortress had struck Dalyan down in the first place. The device had been attempting to steal the Fortress' memories. The Fortress had merely been defending itself.

But that bolt of electricity had gone through Dalyan as well, stopping his heart. Right in front of her. Freja, as their infirmarian, had known what to do, what to ask of the

Fortress, and it had shocked Dalyan back to life; but they were still unsure of the ramifications of the abuse he'd taken. He lay in that bed now, his hair wrapped back to keep it away from the stitches in his scalp. Freja had set a bolster behind him to keep him from rolling onto his back. He looked terrible.

Amal took Dalyan's limp hand in her own. His hand flexed once against hers and then relaxed.

Jan was sitting with her, half dozing. Like Amal, he didn't wear his uniform for this vigil. They'd both changed into the loose and faded black garb they wore for sparring practice or after a long shift. A bit more sensitive to cold, Amal had added an old black sweater that had once belonged to their father. She and Jan hadn't been able to wait and watch like this when their family died, one by one—their father, their elder brother Samedrion, and Amal's husband Anton—from influenza six years before. Amal still resented that, but this vigil over Dalyan would not end the same way. She was determined to believe that.

At first there had been eight of the twenty-sevens in the room, a testament to the fact that in the short time Dalyan had been with them, he'd become popular with her yeargroup. They'd accepted him among them. Now the others had gone on about their duties, with Jan covering some of Amal's: meeting with her secretary, meeting with townsfolk who sought a judgment on the ownership of a number of sheep, and dealing with the demands of the elders.

When their father and elder brother had died, the Horn elders had asked Amal and Jan to choose between them which would take over the provincial seat. Since Amal, with her darker skin, looked far more Anvarrid, she'd been the natural choice. Jan's Family-born mother had given him paler Family skin, so even though he shared Amal's dark hair and eyes, he would have a harder time being accepted by the senate. Some things had to wait on Amal, but Jan willingly helped with what he could. That had been vital over the last two days.

Dalyan's eyelids fluttered, and he squeezed his eyes shut.

Heart racing, Amal leaned closer. She wanted to reassure him he was safe, to apologize for the Fortress' actions, to judge for herself whether Dalyan was there inside his head. That it *was* Dalyan, and not some other version of the long-dead man from whom the Cince had copied him. She wanted . . .

"Where . . ." he whispered in a strained voice.

"You're in the infirmary," she told him. "I'm here with you."

One eye opened to a slit, his dark blue iris edging toward the sound of her voice. "What?"

She touched his cheek, careful to stay away from the bandages about his head. "Can you hear me?"

His jaw clenched. "Can you stop it. The noise?"

"Are your ears ringing?" Amal asked. Freja had rattled off a long list of possible symptoms Dalyan might experience following his electrocution, ranging from mild to terrifying.

"No," he rasped. "The noise . . . the . . ."

Amal listened, but this end of the infirmary, with its individual rooms, was nearly empty. There was nothing. It had to be in his head.

"Everyone is loud," Dalyan finished.

"Amal, leave the room," Jan ordered from behind her.

She glanced at her brother. *How can he ask me to leave now that Dalyan's awake?*

A hiss of breath made her turn back to Dalyan.

"Please, stop it," he whispered.

Jan forcibly lifted Amal from her chair. He dragged her out into the main room of the infirmary with him. "I want you to go to the other end of the infirmary. Talk to Freja. Try to be calm. I'll talk to him."

"Jan, I don't know what..."

He folded his arms over his chest, jaw clenching. "Now, Amal."

Jan wasn't going to be dissuaded. Amal took a couple of deep breaths. "Don't hurt him."

"I don't intend to." He waited for her to leave.

Amal gave up and went, hoping Freja would give her a sympathetic ear.

When Jan came back into the room, Dalyan flinched at the roar of concern. He was sure now—*that* was what he was sensing. Concern. He couldn't figure out how to stop it. It made him want to crawl under his covers, but he ached too much to try.

It wasn't a sound.

It wasn't something he could see.

It reminded him of the heaviness of air right before the rain. It was everywhere, but mostly around Jan. Dalyan squeezed his eyes shut, hoping that could hold it back.

"Breathe," Jan said softly. "Just breathe. In and out. Concentrate on that."

Jan sat in Amal's abandoned chair now, facing him. Dalyan could tell that without opening his eyes. Amal's brother was breathing audibly, setting a rhythm Dalyan could follow. The heavy sensation faded, becoming a backdrop to the quiet of the room. Jan had calmed himself, and that oppressive cloud faded along with that effort.

"You know what's happened, don't you?" Jan asked.

If I deny it, he won't believe me. From nearly the moment they'd met, Jan had insisted that Dalyan must be a latent sensitive, someone born to share others' emotions, but for some reason Dalyan had failed to develop that trait. "Is this what it is to be a sensitive?"

"Yes," Jan said. "My younger daughter, Sara, is going through this breakthrough now."

"She's six, isn't she?"

"Yes. Children usually go through this gradually, like a flower budding, but I think you've been thrust into full bloom. That must be uncomfortable, like running into a wall."

Trust Jan to know how to express this . . . chaos. "What happened to me?" he croaked.

"They took that thing out of your head," Jan said. "You don't remember anything?"

"I remember . . . coming down the stairs. Now I'm here."

The faint sound of a chair scraping and the rustle of fabric told Dalyan that Jan had moved closer. "The thing in your head," he said, "it attacked the Fortress. The Fortress retaliated by hitting it with a bolt of electricity."

Electrocution. Dalyan fought to keep his breathing slow. That explained all of this, his buzzing ears, the aches throughout his body, and the burning on the side of his head. Memory gap, that was a symptom of electrocution as well. All those symptoms were things Dalyan knew, even though he'd never been taught them. "It electrocuted me? How am I still alive?"

The Anvarrid language's word for electrocution was *imp-bitten*, and Dalyan couldn't think of any better term. But there were better words for it . . . in some other language. One he couldn't recall.

"It brought you back," Jan told him, still calm. "By electrocuting you again, I think. Freja can explain it better than I. Do you want the details now? Or later?"

"Later," Dalyan said. "Can I get something to drink?"

A sharp reaction came from Jan, unidentifiable to Dalyan.

"I'm sorry," Jan said quickly, suggesting an identity for that emotion—embarrassment. "I should have thought of that." His hand touched Dalyan's shoulder, a silent hint to sit up.

Once Dalyan was sitting, he opened one eye. Jan perched on the edge of the chair next to the bed, looking more disheveled than usual. His longish dark hair didn't look like it had been combed in a couple of days, and his thick beard showed signs of him worrying at it. He held a cup to Dalyan's lips.

Dalyan swallowed a trickle of cold water. It felt wonderful. He managed to snake a hand out from under the blankets and was relieved to see it was whole. He took the cup in his own shaky fingers. "Thank you."

Jan sat back and heaved a sigh. "I'll talk to Amal, make sure she knows she needs to get her emotions under control before she comes back in here. She can do that; she was just very worried about you."

Worry? It had felt like a horse sitting on his chest, far heavier than Jan's concern. "Was that what that was?"

"Yes," Jan said. "Amal's a worrier. Freja's not. I'll have *her* come in and she can tell you whatever you need to know about your condition. Are you awake enough to do that now?"

"Is there any way I can get to a toilet?"

Jan rose. "I'll go ask Freja's permission."

He left the small room, and for a time Dalyan mentally catalogued his aches and pains, comparing them against his need to relieve himself. The latter had nearly won out before Freja came through the doorway, brisk and blessedly impersonal. "You're not getting out of that bed for another day," she announced. "We have ways of taking care of bodily functions that don't involve standing."

That was what he'd feared.

Amal rounded on Jan as he came walking over to join her. "What was that all about?"

"You were hurting him." Jan laid his hands on her shoulders. "I'm sure his head aches enough without your worry pouring all over him. You need to get your emotions under control before you talk to him again."

She stared at her brother. He was speaking of Dalyan as if . . .

"Yes," Jan said, "taking that thing out of his head made him a sensitive, like he should have been from the start." His hands dropped away, turning her loose.

Amal stepped back, trying to collect her consternation and tuck it back inside. She folded her arms, a chill in her chest that wasn't the normal cool of Below. "That wasn't *taking it out of his head*, Jan. That was an attack. It wasn't supposed to be violent. Could that be what triggered it?"

Jan spread his hands wide. "I have no idea. He doesn't remember what happened."

Amal closed her eyes, nodding. "Freja said he might not."

"She's with him now," Jan said.

Of course Freja was with him. She was an infirmarian. Amal felt jealousy licking at her innards, even when she knew it was idiotic. She wanted to be the one in there with Dalyan. She turned back to Jan, who would know exactly how she'd reacted to his words and would still love her anyway. "So what do I do? How do I make this easier for him?"

"Sit with him for now. Keep your emotions under control. I will talk to the chaplains and find out what experience they have with sudden onset like this. They'll know how to make this easier for him."

That was all sensible. She could have suggested all those things herself, only they sounded more reasonable coming out of Jan's mouth. "How long?"

"No more than a couple of hours," Jan promised.

A sensitive. It wasn't the result the elders had hoped for, but they might be reconciled to his presence here anyway. Amal nodded and left Jan, heading back toward the small room where Dalyan waited.

The elders had hoped that by removing the device in his head, the memories that should have been created with him would resurface—memories of a man who had helped create the Fortresses and who might even be able to repair the long-abandoned Fortress of Salonen. That might come at the cost of the Dalyan they knew, of the Dalyan Amal loved, because memories influenced one's personality. So even though the device had been removed catastrophically rather than carefully, Amal feared that the man she'd known was lost.

CHAPTER 2

DALYAN WOKE, lying on his side this time, not his back. Freja had given him something for the pain in his joints and head. He felt bleary, but the aches had receded. Other than the strange sensation of the skin behind his ear being far too tight—they'd had to cut out some damaged tissue—and dire warnings of what might happen if he popped the stitches, Freja had pronounced him in surprisingly good shape for someone who'd been dead, however briefly.

Amal lay on the bed behind him, her cheek resting against his back. Her arm was tucked around his waist, and for the moment, he couldn't *sense* her. That feeling of being smothered under the weight of her emotions had vanished, a relief.

They weren't in the same room as before. It was very similar, a small box of a room with a couple of beds and plain gray walls. But now they'd moved him—and Amal—someplace where he couldn't feel the emotions of anyone else. It was as if the two of them were completely alone in the world.

"How do you feel?" Amal asked softly. It sounded loud anyway, likely because it was so silent here.

"Where are we?" he asked, proving that his voice was functional, although raspy.

Amal drew away from him, her arm turning him loose. Her mind stayed very calm. "Stay there," she said as she got up from the narrow bed.

Dalyan obeyed, although he was beginning to worry about finding a toilet again.

Amal came around and sat down on the edge of the other bed. "They've moved you to Eight Down," she began. "This is a closed floor. No one lives here. It's where people come when they need to get away from everyone else. When they're like you, their minds overwhelmed."

"We're alone here?"

"More or less. There's a sentry in each hall, and possibly a few unruly children stashed elsewhere, but very few people come here."

"Am I allowed to get up?" he asked.

A burst of emotion greeted that question. He wasn't sure what it was, though—not quite. He kept his eyes on Amal's face, but her expression had already turned impassive again. That was what he'd been taught of the Six Families, that they held in their feelings to protect the sensitives.

Which I am now.

"Yes," Amal finally said. "Freja said you could get up and move around, but not too much."

He pushed himself up to a sitting position, and was relieved when Amal helped him the last few inches. The sheet fell, revealing that they'd dressed him in a pair of the loose trousers they all wore to sleep in here. Good to know that, too. But the effort of sitting up left him dizzy, so he sat blinking while Amal's worry ebbed and flowed around him, slipping past her control. He felt her tuck it up like a blanket and sit on it as his dizziness passed.

"What about a toilet?" he asked.

Amal laughed. "Can you manage that on your own?"

He hoped so. "How far?"

"Right next door. This is a residential hall, after all."

He felt a moment of dull surprise on realizing again that he was in their Fortress, the place they'd been so determined to bar him from. That would take more analysis later. With Amal's help, he got on his feet.

His right ankle hurt, as Freja had promised. The bolt of electricity that killed the thing in his head had exited his body at the ankle, leaving a nasty burn, although it wasn't nearly as bad as his scalp. Once Amal opened the door, he limped out into a hallway and his chest went tight. He fought for a moment to control the panic that set his heart to fluttering.

"What is it?" Amal asked, her worry blooming again in response to his.

He'd been unconscious when they brought him down here, so he'd seen only the small plain room in the infirmary and the small plain room he'd just woken in. Neither had bothered him, but this gray hallway, stretching on and on, provoked a flash of terror, as if he'd somehow been sent back to the facility and the past two years had been a dream.

Amal's hand tightened on his shoulder. "Calm down. You're safe here."

He could feel it, then. She was trying to calm him by calming herself. He matched his breathing to hers and concentrated on that as they stood in the silent hallway. "This is Horn Fortress?"

"A part that's not lived in," she reminded him, "so it's impersonal. No painting on the walls. I didn't realize that would bother you."

He took a deep breath. "I didn't, either."

Dalyan forced himself to look down that hallway again. It wasn't eternal. There were only a dozen or so doors between them and the main hallway, not as far as he'd thought. He turned to look the other direction. The room they'd been in was close to the end of the hallway. "I'm fine now."

Amal kept her worry tucked away. She showed him where the water closet was—more of a group latrine, he decided once he'd stepped inside—and when he emerged feeling better, she led him back to the small bedroom. She closed the door while he sank down on the edge of the bed, his head throbbing, now, and ankle smarting.

He scooted over to the end of the bed next to the wall and leaned his head against the cool surface. He didn't want to lie down for fear that he'd just fall asleep again. "So what happens now?"

"The plan is for me to stay here with you for a day or two while you become accustomed to my emotions. Then we'll try you with a few other people until you feel you're ready to go back out among the regular world."

She'd kept her emotions in check throughout that speech, leaving him unsure whether she was annoyed or not. "Do you have time for that?"

"I'll make the time," she said.

Dalyan shifted against the wall. The room had two beds in it, plus a chest and desk, both shoved against the far wall. Crowded. An inner door, behind the bunk she sat on, led elsewhere. "Where does that door go?"

"These are family quarters. A room for someone with children. They pulled this bed out of the nursery room behind me."

That explained why it was smaller. The bed he'd lain in was large enough for two, but that one was narrow. He leaned his head back, feeling that tight spot stretch as he moved. He held in a grimace, then realized Amal would have felt his reaction anyway. "What do I do now?"

"Freja wants you to sleep as much as possible," Amal said. "If you're hungry, though, I can find a sentry and send him to get us some lunch."

"I am hungry." Dalyan wasn't sure his stomach could keep anything down, but he wanted to try. He felt a bit hollow inside.

She left the room for a time, during which he surveyed the bland walls about him, the gray blankets, the old worn wood of the bed frame. It was plain, but calming, he supposed. That was what everything in the world of the Family seemed to be about—calm.

Because otherwise they think their minds will snap.

He understood that need for calm now, for the mental stillness that surrounded him. He would have to learn to deal with the emotions or live the remainder of his life on this boring hallway on an empty level.

Amal came back into the room, a faint smile on her lips. He could sense her emotion, something warming and soft. "Are you *amused?*"

"Good guess." She sat again. "They'll bring us some food shortly."

"What's amusing?"

That increased the sense of the emotion he felt from her, but then she drew it back. "You've refrained from asking about the puppy."

And that amused her? It had been in the corner of his mind since he woke, but he'd decided not to ask. "I assumed you would make certain she was well cared for."

Amal inclined her head, as if she appreciated that forbearance on his part. "I have to confess, I forgot her for the better part of a day, but Nohr and Mikks have been taking care of her. She's weaning off the milk a little faster than the other pups, but she seems fine to Sidana."

He tried not to spread his relief about, although surely Amal felt it anyway. "Thank you."

"I did promise to see to her." Amal touched his knee, one of the spots that didn't ache. "Anything else?"

His brain felt foggy. "I can't seem to focus right now."

"That's what Freja expected," she said. "Now, while you're awake, Jan suggests that you consider my emotions, and if you're unsure what I'm feeling, just ask me."

That seemed simple enough. "So I have to learn to identify emotions?"

"Most sensitives do it when they're children. You're simply running late."

A cloud of something surrounded his perception of her, not visible, but heavy, like he'd sensed when he'd first woken. "You're concerned."

"Yes," she said. "I know this must be ... baffling. It must be scary. And I wish I could make it better."

"I understood that part." His head was aching again, but he didn't want to sleep away his days. "Can you just produce emotions on a whim?"

She smiled softly. "To some extent. If I remind myself of how I felt when something happened to me, I can usually reproduce that emotion."

"Should we try that?"

She closed her eyes, and a split-second later he was consumed by a terrible rending ache that tore at his heart and lungs, stealing his breath. As quickly as the pain grabbed him, it faded, leaving him shaken. "What was that?" he whispered.

"That's what I felt when I saw you die, Dalyan," she said. "I think about it and ..."

He felt the emotion building again, but she took a deep breath, let it out, and the feeling eased away.

". . . and I relive it. That's one of the worst emotions. I think *anguish* is the best label for it."

"It's like when I have that dream," he said.

She caught her lower lip between her teeth, and he could sense something, an emotion quickly snatched back. Not quite worry or concern, although there was a touch of that as well, but something redder, uncomfortable.

"What was that?" he asked.

Her cheeks flushed, her eyes flickering down toward the blankets. "I'm sorry. I . . . I know it's not the point, but I get a little jealous when I think of that."

Ah, the elusive Katja I dream about. He hadn't guessed before that Amal might be jealous over a long-dead woman he'd never even seen in his dreams.

Amal was saved from further explanation, though, when a knock came at the door. She jumped up and opened it, revealing a young sentry with an impassive face. The sentry carefully thought nothing as he handed her the tray of food. Amal shut the door with one foot and brought the tray over to Dalyan. "Looks like they're trusting you with potato bread and . . . smells like mutton stew."

He resisted the urge to comment on the omnipresence of mutton here. Apparently, that happened even in the Fortress. But a sniff of the stew provoked his stomach into rumbling, so he let Amal arrange the tray over his lap. She uncovered a bowl of stew and some potato flatbread. And even though the stew was more of a thick broth than a stew, it still pleased his stomach.

By the time that Freja showed up, Dalyan was comfortably in his bed once again, sitting with his back to the wall.
He and Amal had worked on recognizing various emotions
while he slowly consumed his soup, walked up and down
the featureless hallway a couple of times, and napped. It
was amazing to him how much better he felt already,
possibly for having food in his stomach, although bathing
and shaving would be nice. He had a few days' growth of
beard now—not something he enjoyed.

Freja surveyed the tiny room, her dark brown eyes
hard. "Where's Amal?"

"Latrine," he volunteered.

Unlike Amal, Freja had the pale blond hair commonly
associated with the Six Families, tied back in a handful of
less-than-perfect braids. Her black uniform bore the elabo-
rate chest trim that indicated she was an infirmarian, even
though she also acted as one of Amal's guards. She might
be petite, but Dalyan had little doubt that Freja could hurt
him severely if she wished. She looked him over and nodded
once. "And you're following my instructions?"

He hadn't been at his best when she'd lectured him,
and there had been so many rules. "Which ones?"

"No sex," Freja said bluntly. "Nothing that overstimu-
lates you."

"We've walked up and down the hall," he said. "That's
the worst of it."

Freja sat on the other bed. "How's your ankle holding
up?"

"It's uncomfortable, but I'm trying not to stretch it. I'm
being careful with my head, too, before you ask."

She snorted, and he realized that carried a hint of
humor with it, although he wasn't sure why. Freja's emotions were different than Amal's. They were held close, small,

and sharp. Amal's were more full-bodied. "Fine," Freja said. "And what's going on inside your head?"

"My thinking's clearer now, if that's what you mean."

"That's good, but I meant your sensitivity. Are you uncomfortable with this arrangement?"

What arrangement? "I don't understand."

"Is Amal being overpowering?" Freja clarified. "Are her emotions causing you discomfort?"

Ah, that was what she meant. "No. I'm fine with this arrangement. But I can't help but think she needs to be elsewhere."

Freja snorted, letting him feel more of her amusement this time. "What about your memory? Anything pop up that you don't remember from before?"

The whole reason he'd come down to the Fortress was the hope that removing the device from his head would enable him to recall the memories of the old man upon whom he'd been based. That long dead man, Jukka Salonen, was the source of Dalyan's physical pattern. That man's knowledge and, supposedly, his memories should also have been passed on, but somehow when the Cince added the device to Dalyan's head during his creation, they'd ruined his access to those memories. While he did have much of the old man's knowledge, that wasn't the same as having his memories. "No, nothing different. I'm sorry."

"Don't apologize for it. Not your fault." Freja rose. "I'll come back tonight and check on you. Sleep is good. No climbing stairs. No unwise exertion. Understand?"

He almost laughed. "No sex. I understand."

Freja opened to door to find Amal standing there. "Is there anything you need?" she asked Amal. *"Anything?"*

Amal glanced at Dalyan as if she'd missed some subtext, but he felt the same way. Freja often mystified him. "Uh, no. We're fine."

"I'll see the two of you later, then." Freja stepped over the threshold, forcing Amal to back out of her way, then walked on down the hallway without another word.

Amal stepped over the threshold into the room and sat down on the bed Freja had abandoned. A faint air of hurt surrounded her, combined with confusion. "Freja's upset with me."

"She was waiting for you to say something."

"I can't say it if I don't know what it is," Amal said, throwing up her hands. "I know she's . . . not exactly angry, but she is frustrated."

Dalyan thought the air he now sensed around Amal would be described as *helplessness*. "Should you go talk to her?"

"No. Whatever it is, she's not ready. And I'm supposed to know what this is about." Amal's shoulders slumped. Freja was her closest friend, but his presence had strained their relationship.

Before he'd gone down into the Fortress, Freja had apologized to him about being petty and childish where Amal was concerned. She'd said that Amal had never kept a secret from her before. That secret Amal held—that Dalyan was created rather than born—was what had provoked Freja into involving the elders and, ultimately, getting Dalyan killed by the Fortress. Then again, Freja had been the one to order the Fortress to bring him back to life, so in Dalyan's mind, she'd more than made up for any misstep.

"She says she'll come back tonight," he told her, unsure what Amal had overheard. "I think I'd like to try to sleep a bit, and then we can try the sensing thing again."

It wasn't a matter of trying to sense things any longer; it was identifying all the emotions he did pick up. That, he suspected, would take years to perfect.

Amal hadn't expected to be this restless. Dalyan dozed on his bunk while she read the files Gyda had sent down for her to review. Most concerned the harvesting and shearing schedules for the end of summer. Itinerant workers would migrate up to the Horn to help, since their harvest fell before the lowlands harvests, and then leave; so small towns of tents and lean-tos would pop up across Horn Province. Keeping those workers in check was always a challenge, especially when it grew cold and they wanted to chop down trees to burn. Even though there were huge forests in Horn Province, they still considered wood a precious resource.

Additional workers would also be needed to handle the arrival of the tithe in a few months. Most of the tithe from the five other provinces arrived after the harvest was complete, allowing the Horn's citizens to do most of the work, but there were usually some needed to handle the horses that pulled the wagons. Since the Horn currently didn't *need* the tithe, it was a temptation every year for her to refuse it, freeing up warehouses in the town and across the province. Then again, if she did that, they might find themselves short some time in the future. So every year they handled the extra work. Most of the clerical duties involved fell to the quartermasters, but there were always some that only Lady Horn could handle.

Amal signed several contracts for warehouses, closed that file, and set it aside. She rubbed her eyes and turned to watching Dalyan sleep. Having a few meals in his stomach had improved his color. He was probably going to be more wakeful in the coming days, meaning more time sitting with her and talking.

Watching him die had told her something undeniable about herself: she was in love with him, rather desperately so. Before this had all happened, she'd even considered him as a potential second husband. She doubted he would be receptive to the idea: he was far too concerned about what the elders thought of her. She wasn't.

On the other hand, she wasn't sure she was ready to marry again.

Freja had said once that she and Anton hadn't had anything to talk about other than their son. Even though Amal had denied it, she had come to admit—privately—that Freja was right. She and Anton had worked disparate shifts, they'd had different friends, and Anton hadn't been interested in compromising on those things, so they'd drifted apart.

If she were to marry again, Amal didn't want the same thing to happen. Even though Dalyan had told her he loved her, love didn't always translate into a will to stay together, or a disposition to work together.

Amal watched Dalyan as he slept. He had changed his schedule to spend more time with her—something Anton had never done—but that had only been one week. Was that something Dalyan would regularly do? Would he be willing to compromise to stay with her?

Because if he *were* to marry her, he would never go to Salonen. And if she brought it up, if she asked how he felt about that and the answer wasn't what she wanted to hear, there would be no way to bury the topic again.

"What are you worrying over?" he asked, eyes slitting open.

And now she'd woken him with her fretting. Amal sighed and calmed her mind, tucking her qualms back into hidden places. "I apologize. I've been looking through requests for the harvest, and I need more manpower."

"What happens then?" He sat up slowly, easing his back against the wall again. "I mean, I doubt you're actually handling any of the farm tools yourself, so what do you have to do with the harvest?"

And so she told him, watching his reactions to determine when she'd bored him. But his interest never waned, and they passed a couple of hours productively discussing her manpower issues. She was a little surprised when Freja showed up again. They hadn't even stopped to send for dinner.

Freja tsked at Amal for keeping him waiting, but otherwise seemed to be in a better mood—or less mysterious one—this time. She checked the stitches on Dalyan's scalp, applied more unguent, and replaced the loose bandage on his ankle. Then she turned to Amal.

"Signe is calling for a meeting in the morning. She wants you there. I can ask Jan or Nohr to come down to sit with Dalyan," she said.

"I could just read a book," Dalyan inserted. "Or if I had my sketchbook . . ."

"Let me see your hands." Freja gazed critically at his hands, likely watching for tremors. "Fine. I'll have Nohr go through your things, see what he can find."

"Thanks," Dalyan said.

"We've set aside a room for you on Six Down," Freja told him. "When you think you're ready to handle more than one or two people, we can move you up there."

They're already moving him? Amal reined in her surprise. She sensed equal disbelief from him, so at least this wasn't something they'd discussed, but hadn't told her.

"I'll keep that in mind," Dalyan said.

"And don't forget," Freja told Amal, "Signe wants you in the elders' hall at eight."

Freja didn't wait for an answer, simply stepped back over the threshold and walked away.

Dalyan raised his eyebrows, and then hissed when he discovered that hurt. "Ow. Six Down? Is that where the twenty-sevens live?"

Amal nodded, distracted. If they planned to take Dalyan up to live with her yeargroup, then he wouldn't be living in the Keep in a room next to hers. She hadn't thought of that.

"What about Nimi?" he asked then. "She can't live down there, can she?"

"Uh, no," she answered. *Another problem.* "Humans only, I'm afraid."

"Can I refuse?" he asked, worry creeping out about him now. "I thought when I was better I would go back up to the Keep."

"This is the first I've heard of this plan," Amal admitted. "I'll ask around in the morning. I'll go get a sentry to bring us some food now."

As she walked down the hallway in search of a sentry, Amal fretted over the idea. She'd assumed they would stay on Eight Down together. Dalyan couldn't leave the Fortress at all, not until the infirmary cleared him to climb stairs. An elevator could be used to move him between levels of the Fortress, but only feet would suffice to get him up the grand stair between the Fortress and the Keep. But moving him up to Six Down meant she would return to her own bedroom. If Dalyan spent his nights down in the Fortress, he wouldn't be sharing her bed up in the Keep.

Either way, it seemed like someone wanted to keep them apart. It was hard not to take that personally.

The next morning, Dalyan endured another inspection of his head by Freja, who sat back and scowled at him when she was done. He wasn't sure what emotion she was exhibiting, but it reminded him of suspicion. "What's wrong?"

"You're healing very fast." Her eyes narrowed. "Faster than I expected."

"That's good, isn't it?"

"A bit strange, but I guess I shouldn't be surprised. Your skin is younger than you are."

Dalyan pinched the bridge of his nose. That made sense. Although his body was a man's, he'd only been created eight years ago. That meant only eight years of wear on his skin. "How long until I'm back to normal? Until I'm not tired like this?"

Freja made a harrumphing sound, surely learned from someone much older. "Electrocution, particularly as it happened to you, is unpredictable. I wish I could give you a definite answer—*in two weeks you'll be back to normal*—but I can't. It could be five days, or it could be never, Dalyan. That depends on you. However, given your current progress, I'm optimistic."

A long-winded way of telling him she didn't know. "Getting some food in my stomach helped most. I would like to bathe, though. And shave."

"Maybe tomorrow." Freja proceeded to ask him another batch of questions about his bodily processes and then, thankfully, she moved on to his memory, where he had nothing new to tell her. She shrugged, as if his lack of memories didn't matter much to her. "Jan's going to come down in a bit, chat while Amal's upstairs. Will that work?"

"I think so," Dalyan said.

"Kick him out if he overwhelms you. Understand?"

"I understand."

CHAPTER 3

A MAL RUBBED HER HANDS over her face, waiting for the meeting to start. The elders had their own gathering place, a large room to one side of the chapel that the Oathbreakers were apparently borrowing this morning. The room had a border of black and blue flowers around the top of the wall, but otherwise was stark and plain. Wooden chairs—some with pads left in them by the regular users—lined up facing the table where she sat. It was always a bit chilly in this room, but Amal suspected that was mostly her own perception. She always seemed to be in trouble when she appeared here.

Villads showed up, walking slowly this morning. White-haired and stooped, he pressed a frail hand on her shoulder as he passed and then sat in one of the chairs facing hers. "Do you know what we'll be discussing?"

Amal swallowed. She had a dull headache from sleeping awkwardly on the narrow bed she'd shared with Dalyan. "My rashness, I assume."

Villads chuckled, a papery sound, and then coughed. "Not exactly. We need to talk to the other Oathbreakers. About him."

She'd dreaded that. Not only would she look like a fool in front of all the other Family's Oathbreakers, they might insist on interrogating Dalyan themselves. Or having the Daujom—the king's investigators—do it. "I see. Is that Signe's decision?"

"Signe wants to *discuss* it." Signe had walked into the room while Amal's attention was on Villads. She sounded testy this morning, making Amal wonder if they were all out of sorts. "It's time for some changes, and we need to lay groundwork before we go any further."

Amal hoped those changes didn't involve removing her from the engineers. "Is Theo coming?"

Theo was the fourth of the Horn Families' Oathbreakers. He usually worked the long day shift, making him the one of them Amal rarely saw. He was also Villads' son, old enough to be Amal's father.

"He'll be here shortly," Signe said as she sat in one of the unpadded chairs, her usual seat. She liked uncomfortable things. Despite being close in age to Villads, Signe had been treated better by time, leaving her with a straight spine and a touchy temper.

"Why are we meeting here?" Amal asked—usually they met on Ten Down.

"Because we're including the infirmarians now." Signe flared with displeasure, but it was short-lived. That could be because she disliked infirmarians . . . or simply hated to come up to One Down.

"Why?" Amal asked.

"Because they're angry and Elin's been lobbying the other elders for a stake in the matter." Elin was the Head Infirmarian and thus sat on the elders' council.

As Signe spoke, the remainder of the group arrived. Theo came and sat next to his father. To see them together was to see aging in process. With pale hair and a rangy build,

Theo looked startlingly like Villads, only healthier and younger. A pair of infirmarians were the last to enter. Amal wasn't entirely surprised to see that Freja was one of the two, even though Freja hadn't mentioned it the night before. That explained why Freja had been the one to tell her about the meeting.

The other was, unfortunately, Laurits, from the twenty-ones.

Amal squelched the desire to groan. A few months back, he'd been introduced to her as a potential husband.

Laurits was, according to Freja, absolutely brilliant. He was also handsome, and therefore bore the resultant curse of believing himself what every woman wanted in a man. Amal had the impression that, when directed to introduce himself to her, he'd assumed the post of consort to Lady Horn was his for the taking. They had shared only one meal because she decided the young man was overly sure of himself. Almost obnoxiously so. And he'd kissed her. It hadn't been a terrible kiss so much as he'd never asked her permission. In response, she'd hooked his legs out from under him with one foot and left him lying on the stone floor of the main hall of the Keep.

Despite having spent a great deal of time in the infirmary lately, Amal had managed to avoid the young man. She glanced over at Freja, who shrugged with one shoulder. Freja would have suggested to Elin that someone else might be a better choice, given that Amal was here, but Elin probably wasn't all that fond of Amal right now. And given that Freja was angry with her about something, Amal doubted Freja had fought the decision very hard.

"Since we're all here," Signe began, "I'll remind the infirmarians that things stay within this group. Engineers have been working with the Fortress since the first days. You're children next to us."

"Why is that the case?" Freja asked. "If Horn has the ability to create humans, then logically it can do more to help heal them than is currently allowed."

Signe turned a hard face on her. "We have always known that the infirmarians would be angry when they learned how limited they were. But the Oathbreakers know the truth about Sorensen, and we keep in mind that even the best of intentions can kill."

Freja licked her lips. "Sorensen?"

"Our sister Fortress," Signe said. "The one that spoke the same language as Horn."

Amal shifted uncomfortably in her chair. Apparently, Signe was going to start off by telling the infirmarians the brutal truth to emphasize the logic behind the Oathbreakers' decisions.

The Six Families had once been Eight. The Salonen had been the only one who spoke their own very different language. The Lee, Andersen, Lucas, Halvdan, and Jannsen Families all spoke one of two very similar tongues. And, long ago, there had been a Family that spoke the same tongue as the Horn.

"The Fortresses remember everything," Signe began, "and when one of them dies, all the others know. Horn remembers Sorensen's death, a death brought about by the hands of well-meaning infirmarians."

Freja sat up straighter. "How?"

"Centuries ago, the Sorenson infirmarians sought a way to cure a disease, and they hoped to use one disease to kill another, like a farmer burning one field ahead of the path of a fire so the flames can't jump to the next field in line. They used an old sickness to create a new one, but that new sickness changed in an unexpected manner and infected everyone within Sorenson. A handful of the Family was outside, locked out. Those within the Fortress died quickly, most within two weeks. The engineers in Deep Below were among the last living. They ordered the Fortress to burn itself out so the new sickness wouldn't spread anywhere else."

Freja had paled, horror seeping all about her now, easy for Amal to feel. Laurits, Amal could tell, doubted the truth of the tale, but Freja ... Freja had been among those infirmarians who went into the Keep to treat those infected with the influenza that killed Amal's family. Freja had seen terrible contagion first-hand, and had become infected herself, but was one of the few who survived.

Laurits glanced at Freja then as if just noticing her horrified expression. He wasn't a sensitive, Amal recalled, and probably missed half the undercurrent.

"For that reason," Signe went on, "we've limited the infirmary's capacity. Until there's a way to prevent the infirmarians from repeating that mistake, we have no choice."

"You don't trust us ..." Laurits began.

"It's not a matter of trust," Signe said firmly. "When we deal with the Fortress' memories, we're dealing with knowledge far beyond our capacity to understand. We're infants set loose in a room full of loaded firearms."

Laurits sat back. At least he was smart enough to recognize that he wasn't going to argue Signe off her position. He glanced at Amal, who gave him a flat stare in return. She was behind Signe on this issue.

"Will the infirmarians be included in all our discussions in the future?" Amal asked. "Or only ones that concern them?"

"How will you decide which discussions concern us?" Freja asked in turn. "What happens if a planned discussion didn't, but the topic changes? Will you send someone up to the infirmary to fetch whichever of us is on duty?"

Ah, that's right. Amal recalled now that Laurits served night duty while Freja had the day.

"It's either all or nothing," Signe said smoothly. "One of you comes every time we meet, even if we're just talking about wall plates."

"What are wall plates?" Laurits asked.

"Not now," Freja said to him. She turned back to Signe. "Fine, that's acceptable."

"We need to start planning what we'll tell the other Families about this man, Dalyan," Signe announced, effectively starting the actual meeting. She opened out a leather notebook and tugged a pencil from behind her ear. "To address the problems he presents, we'll have to go back to the very beginning."

Amal hoped they weren't going to go back to the days of the Founders or this meeting would be interminable.

"Our first issue is where the pattern came from and how that pattern got into Cince hands."

"Since you checked his pattern against the patterns of the Salonen Originals," Amal said, "I assume that Horn has all the patterns from *all* the Families in its memories. Is that also the case in the other Fortresses? And is it possible that other peoples outside the Six Families have access to that information?"

Signe shook her white head. "Horn says that outsiders shouldn't have the patterns. Then again, there was a mess during the invasion, and some odd things have ended up in Pedraisi hands. It's possible that someone sold a pattern to the Cince that long ago. But I doubt it. I think we're looking at a far more recent theft."

"How hard would it be to steal a pattern?" Amal asked.

Signe snorted. "From us? Difficult. Horn knows when its memories are tampered with. The problem is those six other Fortresses. During the invasion, each Fortress was stripped of many of its capabilities. It's possible that someone could have reached into a Fortress' memories, and that Fortress simply lacked the self-awareness to protest it."

"You're including Salonen in that count?" Theo asked.

She turned to him. "We have to assume there's a chance—however unlikely—that someone's gotten into Salonen."

"If it's alive," Amal pointed out, "it should be able to defend itself like Horn did."

"It probably wouldn't in this case. Horn was defending itself against an all-out assault," Villads said. "Stealing one pattern is like going to the mountains and stealing one snowflake. The mountain won't notice that. But it's not likely to have been Salonen, anyway. Not if that's what they're trying to get *into* now."

That made sense. That left five Fortresses. "Can the other Fortresses ... look through their memories to see if one's missing?" Amal asked.

"Yes," Signe said. "But it will take time. To use Villads' example, we're asking them to look through every snowflake on the mountains, and I have doubts over whether the others have the capacity to do that and still carry out their basic functions."

"But they might," Amal said.

"What we need is basic, old fashioned, interrogation," Signe said. "Your lover's pattern was chosen deliberately. Plucking one pattern out of thousands and getting one who had his knowledge and skills? Not an accident."

Amal felt her cheeks flushing. Trust Signe to call Dalyan *your lover,* and do it in front of Laurits. Not that Amal cared what Laurits thought, but she had no idea whether he was a gossip. "So you think it was someone with knowledge of the Originals."

"I can't see any way it wasn't one of the engineers," Signe said. "A slim chance of being an infirmarian, but they don't have access to the parts of the Fortress where that information can be found."

"And how does one steal a memory?" Laurits asked.

"Put it into a device and carry it out," Signe told him.

Laurits glanced at Freja as if asking her to verify that claim. She ignored him.

"It's a physical act," Villads said, "and the engineers in each Fortress probably have a good idea which among them could have done it. Given the boy's age, we know it was done at least eight years ago."

The boy, in this discussion, being Dalyan. That was slightly better than *your lover.* "So I'll ask all the Oathbreakers to question their people," Amal said.

"Once we have an idea where and when it happened," Signe said, "it's less of a drain to have the Fortress involved search for exact details."

"And to determine whether any other patterns were stolen," Amal finished, nodding.

"Yes," Signe said. "And that's the easy part. Because you're going to have to force a decision, Amal. Not immediately. It would be irrational to expect them to come around quickly. But as soon as possible—a few months at most. The other Fortresses *must* be brought back to full function. Otherwise they can't defend themselves like Horn did. If the Cince stole a Salonen, they could have stolen a member of each Family, giving them access to every Fortress. If one Cince operative gets over the threshold into a Fortress, there's no telling what they could steal."

"Is there any chance of working *with* the Cince?" Laurits asked.

"No." Freja cast a withering glance Laurits' way, accompanied by a burning wall of scorn.

Now Amal knew where Freja stood on the idea of including Laurits.

"It's not a stupid question," Laurits insisted. "Our people have always considered the Cince enemies. Perhaps it's time we consider negotiating with them."

"No," Freja repeated.

Amal stepped in. "The Cince have never shown an interest in negotiation. They take what they want, and they're not unwilling to use brutal methods to do so. I agree with Signe—our best defense at this point is to bring the other Fortresses up to full function."

"Why hasn't that been done before?" Laurits asked, apparently determined to be the stubborn member of the group.

"The Cince," Amal told him. "We've wanted them to think the Fortresses are so stripped down that they're not worth attacking, not worth invading again."

"They've never invaded us," Laurits protested.

Amal took a deep breath, willing herself to be calm. She didn't recall a time when she'd ever thought that, but she was Anvarrid and an Oathbreaker, and thus knew more of the story than most did. "Before the Anvarrid came here," she told him, "they were driven out of their territorial lands by the Cince. As a part of the treaty that settled that war, the Cince ceded Larossa and Pedrossa to the Anvarrid as a new ... homeland. The Cince had never had any claim to either country, but they convinced the Anvarrid there was treasure here, so the Anvarrid invaded Larossa. They managed to empty most of the eastern Fortresses of everything the Families had. Every stick of furniture, every book from their libraries, every bit of cloth and food in storage. Almost all of that was sold to the Cince, along with a great many Family personnel. *Brutal* is a mild description of the Anvarrid army's actions toward the Families."

Laurits seemed sobered by this reminder. The Anvarrid had never reached the Horn, making that story one her people sometimes forgot.

"What worked in the Families' favor was that the Anvarrid hadn't forgiven the Cince for driving them from their homeland, and thus they wouldn't allow any Cince into Larossa once they'd secured its borders. That bought the engineers time to strip away the Fortress' memories and functions, making them less of a target for the Cince in the future."

"Then why bring the Fortresses back to full function if that will draw the Cince's attention?"

Signe scowled at Laurits. "Because, stupid boy, the Cince *already* have their eyes turned on us. Playing dead is no longer an option."

That silenced the young man, for which Amal was grateful. The four Oathbreakers had known each other for years and rarely needed to explain anything to one another. They all had the same knowledge base. Adding Freja and Laurits to the group meant they would be doing this more often from now on. Amal suspected that Freja simply had the sense to hold her demands for an explanation until later, in private.

"The other Families are going to have fits about this," Amal said. "Not Lee or Andersen, but the Lucas are going to worry that it violates the treaty." It *did* violate the treaty, although only the linguistic sense. The Fortresses, once wakened, would start speaking aloud again, effectively making every member of those Families into Oathbreakers since they were not to do anything—read, write, speak, and very possibly, *hear*—in their ancestral tongues.

"Could the Fortresses be taught to speak Anvarrid?" Laurits asked in a quiet voice once Amal explained that.

Freja answered before Amal needed to. "No. The Fortresses each speak their ancestral languages because they were intended to help our people preserve our heritage. Same reason we have lists of permitted names. So we don't disappear into the larger cultures about us."

Amal suppressed a wry smile. Freja knew that because as a child she'd wanted to know why Eldana could have an interesting and different name while *she* was only named after her grandmother. Sidana, born in a foreign country, had asked special dispensation to name Eldana for her own mother back in the Orinoso Islands. It was a dispensation that didn't last beyond that generation, though, as Eldana and Magnus had chosen traditional names for their twin sons.

"And Anvarrid is a wretchedly inadequate language," Amal added. "It can't handle many of the concepts the Fortress wants to discuss with us. To force Horn to speak Anvarrid would mean limiting its ability to express itself. That's a path we don't want to go down."

"Jannsen isn't going to cooperate," Theo said darkly.

"You never know," Signe said. "If Amal can make it sound like a way to protect their racial purity, those idiots might do it."

Amal pressed her lips together, not wanting to say anything at this point. The Jannsen had recently fought an internal war over the idea that sensitives were not pure-blooded, but rather a stain left on their bloodlines after the Anvarrid invasion. It was a patently false idea, not supported by the evidence of history. It was hard for Amal to grasp why anyone would believe it, and yet the Jannsen did. Presenting them with Dalyan, a sensitive, and saying that he was one of the Originals would set their backs up. She had no idea how she could convince them.

And there was no way to be sure what the Halvdan Family would do. They were quiet and kept their own counsel most of the time. They were never unreasonable, like the Jannsen. The Halvdan merely did things at their own speed, when they were ready to do so.

The conversation went on around the topics that they needed to discuss with the other Oathbreakers, Signe taking notes, her eyes narrowed at Laurits as he asked a question here and there. She clearly didn't approve of his inclusion in the group. After a few hours, Signe called a halt to the meeting, claiming they couldn't get any further with their plans without involving Dalyan.

Since he was the prime piece of evidence to be presented to the Oathbreakers, Amal knew he would have to be included eventually. She was relieved when they all rose to leave. She tried to catch Freja's eye, but Freja left without speaking to Amal. Unfortunately, that wasn't the case with Laurits. He stopped Amal by the doorway with a brief touch of one hand on her wrist.

"I owe you an apology," he said. "The last time we met, I was overly familiar."

Amal blinked at him, confused. Did he think that he still had a chance of winning her over? Or perhaps now that he knew she'd taken a lover, he thought she would be less discriminating in the future. "I appreciate the apology," she finally said. "Don't try it again."

He laughed softly, making his handsome face seem . . . likable. "No, I won't make that mistake."

She doubted he'd learned his lesson.

CHAPTER 4

UNABLE TO CATCH UP with Freja, Amal tracked her to the infirmary. When she came through the large door into the main infirmary, she spotted Freja already talking to a patient—a child under the watchful eye of his yeargroup sponsor. Freja sat next to the child, one hand across his forehead. The boy looked queasy, and Amal hoped she didn't have to watch him be sick. Fortunately, Freja sent the boy away with a few words to his sponsor.

Then her eyes settled on Amal as she approached. Her demeanor stayed cool, professional. "What is it?"

Usually with Freja, the direct approach was best. "I don't know why you're angry with me this time. Whatever it is you think I'm keeping from you, I'm not."

She'd figured that much out—Freja thought she was keeping a secret again.

Freja came a little closer. "I've figured that out, Amal. You actually don't know. That doesn't mean I'm not jealous."

"What are you talking about?"

Freja shook her head. "It will work out eventually. About Laurits..."

Amal rolled her eyes. Only a little, though.

"He wasn't my choice for this," Freja said quietly, "but he *was* Elin's. I have no doubt he's smart enough to handle what we're delving into, but we both know there's another reason for including him."

Amal was afraid of that. "I'm not interested."

Freja shook her head. "That won't stop him from trying to win you over. He's the elders' favorite."

"He's a twenty-one," Amal protested. "Do you remember what we were like as twenty-ones? How different we are now?"

"They want him as your consort," Freja said. "Or at least several of them do. Over Dalyan."

She wasn't surprised to hear there were elders wanting to end her relationship, such as it was, with Dalyan. "Which ones?"

"Elin, I know," Freja said, "but definitely Vibeka and Victor. Remember, Laurits is Vibeka's son."

"He is?" Amal tried to recall whether anyone had told her that earlier. Vibeka was in charge of the guards, and her twin brother, Victor, in charge of the quartermasters. They were included among the elders, not due to age, but because they held influential positions.

As Lady Horn, Amal could do as she wished, but Jan worked directly under Vibeka, as Freja did for Elin. She hoped that both elders would behave professionally if she didn't choose Laurits, but that didn't always happen. She sighed.

Freja set a hand on Amal's elbow. "Don't let that sway you. But remember, handle him *tactfully.*"

"I'll remember that," Amal said. "Thanks."

"And the other thing," Freja said. "I'm just being petty. Ignore it."

Amal wished she could, but once Freja had gotten a thistle in her brain, she rarely let go. Freja turned stubborn about odd things. "I'm going to go back and check on Dalyan," she said simply.

"Do that," Freja said, tilting her head toward the infirmary's open doors. "We'll talk later."

Dalyan had spoken with a subdued Jan for a while before it occurred to him that Jan was intentionally keeping his emotions in check to avoid causing him discomfort. Once he'd made clear that he could handle Jan's normal emotions, Jan relaxed and they'd had a pleasant chat where they discussed what would happen once he was moved upstairs to the hall shared by the twenty-sevens. Apparently, that was happening faster than any of them had anticipated. What Jan didn't say was why.

Jan had brought paperwork, though, making Dalyan's adoption by the Horn Family official. Dalyan signed where told, mostly because Jan expected him to. He hadn't had time to work out the full ramifications. He would have his own quarters in the Fortress, something very similar to the room he occupied at this moment. The twenty-sevens lived on a hall intended for young families, and therefore most had a small nursery room like the room he was occupying now. Also, because he'd been injured, he wouldn't be required to work in the sheds until the infirmary released him. He was, however, supposed to start having lessons with Villads or one of the other engineers.

And finally, as part of the twenty-sevens, he would have to report to Magnus, who would be his *First*. Sidana and her husband, Milas, would be his sponsors. Effectively, his parents. And Eldana would be his sister. He didn't know how much they would include him in their family, but the idea of having a family at all was hard to grasp.

He was *officially* going to be one of them . . . a strange thought. He could feel Jan *wanting* him to feel safe, to feel protected, and for once, Dalyan did.

It was exciting, as if he was finally fitting in to this world. Then Dalyan felt his excitement fading. They hadn't come up with an answer for one of his main concerns since Freja first mentioned moving him to Six Down. "What about Nimi?"

"The only solution I can think of is for her to stay with Amal," Jan said, "in Amal's quarters. That way she'll be safe at night, and someone can collect her during the day."

Currently Nimi was still with her mother, even if almost weaned. But Dalyan had looked forward to having the pup stay in his room upstairs. He'd even arranged with the servants to obtain a basket with an old blanket for her to sleep on.

Amal had promised to take care of the puppy, more than once, if something should happen to him. Even so, Dalyan hated the idea that he was forcing his puppy off onto Amal, who had never actually wanted a puppy. *We don't keep pets,* she'd once told him.

Dalyan pinched the bridge of his nose.

"It will all work out," Jan said, patting Dalyan's knee, pushing that sense of feeling safe at him again. "And she's adorable. I've been up to see her."

Dalyan laughed at that mental image. "I didn't realize people were visiting her."

"Nohr wants a dog now," Jan said, amusement spilling warmly around him. "This is how society falls apart."

"It's how society changes," Amal said from the doorway. "One person discovers they like dogs, and that idea spreads like a contagion."

How long was she listening? Amal stepped over the threshold into the small room. "Jan, um ... about the meeting."

"This morning? Freja went?"

"So did Laurits," she said. "They've chosen him to back up Freja."

Dalyan could tell that wasn't a good development.

Jan shook his head. "They haven't given up, then?"

"Apparently not," she said. "Freja reminded me to be tactful, but I have no intention of giving in to their recommendation."

Dalyan gazed up at her, but she was focused on her brother.

"Vibeka won't like that," Jan said, "but she has no business putting him forward anyway. He's too young. Don't worry about me."

They fell silent, and Dalyan suspected they weren't comfortable discussing the man working with Freja in front of *him*. His mind provided a bit of information Amal had shared with him when he'd first discovered that others were gossiping about the two of them. The elders had been introducing her to young men from the Family in the hope that she'd choose one as her next husband. Jan rose, carefully folded up the adoption paperwork, and left Dalyan alone with Amal again.

"I should explain," she began.

"Is he the twenty-one who made you feel old?"

Amal laughed shortly, sinking down on the bed Jan had abandoned. "You have a good memory. Yes."

"What does it mean? You told Jan, so there's more than just awkwardness involved."

Amal set each foot up on the bed in turn and unlaced her boots. "Freja said that some of the elders still want me to contract with him. Unfortunately, he's well-connected. He's the son of one of the elders, the nephew of another, and apparently, the favorite of Freja's superior."

"Vibeka is his mother, right? She's the elder in question, the one who supervises the guards, like Jan?"

Amal set her boots on the ground and folded her legs beneath her. "Yes. And while I'd rather not annoy her, I'm not going to marry her son."

This was dangerous territory for him. He didn't truly understand the structure of the Horn Family. It was possible they could make Amal's life unbearable. He simply didn't know.

Her eyes lifted when he didn't say anything. "This has nothing to do with you, Dalyan. I didn't like Laurits when I first met him, and I'm not impressed now. Certainly not enough to share a bed with him."

"But the elders see me as interfering," he guessed.

"Some do, I think." She abruptly unfolded her legs, got up, and clambered onto his bed. She managed to lie down on the far side of him without doing any damage to his head or ankle. When she settled, her face pressed against his back, she whispered, "I'm not sure how far they might go to be rid of you."

That suddenly made sense of the rush to move him upstairs. He could feel Amal's worry now, even though she was trying to hold it in close. "Should I leave?" he asked. "Would that be safer for you?"

"I want you to stay," she said. "I . . . want to try to make this work. I think, in time, I can win the elders over to my side."

Freja had been insistent that he not lie on his left side, but he was going to defy that. For a little while, at least. He managed to turn over without knocking Amal off the far side of the bed. "Amal . . ."

"I love you, Dalyan," she said, surprising him. "There's nothing like having someone threaten me to get me to speak my mind. If Vibeka thinks I'm going to cave in and accept her son, she'll have a fight on her hands."

It wasn't love she was feeling now; it was determination. He could feel her resolve, hard and fiery, and reminded himself not to try to coerce Amal into anything. Clearly, that didn't work. "So what do I do? How do I make this simpler for you?"

She sighed. "I don't know. But ... don't ever believe you need to step aside so someone else can take your place. You'll probably be told you should. Don't. No matter what. If they want to draw you off, they'll tell you it's for my benefit, my safety. Something like that. Don't be noble and walk away for my sake. Because I will be very angry if you do."

He could see that scenario coming up, a well-meaning elder telling him it was for Amal's own good, that she was simply being stubborn, and that he needed to save her from herself. All of that presupposed that Amal couldn't make a valid decision. He knew better. "I won't."

"I haven't decided if I want to marry again," she said softly. "But so far, you're the only man I've found tempting."

That was flattering, at least. "If I'd recovered the memories I was supposed to have, do you think the elders would feel differently?"

She stroked two fingers down his cheek. "I've no idea. Does your head hurt?"

Her emotions altered, fading from single-mindedness to desire. Not a burning desire, but he could tell the focus of the discussion—in her mind—had changed. "Do you realize the door is still open?" he asked.

He felt a quick flare of alarm from her, but then she shook her head. "I'll leave it that way. It'll keep me out of trouble."

She shifted closer and kissed him, the first time since the day the Fortress had struck him down. Her lips were soft on his. Her emotions surrounded him, warmth and comfort and pleasure sliding against his skin. Dalyan gasped and pulled back.

Amal's emotions changed abruptly to worry. "Did I hurt you?"

"No," he admitted. "I was surprised. The feelings were overwhelming."

She laughed softly and leaned her head against his chest. "The two-sensitive problem," she reminded him.

He'd learned that the first time they had sex—the emotions had echoed back and forth between them, the excitement built too quickly, and it had all been over within a couple of minutes. He knew from experience that it usually took women longer to reach their climax, but with Amal being a sensitive, she essentially shared his. It was a relief, in a way, but also a challenge to keep their emotions from spinning out of control. Now he could discern what her emotions actually were, though, and it added a depth to the arousal that he hadn't felt before. He looked forward to exploring the problem in detail once Freja gave him permission to resume more normal activities.

Thinking of that, Dalyan wrapped one arm around Amal and edged the other under her pillow. Amal sighed, a contented sound. "I want to pretend that it will all be easy," she said. "That no one will care what we do. That they'll leave us alone."

Dalyan pressed his lips to the top of her head. "Me, too."

Amal woke alone, and for a moment couldn't recall where she was. Then she recalled that she was here to look after Dalyan, who wasn't there.

She hadn't meant to fall asleep in the middle of the day, but evidently she'd needed it. For a time she contemplated simply staying huddled under this blanket that smelled of him, but she needed to update Jan on her plans. She dragged herself out of bed, straightened her clothes and her braids, and went to find Dalyan.

It wasn't far to go. He was out in the hallway, walking. Freja had come down to see him at some point and instead of disturbing Amal, they'd simply taken the daily exam out of the room.

Even from the far end of the hallway, Amal could see that he was moving quite normally. Freja watched his ankle closely, but when they arrived at the doorway, she conceded that it looked good. She glanced over at Amal. "I'd like him to move upstairs today. It will be hectic with the children, but we'll make certain they understand he's still delicate."

Dalyan rolled his eyes. "I told her I could take the stairs."

"No, he needs an elevator," she told Amal. "In fact, it might be easiest to move him right now, if you're willing to do so."

Because I can access the elevators. "Of course," Amal said. "We just need to pack up his things." It was a few days earlier than they'd planned, but Freja had said more than once that he was healing well.

"I'll drop the linens for the laundry," Freja added. When Amal moved to step over the threshold into the room, Freja stopped her. "I want him to have a few nights sleeping alone, Amal."

"It's a new place . . ."

"And he knows all of us. I've cleared him to sleep on his back. I want him to take up as much space as he needs. He'll sleep better that way."

Amal felt her cheeks flush. "Fine."

"It's only for a few days, Amal. Probably going to take those stitches out soon, so that will make it faster."

Amal knew it was for Dalyan's good, but it felt like she was being pushed away. "Can I still come down this evening, sit with everyone?"

"I wish you would," Freja said. "We haven't seen you much, so we can all catch up. And that would ease the transition for him."

Amal followed Freja into the bedroom, helped collect Dalyan's things and her own, and then helped Freja strip the beds while Dalyan waited outside. Once done, Amal picked up her own satchel and Dalyan's and headed with him toward the elevators while Freja carried the laundry in the opposite direction. Amal waited until Freja had dumped it off on the sentry at the end of the hall and jogged back to join them. Then she touched the plate next to the elevator and asked Horn to open the door for them. After only a moment, the doors slid apart, revealing the elevator.

Amal always felt guilty for using an elevator when her feet would get her somewhere, but since Dalyan was forbidden to climb, she wouldn't report herself.

Dalyan glanced about the wide space. "Are they all this big?"

This particular elevator was made for moving supplies—the quartermasters' purview. "No," she admitted. "This one is for transporting supplies from the tithe to various levels. Fabric, foodstuffs, occasionally furniture. Big things or high quantity. I would have used one of the engineers' elevators, but this one's closer."

"And I insist," Freja added, arms folded over her chest. "If Victor takes offense, tell him that."

Amal doubted the quartermaster would say anything, no matter what their current differences. The door closed softly, and then Amal felt the elevator move upward. It opened on the main central hallway of Six Down, the level on which the twenty-sevens lived. Freja stepped out quickly —she hated the elevators—and Dalyan followed.

He stopped only a step outside, prompting Amal to push him gently out of her way. While he gaped at the paintings on the walls, she exited the elevator and told Horn to lock it. She didn't want a child to find it unlocked and ride up and down all afternoon.

"It's beautiful," Dalyan pronounced. He was looking at the patterns painted on the upper edge of the walls, above most people's reach.

This hall bore a pattern of stylized flowers, painted in blues and blacks against the gray wall. The blossoms weren't realistic, but softly curved imaginings of someone who'd only heard about flowers in stories of a distant past. They were intended to decorate the halls, adding some liveliness to what was, quite honestly, a visually monotonous place to live. They also provided a focus for youngsters still learning to control their emotions. They could trace the patterns with their eyes while they counted or recited poetry to themselves; that calmed most of them.

Because they were on the front end of the Fortress—the end directly under the grand stair—the hallway stretched away from them for a quarter mile or so. This floor was residential, housing yeargroups in their mid-twenties to mid-forties.

"We're three halls down," Freja told Dalyan. She laid a hand on his shoulder to steer him in that direction.

He walked steadily enough with Freja, allowing Amal to trail with the bags. Freja stopped at the guideline before turning into the twenty-sevens' hall. The guideline was a foot-wide strip of floor with a pebbled texture rather than the smooth floor everywhere else. "This rough line is the guideline. You don't cross a guideline without permission," Freja said. "Not unless it's *your* guideline."

"And don't step on one," Amal added. "Not intentionally."

"Because that's a slight?" he guessed.

"Exactly," she said. "We don't go swiping our feet on the twenty-eights' guideline. It's rude."

"I understand." Dalyan gazed down the twenty-sevens' hallway, peering up at the black and white wall patterns there. "Are those birds?"

"Yes," Amal said. They were even more stylized than the flowers, all swooping lines and sharp, curved beaks and talons. "Gyrfalcons. For Jan and I."

"Ah," Dalyan said, suddenly smiling. "Your House crest."

He had been trained as if he were Anvarrid, so it didn't surprise her that he knew about the crests. The Anvarrid invaders had even painted their faces to resemble falcons, although that had only been in the loosest interpretation. "Yes, our House was one of the Falcon Houses, so whenever Jan and I move, the yeargroup has falcons painted on the walls."

His brows were drawn together. "What does a gyrfalcon actually look like?"

"Black and white," Amal said. "Sort of. We don't hunt them here. Once a decade or so, someone from the Western Kingdoms brings us a captured one. After they leave, if the bird can fly, we let it go and hope it can find its home. Cruel to keep one here."

"Enough about the birds," Freja said impatiently. "Let me show you your quarters."

Dalyan stepped over the guideline into the twenty-sevens' hall, following Freja. On either side of the hallway, the common area opened out, with couches and chairs and shelves, most old and worn, but kept carefully clean. This was where the twenty-sevens gathered at night to be together. At the moment it was empty—most adults were at duty posts now and the children under the eyes of the carers. Any adults left on the floor were likely sleeping, having come off night duty. Once they'd passed the commons, private quarters lay on either side, doors closed save for one near the end. That door stood open, and it was there that Freja led Dalyan.

He stopped before the doorway. "This is my room?"

"Rooms," Freja said. "You're of an age to have children, they assume, if you're on this hall. Go on inside."

Dalyan stepped past her, over the threshold, and into his own room.

"Now you can invite me in," Freja said. "Or Amal, at least, since she has your luggage."

Amal had begun to wonder when either of them would remember that she was carrying everything.

"Oh, I'll take that," Dalyan said, holding out a hand.

"We don't do that," Amal said. "It's unlucky. You either come out and get it, or I'll bring it in. Don't pass anything over a threshold." She could almost see Dalyan thinking, as if trying to recall whether he'd ever seen her do so. He probably hadn't. The taboo was so ingrained that Amal never even gave it a second's thought.

"You should come in, then," he said, flushing with embarrassment.

Amal stepped into his room and set his satchel down on the bed.

Freja didn't follow. "Amal, can you get him settled in? And then let him get some sleep. He'll find it overwhelming when the children come back. I'll look at your scalp again then."

Amal didn't argue. She let Freja head back to her duties as Dalyan sank down on his chair. He hadn't wanted to admit he was tired, Amal guessed. She set her own bag down and sat on the bed. The room already had a desk on one side with a shelf above it, a pair of wooden chairs, a bed, and a chest for his clothing. A second door led to the nursery room. "So, this is yours now."

"It's not painted," he noted.

No, the walls were plain. Given his skilled sketching, she suspected he might come up with something amazing. "Paint can be acquired from the quartermaster, although I suspect there are plenty of bottles and brushes stored in a locker on this hall. Ask Magnus."

"I get to paint it myself?" He seemed shocked.

"It's your room," Amal said. "You may leave the walls blank, or you may paint them, although you can't just paint anything. If you come up with an idea, check with Magnus or Freja. They're your First and Second now, and you have to get their approval for a lot of things."

Magnus would explain all that to him later. Amal suspected that Dalyan could use a nap if he wasn't too wound up.

"I didn't realize I would report to Freja," he said.

"I have been reporting to Freja most of my life," Amal admitted, letting her amusement flare up so he would know she wasn't angry about that.

He smiled again. "That day on the glacier when you were injured, I thought it was odd that she could order you around."

"I can defy her," Amal said, "but she'll make me pay later."

"That I believe." His eyes glanced down at his house shoes. "I don't know what to do now."

Amal laid a hand on his knee. "This is not permanent. Nothing that happens today or tomorrow will change your entire life. You're here so Magnus can keep you safe, so Freja can keep an eye on you. Just rest, and try to enjoy being among the group. If you need to, come back to your room and shut the door. You don't need permission to do that."

He nodded. "And why does Magnus need to keep me safe?"

"I don't think anyone would hurt you," Amal said, "but I wouldn't be surprised if people came to talk to you . . . try to influence you."

"You mean the elders who don't want me around you."

Amal pressed her lips together. Trust Dalyan to pick up the detail that no one had spoken aloud. Amal hadn't discussed it with Freja or Magnus, but she knew exactly what had gone through Freja's mind. And Magnus' and Jan's. "I don't want them to bother you. Neither does Freja. So to get to you now, they'll have to go through every twenty-seven first."

"I'll sleep a little better knowing that," he said.

"Me, too."

CHAPTER 5

AMAL RETURNED TO her office to work that afternoon since she knew Dalyan was in a safe place. It turned out that Sofie was on the hall, and was sitting in the common area drinking tea by the time Amal left. Since Sofie stood sentry duty at night, she was often there in the afternoon. She promised to keep an eye on the hall, just in case anyone decided to visit Dalyan.

Fortunately, Gyda had kept everything organized over the last few days, and Amal spent a while signing and stamping documents before moving on to reading Gyda's notes about the latest preparations for the tithe. A new warehouse was being built in Farden, a town at the foot of the mountains, intended to hold part of the tithe for midwinter distribution. She made a note asking Gyda to find out where the funds for the supplies and workers were coming from, and left that atop the folder. More files talked about needed road improvements, something that *would* have to come out of provincial funds. The problem with improving the roads was that winter would simply destroy them again. It was a continual expense.

Deciding she'd done enough, Amal closed her office and made her way up to the Keep to change clothes. When she reached the residential hall of the Keep, though, she found her bedroom door standing open, with Nohr sitting on the floor inside.

Nohr had blonde hair that was braided back from his face and a heavy beard that he kept neatly trimmed. He looked ridiculously huge sitting on her floor with the puppy. He glanced up when Amal coughed discreetly into her hand. "I'm trying to explain to her that this is her basket," he said. "She wants to get on the bed, I think."

It was amusing to watch such a large man being bested by a puppy that didn't even have the proper number of legs. Nohr put the puppy in the basket, and the puppy promptly clambered out and made her way to the bed. Then she raised her single foreleg and tried to jump up onto it. Given her size, it would take a few more months before *that* would work.

Amal set her satchel down on the end of her bed, and glanced down at Nohr's uniform, which bore a liberal sprinkling of white hair. She felt a surge of despair. "She's leaving hair everywhere."

Why did I not realize that would happen?

Nohr grabbed the puppy and set her in the basket again. "She doesn't know that I deal with children all the time. I can do this longer than she can."

That was true. "Do you plan to stay here all night?" Amal asked.

"Ha, no." He grinned. "I'm off duty, Amal. I was just waiting for you. I brought you the pup because Sidana said she's not suckling any longer. Or rather, her mother has stopped letting her."

They'd worried that would happen. Amal sighed. She was the one who would have to take care of the creature in Dalyan's stead—feed her and do everything else. "Will she . . . pee on my rugs?"

Nohr rattled off a series of commands that, according to Sidana, the pup *should* learn, although Amal had her doubts. She'd never trained one of these creatures. They weren't like children. She was going to have to take the puppy outside several times a day. First thing in the morning and before bed. And the puppy apparently chewed things. Amal picked her lovely embroidered house shoes off the floor and put them on her desk. "What else?"

Nohr crossed his arms over his chest. "Be nice to her."

Oh dear. Not only did Dalyan love the little beast, but apparently she'd won Nohr over as well. "Fine."

Nohr rose and, chuckling under his breath, strolled out of her room leaving her at the little beast's mercy. Amal stared down at Nimi, who proceeded to walk-hop over to her and place her one white forepaw on Amal's black pantleg. The puppy made a yipping sound and, unable to steel herself, Amal leaned down and picked her up. "You are going to be an annoyance, aren't you?"

Nimi's head tilted, triangular ears perking up. Her tail had filled out some since the last time Amal had played with her, another source of white hair. Amal sighed and sat down at her desk, clutching the puppy close. She would just have to live with it.

Dalyan woke in the late afternoon—a fact he only discovered after visiting the latrine. He made his way down to the common area and found Sofie there. The stocky sentry wore casual clothing at the moment, loose trousers and a shirt and sweater. He'd only talked to her a couple of times before, but her wry sense of humor made her likable. Bearing in mind that he would be living in the same hall with her, he apologized for his unbathed state and then asked where she'd acquired the tea she was drinking. She showed him a rack with a couple of tea warmers on one side of the common room. He poured a cup of tea into an old, chipped cup and, when she gestured, went to join her on one of the many sofas.

After half an hour spent chatting, he had a better understanding of the yeargroup, their structure and schedules, and the military in general. Sofie was a woman of few words, apparently. She knew how to pass information succinctly and without expending a great deal of emotion. Others began drifting back to the common area, heading back to the quarters to change out of their uniforms into more casual clothing like he currently wore, and some to bathe. The shifts were changing, Sofie explained, and many of the twenty-sevens and their children would soon be returning from the carers.

"You might want to retire to your quarters until the children are upstairs eating," Sofie suggested then. "I hear that you're adjusting to being a sensitive, and our lot is pretty young."

Meaning they lacked emotional control, unlike Sofie herself. Dalyan rose, cup of cooled tea in hand. "Can I take some tea back to my quarters?"

Sofie smiled. "Yes, they're your quarters. But if you spill in the hallway, you have to clean it up. Also, it's up to you whether you leave the door open or closed."

Dalyan thanked her, refilled his cup, and headed back to his quarters. Although a couple of shadows passed his door, no one peeked inside until Freja came by, as promised, to look at the stitches on his scalp. She leaned over him where he sat, tugging gently at his hair. Then she stood up straight again. "I'd say another day on the stitches, but I will clear you to bathe now. You can use soap on your scalp. Don't rub the stitches themselves. Understand?"

He licked his lips. "Um ... are there other people in the showers?"

Amal had shown him the latrine and the showers here, a large shared bath. He wasn't sure he was ready to bathe among all these people.

"You're going to have to get over that," Freja told him. "For tonight, wait until we take all the children up to the mess for dinner. We'll bring some food back down for you. I'll let you know when we leave."

A short time later he was standing in the showers, washing off what felt like a month's worth of grime. It felt glorious to wash out his hair. Then he wrapped himself in towels that were, according to Amal, his. He made his way back to his quarters, dressed, and gently dried his hair before Freja returned with a tray in her hands. "Personal service," she said. "Aren't you lucky?"

"I do appreciate it," he said. "I feel much better now."

"Less smelly." She proceeded to peer at his stitches again and pronounced her approval. "Bring your food down to the commons and eat with the adults."

He decided that was an invitation, not an order. He followed in her wake, carrying the tray. The others—he thought he could recall all the names—greeted him sparingly, clearly an effort to keep from overwhelming him. He sat down on one of the sofas to eat, balancing the tray on his lap. Jan settled across from him, but the others kept their distance. From one of the couches, Nohr was monitoring the handful of children still awake; Mikks wrote in a small leather book at one of the tables, leaning his head on one elbow and rumpling his short blond hair. On the next sofa over, Freja sat with Juliane—a tall and fair woman, slender despite having recently given birth—chatting about the baby.

"We're mostly going to leave you alone," Jan said. "You can interact with people when you feel ready."

"It doesn't seem unbearable," Dalyan noted between bites of stew. The children were dashing back and forth along the hallway, playing some sort of game that involved a fist-sized ball. They were visually distracting, but not loud, so Dalyan suspected they were intentionally quiet. Nothing here was too distressing, as far as he could see.

"You're adapting quickly," Jan said. "Since I'm the broadcaster of the group, I'll be the first to annoy you. If the ambient becomes problematic, it's customary to whistle."

The *ambient* was the term they used for the collective emotional environment in a place, whether it was a room, an entire common area, or the Fortress in general. Jan whistled, a simple two-note whistle, going up on the end. Dalyan had heard that before somewhere. It filled in a space in his grasp of Family habits. "I can do that," he said. "It's strange, though. I feel . . . I feel like I've been missing this. Does that make sense?"

Jan's expression didn't change, but Dalyan could sense his confusion as a dense cloud around him. All of Jan's emotions seemed that way now—thick and nearly opaque, the strength of emotion that could almost push others before it. That must be what Jan called being a broadcaster.

Dalyan tried to explain. "Have you ever had a headache or an injury, but you didn't realize how much it hurt until it was gone?"

Jan nodded, but his confusion didn't clear.

"It's like that. I was created and lacked this, but I didn't realize until it came back how much I was missing it. I constantly felt unsure of how others were reacting, but I think that's because the knowledge in my head was created by someone who was a sensitive. He, and therefore I, would have *expected* to grasp others' feelings . . . only I didn't."

"And now you do," Jan said.

"Now I'm starting to think that's what I was missing all along."

Jan's confusion had ebbed away. His mind turned inward, as if he was contemplating that idea, teasing out the ramifications. "I'm told latents often feel that way," he finally said. "That they're missing parts of conversations. Is that what you mean?"

"Not exactly," Dalyan said. "If I understand, a latent has never had recognition of others' emotions. I mean that the man on whom I'm based did, but it was lost during my creation. So it's not something I've never had. It's something that was misplaced, and now found. It's familiar."

"Sorting out who you are and who the other man is must be confusing."

Dalyan chuckled. "No. It's only confusing when I try to *explain* it."

It was Jan's turn to laugh. "That, I understand."

Dalyan took another spoonful of stew. From the corner of his eyes, he saw the children in the hallway migrating toward the main hall. Jan turned to gaze over his shoulder, and that was when Dalyan saw the source of the distraction. Amal walked toward the common area. A dark-haired girl stopped and hugged her—Sara, Dalyan recalled, Jan's daughter—but then Amal waded through the children to the commons.

She approached the sofa he sat on, clutching a satchel close at her side. "May I join you?"

Dalyan wondered at the anxiousness he sensed from her, so he quickly agreed. Amal sat next to him, arranging the satchel carefully between them. She kept one hand on it. Her anxiousness abated a bit, but didn't fade completely.

"You look well," she told him.

That seemed strangely awkward, too. "I'm sure I smell better."

She flushed, amused. "Yes, you do."

He took a final bite of the stew and asked Jan what he should do with the bowl, tray, and spoon.

"I'll take them today," Jan said, reaching across to grab the tray. "but later I'll show you where they go." He rose and left the commons, tray in hand.

"There are elevators that take everything back up to the mess," Amal offered, leaning closer. "Most people eat in the mess, but there are always exceptions, like not being allowed to climb stairs."

That made perfect sense. "So what do we do now?"

Amal made a gesture that encompassed the whole commons area. "We enjoy being together. This is why we have a yeargroup, so that we always have companions, family, around us. We spend off-times together. This is . . . what life is about," she said. "Being together."

Dalyan thought of his years alone in a cell, of his time alone in the mountains. When he'd first come to the Horn, they'd worked hard to keep him from feeling isolated, and he'd initially mistaken it for distrust. It wasn't until he discussed it with Amal that he'd understood they wanted *this* for him, because they couldn't imagine their lives without it. "And if I do want to be alone?"

"You can go to your quarters or sit by yourself." She gestured with her chin toward Mikks, who still wrote in his journal. "Or you can, if you absolutely need to, go down to a silent floor, although you need to tell someone before you do."

So they wouldn't worry, he guessed.

The dark-haired girl came and took over the spot that Jan had left. She peered at Dalyan with serious eyes. "I'm Sara. Father said you were hurt."

This was, he realized, the first child he'd spoken with here. He didn't sense much emotion from her, making him wonder if that trait had come from Freja, who held her emotions close. "I'm Dalyan, and yes, I had ... a burn on my head."

Her brows drew together slightly. "Is it ugly?"

"I suppose so," Dalyan said. "Do you want to look?"

The girl nodded quickly. She rose and came closer, and Dalyan turned his head so that she could see the area of his scalp—behind his left ear—that had been burned. She rested one hand on Amal's satchel to balance herself as she peered as his stitches, provoking a quick stab of worry from Amal and a squeak from the bag.

The girl jumped back. Her dark eyes flicked toward Amal's face, then back to Dalyan's, and then she stepped back and sat down with great dignity. "Hmmm."

Dalyan gave Amal a questioning look. "Did you bring..."

"Contraband," she whispered.

"You brought contraband down here?" He already knew the answer. The satchel moved, but didn't make another sound.

Sara gazed at Amal, a calculating expression on her face. "May I look in the bag?" she asked very softly.

Unfortunately, their reactions had alerted Freja. She rose and stood with her arms over her chest. "What's going on?"

Amal pressed her lips together as Sara clearly debated whether to tell her mother or not. In the end, Freja won. "There's something in that bag," Sara said, pointing. "It squeaked."

Freja's irritation flared out toward them, a careful display of emotion so they would know where she stood. "Things like that are not allowed in the Fortress," she said with a clenched jaw. "You need to take it away."

Amal exuded guilt.

"I want to see it," Sara said firmly. "It's already here, Mama."

Without waiting for Freja's further condemnation, Dalyan unlatched the satchel and carefully withdrew the contraband item. Nimi wiggled frantically at the sight of him, and licked his face ecstatically when he lifted her close enough. Sara jumped up from her seat and squeezed between Amal and Dalyan so she could pet the puppy.

Freja thumped the back of Amal's head. "What were you thinking?"

Amal opened her mouth to argue, then closed it.

Dalyan didn't defend himself, either. He scooted over and set Nimi on the couch next to him. Two of the other children approached, but neither seemed inclined to touch the puppy. They stood together a few feet away, likely watching to see if Nimi bit Sara's nose off. Sidana had told him once that *most* Family were moderately afraid of animals.

Sara knelt on the floor, not afraid of risking her nose. Nimi obliged by licking her face.

"Why does it only have three legs?" Sara asked, her brows drawing together again.

"She was born that way," Amal said. "Sometimes that happens."

"It's a girl dog?" Sara squinted at the pup's belly, apparently to verify that claim.

"Yes," Amal said.

Nimi wiggled onto her back to have her belly scratched. Dalyan obliged, and then Sara tentatively followed his example.

"Oh, dear," Jan said from the hallway.

Dalyan resisted the urge to laugh at his expression. "I'm sorry, Jan. This is my fault."

"Too late to deny it." Nohr leaned over the couch and plucked Nimi up to let her lick his face. Then he knelt and held her so the other children could try petting her.

Amal sighed. "I didn't mean for any of the children to see her. They can't keep a secret."

"She'll get white hair on everything," Freja said peevishly. *"Everything."*

"It would have been better if she was black," Amal agreed.

"I've been worried," Dalyan told Freja, hoping to diffuse her anger. "I feel much better for having seen her."

Freja's eyes narrowed. "I'm sure you do."

Amal's hand found his and squeezed his fingers. A sense of ruefulness surrounded her, so he leaned closer and whispered in her ear. "Thank you."

Even if he wasn't the one petting the pup, it did do his heart good to see Nimi well.

Amal left after only an hour in the commons after all the children had their chance to pet a puppy, most for the first time in their lives. Freja might be vexed with her, but none of the other adults had been particularly surprised. Jan suggested that she warn them next time so they could keep the incident secret.

Amal was pleased she'd been able to do something that pleased Dalyan so much. He usually seemed content with, or at least *accepting* of, his lot with them, but few things made him as happy as that silly three-legged puppy. After all he'd been through in the last week or so, she'd wanted to give him that.

Nimi, on the other hand, wasn't content to sleep in her basket after all that excitement. Before going to bed, Amal had dutifully taken the puppy outside, waited until the pup peed, and then praised the beast accordingly. Even so, Nimi seemed no more inclined to stay in the basket for Amal than she had for Nohr. After several repetitions of getting up, putting the puppy back in the basket, and climbing back into bed, Amal gave in. She picked up the pup and put it on the bed with her. "You do realize you can't get down from here, don't you?"

Nimi pawed at the blankets for a moment and then settled, eyeing Amal.

"Your master has a lot to answer for," Amal told her.

The puppy's ears pricked up, but she settled her chin on her paw.

Amal sighed and turned down the lamp on her nightstand.

It was nice to sleep in her own bed. She could stretch out as much as she wanted, one of the perquisites of having quarters in the Keep—the beds were bigger. Even when shared with a puppy. She lay there for a time, thinking of all the things she'd let lapse in the last several days.

She didn't know how much longer before Dalyan gained Freja's permission to do normal things again, like climbing the grand stair up to the Keep. She hoped it wasn't too long. Then again, perhaps her monthly would come and go by then, and not interfere.

She had no idea how Dalyan felt about things like that. It hadn't come up before.

Nimi yipped softly and Amal absently reached out to scratch the puppy's head, a cold stone of worry building in the pit of her stomach.

Her last monthly had come *before* she'd taken him down into the steam shaft to protect him from detection at the new moon. Easy to remember—she'd been relieved it was over because she knew they would be in close quarters down there. The month before that it had come while she and her guard traveled from the capital to the glacier, making the trip more annoying than normal for her. She'd been irritable and tired when they'd found Dalyan, but that had been the last day—the day after the new moon.

When they took Dalyan down into the Fortress to remove the device from his head, it had been three days before the new moon. And that was ... seven days ago? Six?

She'd lost track of time, but the new moon had definitely passed already. Then again, the last two weeks had been so stressful that she might simply have skipped this month. That had happened when Anton died. *Maybe that's all it is.*

Freja became nauseated in the mornings; that was how Freja always knew. But that hadn't happened when Amal was pregnant with Sander. Her main symptom had been an inexplicable weepiness that amused Anton terribly.

Amal scratched the puppy's head.

Freja had noticed. Freja kept track of things like that as a part of her position as Second. She had a fair idea when each of the women in the yeargroup had their monthly. Amal flashed back to the memory of Freja coming to examine Dalyan and then asking whether *she* needed anything. Because Freja knew she should have needed supplies for her monthly, but hadn't asked for any.

And Freja had been trying to get pregnant for months now, so she was jealous.

Amal realized that tears were slipping down the side of her face.

This isn't what I planned.

CHAPTER 6

AN HOUR LATER, Amal had managed to quell her tears. She set one of the sentries to watching Nimi and made her way down the grand stair to the Fortress. Once inside, she headed back for Six Down. She didn't want to have this conversation, but it was necessary. When she reached the yeargroup's hall, though, she found only Magnus there, schedules spread out on a table before him.

Despite not being closely related, Magnus shared Jan's coloring, fair skin and dark hair. He had a less noticeable appearance, though—Jan was taller and broader and shaggier in all ways—and thus Magnus was often over-looked. He was, however, the First of the yeargroup. He was the most competitive of them, with a sharp mind and an eye for detail. This was part of his responsibility as First, to make certain that everyone served their duties and still made time for their family. And at times that meant *he* had to go without sleep.

Amal joined him at the table. "Do you know which room Freja's in tonight?"

Magnus chuckled. "Normally I would say I have no idea, but lately she's been going back to the infirmary after the children all get to bed."

That was the first Amal had heard of that. "Why?"

"To study what's in the Fortress' memories, I think." Magnus set aside the schedule he was working on. "The lack of sleep is making her irritable. I hope she'll cut it back to more normal hours soon."

Amal wasn't sure if Magnus meant that as a subtle push to get her to talk to Freja. She did, however, wonder if that was why Magnus was out here working on schedules when he normally would have been asleep—because Freja was shirking her duties as a Second. Amal rose. "I'll talk to her about it."

"She's already mentioned being taken off your guard rotation," he added. "I thought you should know."

As she walked back toward the main hallway of Six Down, Amal felt a sinking in her stomach. She had to push down the desire to cry again. Lately it had felt like she was losing her closest friend, and that scared her. Freja had been a constant in her life for so long that Amal wasn't sure what she would do without her. The other women in her yeargroup were her friends as well, but none of them knew her the way Freja did.

She counted to stifle her emotions as she climbed the central steps back up to One Down. It helped a bit, but a sentry passing in the stairwell whistled softly at her anyway. She nodded in apology and kept climbing.

When she reached the infirmary, she didn't see Freja anywhere. A young woman sat at a desk, her face lowered as she studied a book. Her black uniform bore the trim markings of an infirmary student. Amal coughed to alert the young woman.

She sprang to her feet. "Lady Amal, how can I help?"

"I'm only looking for Freja," Amal said. "Can you tell me where she is?"

"The new room," the young woman said. "I'll show you."

Amal followed her, wondering if she was just a seventeen. She seemed so very young. "New room?"

The student glanced over her shoulder as she walked Amal toward the infirmary's offices. "Oh, where the infirmarians can talk with the Fortress. It's not new. It was closed off before."

"Ah, we call those control rooms," Amal told her.

The young woman's lips pursed. "So, you knew it was there?"

"In the abstract," Amal said. "I've never gone looking for it." There were at least two control rooms on every level of the Fortress, but most of them had been walled off for centuries. Signe must have decided to have the wall opened in the infirmary, probably to keep Freja from spending all her time on Ten Down in their control room.

"I see," the young woman said, a faint touch of irritation seeping past her control. She pointed down the hallway. Amal had visited this hall a thousand times, hunting for Freja. Where there had been blank wall before, now there was a door. *Yes, that has to be Signe's work.*

Amal thanked the annoyed young woman and knocked on the door. After a long moment, the door opened inward. Freja had her mouth open as if ready to rebuke her visitor, but sighed when she saw Amal there.

"I thought it was Luna again," Freja snapped. "She keeps asking me questions about her reading, instead of just reading the damned book."

Behind Freja, Amal spotted a chair similar to the one they had in the control room on Ten Down. This room had several screens on the walls, all blank at the moment. "I didn't know that Signe had opened . . ."

"Unhid it," Freja said pointedly. "Not opened. It wasn't like we've just been ignoring this door, Amal. There was no door."

"I know." Amal wasn't sure how to proceed. "I wanted to talk to you," she finally said.

Freja's eyes flicked from her head to her toes. "So I was right."

When she'd been pregnant with Sander, Freja had known before she had. "How do I know? For certain, I mean?"

"You're late, aren't you?"

"But Dalyan is supposed to be sterile." He'd told her that the first night they'd been together, and he'd believed every word of it. "He said he was created . . ."

Freja grabbed her arm, dragged her into the control room, and closed the door behind them. "Yes, I know. Sit down."

There was a second chair in the control room, one that lacked the pads on the arm rests that allowed Horn to recognize her. Amal sat there while Freja leaned against one of the walls.

"You remember what you told us about the Originals? That we're descended from them? How could they be sterile, then?"

"Then he lied? No, the Cince lied to him."

"Neither," Freja said. "I talked to the Fortress about it. I'm unclear on a few of the words it's using, but the Originals *were* all created sterile."

"Then how . . ."

"The question is why," Freja said. "Why create a sterile populace when you want them to reproduce?"

Usually I'm the one giving the history lectures. "And?"

"If you were going to take a yeargroup—all eighteens, let's say—and put them in a new place, would you want them to have children nine months later? Because I assure you, that's how long it would take. Eighteens aren't going to refrain from having sex."

"What's your point?"

"There wouldn't be any carers, no adults to help them with the children, no adults to help deliver the babies."

"But they would have *knowledge*. Like Dalyan was supposed to."

Freja crossed her arms over her chest. "Do you think he's ready to deliver a baby?"

Amal shut her mouth. She had no idea whether he would know what to do.

"Exactly," Freja said. "They didn't want the Originals to have children. Not for a while. That's the key. They put a device into their patterns, like the one the Cince put in Dalyan's head, only this one was in the abdominal wall. It leached chemicals into their systems that made them all sterile. And over time, it dissolved."

"How long?" Amal asked.

"Five to seven years," Freja said, "with six being the norm."

Six years. Then Dalyan's would have dissolved about the time that the Cince had sent him toward Larossa on his mission to find Salonen Fortress. Amal licked her lips. Had that timing been incidental? "I see."

"So as far as he knows, he is sterile," Freja said with a shake of her head. "You want to be the one to tell him? Or should I bring it up?"

Amal wanted to cover her face with her hands.

How do I tell him about this? What would Dalyan say? He'd once told her he hated that the choice about having children had been taken from him. That didn't mean he *wanted* children.

And she'd told him she didn't plan to have a child with him. She remembered saying those words. She wasn't even sure how she felt about this herself.

"Can you let me think about it for a day or two?" she asked.

"Fine." Freja didn't look pleased, but Amal could sense that her reaction came mostly from concern. Freja never liked to put anything off.

"I'm worried," Amal said then. "I worry that you're angry with me. I don't want to lose you. You know you're ..." Without warning, she started to cry. Amal pressed one hand over her mouth to hold it in.

"Oh, Hel's tits," Freja snapped. She fished through her jacket pockets until she found a handkerchief. She shoved that into Amal's free hand.

Amal dabbed at her nose and then her eyes. "I'm sorry."

"That was what tipped me off," Freja said. "With Sander, you cried all the time at first."

Amal took a deep breath, pushed down her worry, and handed back the handkerchief. "I'm sorry."

"You've said that twice. Some women cry when they're pregnant. Better than vomiting everywhere, believe me."

Amal laughed; Freja would know.

Freja sat down in the control chair. "Look, I know I've been snappish with you lately, but there's a lot going on. I haven't been getting much sleep, and Laurits is being difficult, and ... yes, I'm still not pregnant. But I've been thinking that with everything else happening now, that may be a good thing. Learning what the Fortress has to tell us, that needs to be my priority now. And yes, I'm upset that the Oathbreakers kept so much from us, and a lot of the time that means I'm upset with you. But you're my best friend, and best friends don't abandon each other."

Amal took Freja's hand. "Thank you."

"Just ... be patient with my moods. Things aren't going as smoothly in my life as I'd like, either."

Amal stretched her feet out in front of her. "Sorry about the puppy."

"What were you thinking?" Freja asked laughingly. "Now all the children want to know when you'll bring her back."

They spent another hour there, chatting about Freja's worries for a change. That left Amal feeling oddly better. At least she wasn't the only one with complications in her life. She made her way back up to the Keep, collected Nimi from the sentry who'd been watching her, and returned to her own bed.

Freja was likely right. She was probably pregnant. Now she just had to decide what that meant for her future.

Dalyan sat up straighter when Signe came to visit him that morning. The woman had a very stern visage, the sort that made him want to admit he'd done something wrong. Even if he hadn't.

She'd brought a satchel of books with her, apparently to begin his tutelage as an engineer. "If you're going to sew on the trim," she said, "you have to do the work."

"Yes, ma'am."

Sewing on the trim was surely a reference to the soutache trim each member of the Family sewed onto their uniform jackets to indicate their posting and rank. He was only now beginning to recognize the different patterns: bars across the chest meant one of the military postings, chevrons were for fightmasters, ornate chest swirls were for carers, including the infirmarians like Freja, and a geometric pattern on the chest—like stair steps that folded back over themselves—that was engineers. And he had already learned that when the time came, he was expected to sew on the trim himself.

With my own hands. That wasn't going to go well.

Signe heaved the books onto the sofa next to her and regarded him across the table, pale eyes narrowed. "I've been talking to Elin, and she says it's completely possible for you to have knowledge without memories attached to it."

He hadn't doubted that. "I see."

"She explained it as in remembering almonds," Signe pronounced. "Do you know how almonds taste?"

"Yes, of course."

Mikks dragged over a chair and sat down at the table with them.

Signe gazed at him with one raised eyebrow. "Are you not on duty?"

"Amal is in her office," Mikks said, "so I'm loose until lunchtime."

"Are you thinking about trying this again?" Signe asked him.

Mikks eyed the books on the table. "You need people, don't you?"

She regarded Mikks with narrowed eyes, and Dalyan thought he could sense guarded approval from her. Had Mikks wanted to be an engineer at some point?

The old woman turned back to Dalyan. "Where did you first eat almonds?"

Dalyan thought back. "In the capital, in a Larossan restaurant. There was a cake with sliced almonds on top."

"Was that the first time ever?" Signe asked.

"I think so."

"How did you know they were almonds?"

He'd been created with memories that let him dress himself, feed himself, and care for himself. But he'd also had a head *full* of details that seemed to crop up unexpectedly. "I just knew."

"That was her point. People have two kinds of memory, she told me: the memory where you learn things, and the memory where you tell yourself stories. The restaurant and eating the cake there—that's the second kind, a story that you can relate. The first type is the facts, the learning, the habits, but the second gives us a framework to put them all together. Without that, we don't know where knowledge comes from, and can't find it when we want it."

"That makes sense." He'd tried to explain his memory not matching his knowledge before in terms of weaving— although one thing he apparently didn't know was the proper terms for making fabric.

"Since you do remember events from *after* you were created," Signe added, "it's not damage to your brain that's causing the lack of old memories. It had to be a flaw in the Cince's creation process."

"Did the Founders *intend* for the others like me to have . . . the second kind of memories?"

"Yes. Otherwise the Originals wouldn't have known what they were supposed to do to set up a civilization. They were each taught specific duties before their memories were inscribed into their patterns, so they could get to work as soon as they were created."

She could talk to her Fortress about these things, and it apparently had a very long memory. That meant he *had* come out flawed, even if he didn't feel defective. "In some ways, it's easier not to have the memories, I think. I have that one dream, and I know that something terrible happened to him—the Founder I'm based on—but I can't remember what, so I don't have to live with the pain of it."

Signe peered at him. "The dream you have sometimes? Amal told me that you have a dream of running down a hallway, and you call out for Katja, but you don't know who that is."

There was *one* event he remembered of that man's life, his single flicker of old memory, relived only in dreams. The emotion tangled with that dream was one of anguish and loss, and Dalyan tried not to dwell on that. "That happened to a man who lived hundreds of years ago, ma'am. His life. His loss. It's not mine, and I don't want to know more."

Mikks sat back, lips pressed into a thin line. He understood all too well how memories could haunt someone. He held his peace, though.

Signe knotted her thin hands together. "Your lack of memories, though, means you don't have a framework to tie your knowledge together. Think of it as walking into a room full of people where you know each person's name, but have no idea if any of them know each other, or what their skills and professions are. How do you know with whom to talk with first?"

If he answered with his first impulse, he would say to speak to the closest person first. That wasn't Signe's point, though.

Supposedly, the man on whom he was based had specialized in disaster recovery—making decisions about what could be saved, and what *should* be saved. Priorities. That was why the Horn elders had wanted the device out of his head, because they hoped its removal would awaken his missing memories and allow him, someday, to determine whether Salonen Fortress could be salvaged. In their eyes, that was his great value.

"So I have to relearn all the connections?"

"Yes," Signe said.

"Any one of us could do *that*," Mikks inserted.

"No, you can't," Signe said. "Or rather, not with the speed that he can. He already knows all the players."

Mikks considered that, his lips twisted to one side, as if he thought it a challenge. "Hmm."

Dalyan gazed again at the pile of books Signe had brought him. "So will those help me make the connections?"

"That's what I'm hoping," she said with a quick nod.

CHAPTER 7

AMAL HAD RISEN earlier than she wanted that morning because her bedmate began yipping. The strange noise dragged her from a sound sleep, and she blearily realized the puppy was trying to get down from the bed. And then it occurred to Amal *why* Nimi wanted off the bed.

She jumped up, thrust her feet into her house shoes, and tucked the pup under one arm as she tried to wrap a throw about her bare chest. She managed to get out of her room and halfway across the main hall before the puppy lost control, leaving Amal with a dampened throw and very little dignity in front of the handful of sentries in the hall at that hour.

It's rather like having a baby. She sighed, took the pup out to the terrace, and once Nimi was done, carried her back to the bedroom with the damp throw still wrapped around her. *Only a baby would stay in the basket if I put her there.*

Once she'd cleaned herself and the puppy to her satisfaction, Amal had decided she might as well get to work for the day. She dressed and, after asking the sentry on duty in the hallway to look after Nimi until Eldana came to collect the pup, headed down toward her office in the

Fortress. She sternly reminded herself to keep her attention on her paperwork, not her possible pregnancy, and managed to work through the tithe preparations Gyda had left for her.

A few hours later, though, she'd begun to wonder if anyone would find a nap suspicious. She might go down to Six Down and see how Dalyan was faring. Or go back up to the Keep to her own bed. *Tempting.*

Unfortunately, that hope was dashed when Laurits showed up. He barely waited for her to acknowledge him before stepping inside and closing her office door. Amal rose, prepared to dump him on the floor again, but he held up his hands and kept his distance.

"Look, I know we didn't communicate well when we first met . . ."

"I'm not interested, Laurits," Amal said. "I won't change my mind."

"I know that," he said. "I don't want a contract with you, either."

Amal sat back down. "Truly?"

Laurits sighed and shook his head. "I didn't say that well. May I sit down?"

Amal gestured toward one of the wooden chairs. "Then why are you here?"

"I'd like to discuss the situation. I've seen you in the infirmary, so I know."

That last bit came out smoothly, but Amal could sense sulkiness behind his words. She pressed her lips together, wondering how the elders ever thought she'd agree to contracting with a man this young. "In the infirmary?"

"With the Salonen man. I saw how you are with him, so I don't know why the elders think you would accept anyone else."

Ah, Laurits was annoyed with the *elders*—probably his

mother most of all—because they were pushing him to pursue a doomed relationship. How much pressure was he under? "Then you understand why I'm not interested."

"Yes. But they're going to keep trying," he said. "If not me, there will be someone else. Some of them don't like the idea of the Salonen man influencing you."

Amal drew in a deep breath, trying hard not to be vexed with Laurits. This wasn't his fault. It annoyed her, though, that the elders had wanted Dalyan under their control so badly that they would risk bringing him into the Fortress to cut a device out of his head, yet turned their backs on him when he didn't regain the memories they believed he had. Dalyan was more than just a storehouse of memories.

And if they learn I'm pregnant with his child? What would they say then? "I can see that."

Laurits' eyes shifted to one side, a tinge of desperation accompanying that glance. "I know my mother and uncle both pushed for me to be put in this group—the special infirmarian positions—so that you would have to interact with me, but Elin agreed because she knows I'm the best candidate for this job."

Amal sat back. *Laurits wants to be taken seriously.*

When she was his age, she'd suddenly become Lady Horn. She'd stood in front of the senate, terrified that they would look at her and only see a child. But the king had stood with her, making it clear to the senate that he expected them to treat her with respect. She'd worried that the elders, the trade groups, and the town council wouldn't take her seriously. Grandfather and Jan had eased her way with the elders, and Gyda kept her on solid footing with the provincial business leaders. Didn't she owe Laurits the same chance?

"Why are you the best candidate for the work?" she asked.

His chin lifted. "I'm smart. I'm learning the language quickly, and I'm willing to work with Freja to help Elin make decisions. I think I can balance out Freja's lack of caution."

Amal licked her lips, holding in prickles of irritation. "Lack of caution?"

Laurits gave a short, bitter laugh. "I went down with Theo and I *saw* the memories the Fortress has of Sorenson. What happened there is terrifying. But Freja wants to dig into the Fortress' memories and start using them to treat our patients. To have the Fortress create medicines and tools and use them without our properly understanding them."

That's exactly what Freja would do. Amal let her vexation flow away. She grasped now why Laurits was here, and this was too important to allow his past idiocy to get in the way.

"We don't even truly comprehend the *language*," he went on, "so how can we understand the ramifications of what we're studying? It's a dangerous path to be on. Surely you see that."

She held up her hand to stop him. That was part of being an Oathbreaker—learning that knowledge wasn't always safe. "I understand. What do you want me to do about it?"

A flash of surprise came from him, quickly buried. "Freja doesn't listen to me. I think that's partly out of loyalty to you and him. Can you talk to her? Tell her that I wasn't chosen because of the contract thing."

That was, in truth, Elin's responsibility, not hers, but if Freja believed Elin was biased, she might not take Elin's words at face value. "I can talk to her."

"That's all I ask," he said, rising. He touched the latch of her office door, but paused. "If . . . someone wanted to cause problems for the Salonen man, I would think that his adoption papers might go astray. End up lost."

"His name is Dalyan," Amal said. "And thanks for the warning."

"That goes for any other kind of contract, as well," Laurits hinted, still holding the door latch. "I don't think anyone would hurt him, but short of that?"

Amal rose. "Tell me."

A frisson of fear flared around him, as if he'd realized he'd stepped into dangerous territory. But he straightened and said, "He's a foreigner and therefore can be picked up by the military. If he *is* adopted, he'll fall under the jurisdiction of the Daujom. A simple letter sent to the right people in the capital would be enough to be rid of him."

"He's a vital witness in a matter of treason," she ground out.

"That's why he's still here," Laurits said. "And no one wants to risk involving the Larossan military because they'd learn things we don't want them to."

"We?"

"The Six Families. I meant that in general." Laurits shook his head. "Still, taking him to the capital is taking him right to the Daujom."

Amal nodded and watched as Laurits let himself out of her office. She hated to think that anyone in the Horn Family would want to be rid of Dalyan badly enough that they would turn him over to the king's investigators.

She sat back in her chair. In the very first days, when they'd found Dalyan trespassing on the glacier, she'd considered turning him over to the king to deal with. She hadn't wanted the complication of having a prisoner in the Keep. She may have said that aloud to Jan, but surely not in Dalyan's presence. And that was months ago, before she'd known him. Now that she did, she was going to do whatever was necessary to protect him.

There is one sure way to keep the Daujom from taking Dalyan from us.

After promising to bring a second set of books for Mikks later, Signe left them, and he and Mikks sorted out the books on the table. Signe hadn't told him which books to start with, but Dalyan had the feeling that was a test of sorts—to see whether he could recognize which books covered the simplest material.

The books were all in the Horn language, meant for the Oathbreakers. Fortunately, at some point in the past an Oathbreaker had translated the sentences into Anvarrid, writing the Anvarrid words in the edges and between the lines. It was almost illegible, but enough that they could make out the gist of the subject. "This is what the engineers have to work with?"

"Yes," Mikks said, nodding ruefully. "Most of the engineers never learn Horn. Or if they do, I never got far enough to know of it."

Dalyan peered at him more closely as he picked through the books. Most of the time Mikks held his emotions even tighter than Freja did, meaning that Dalyan didn't have the crutch of being able to sense how he felt. "Did you want to be an engineer?"

Mikks selected one of the other books, one about walls. "I . . . yes. I gave up before. I was having black episodes. I gave up on *everything* for a while, so I lost my place."

That was one of the things he and Mikks had in common—they both had times when they couldn't trust what was in their heads. Mikks had thoughts he knew weren't his own, ones that he called his *shadows*. "That must have been difficult."

Mikks shrugged. "That was back when I was first having problems. I was terrified that I would turn into my father. If not for Jan and Nohr and Freja, I probably would have. But they eventually drew me out of my despair, and I got my feet back under me."

To most people, Mikks seemed careless and chaotic. In Dalyan's experience, though, Mikks was rigorously disciplined about certain things in his life. If he decided he wanted something, he would likely succeed. "It would be nice to have someone to discuss these things with."

"You have Amal," Mikks pointed out.

"Not the same," Dalyan returned.

"Well, apparently, you'll learn it all much faster than me." Mikks sat back and frowned at the books. "I've read the one on imps. You should start there."

"Imps?"

"The force that moves water and air and light through the walls," Mikks said. "There's no term in Anvarrid that matches the old words, so we use the term *imps*."

An imp was, if Dalyan recalled folklore correctly, a tiny demon. He should have made that connection because the term for electrocution was imp-bitten. Amal had complained once about Anvarrid being a terrible language for materials, and this was a prime example of that. "I'm going to have to learn to speak Horn, aren't I?"

"*Ja*," Mikks said. "The good part is that the alphabet is the same, more or less. The pronunciation is *not*."

"*Ja* is yes?"

"Very good," Mikks said. "Because our Fortress is mostly awake, we hear it talk from time to time, so we all know a few words. The Horn are all Oathbreakers, in our small way."

Amal found Grandfather in his office. When not keeping her from making mistakes, he worked in the records office, on the same hall as the quartermaster's office. The office was a spacious room that held walls of files, the lights always turned up high. The Family kept paperwork on everything, so this was only *one* of the caches of wood pulp she knew about, but this office handled records of birth and death . . . and contracts.

When he spotted her entering the main records room, Grandfather waved her over to his small office in the back. She came to join him, enjoying the smells of old paper and glue. "I need to talk to you."

He closed his office door. "You're not here to socialize?"

"Sadly not," she said. "I wondered if Dalyan's adoption papers had been filed yet."

He settled on the edge of his desk. "No. They went missing somewhere between Sidana and Milas signing them, and here."

So Laurits was right. Amal pressed her lips together. "What should I do about that?"

"Nothing," Grandfather said. "I actually had Jan carry through two copies, so I have a backup."

Amal wanted to cry with relief. Trust Grandfather to be two steps ahead. "So what do I do?"

"Nothing yet," he said. "This is a power play by a handful of the elders who want their way above the will of the majority. If we have to circumvent it, their actions will become moot and they'll avoid trouble, but if we let it play out, they might be discredited."

"We're planning to go to Noikinos as soon as Dalyan is healthy enough to travel. I'd rather take steps to keep him safe *before* we get there."

"And someone arrests him. I understand."

"So . . . what paperwork do I need to make him part of the House of Horn?" It was the one thing that would protect Dalyan from the Daujom—if he was an Anvarrid citizen.

Grandfather reflected an air of smugness, as if he'd guessed she would ask that. "You'll need paperwork from the House law firm in Evaryanos. Then two-thirds of the members of the House will need to sign off on it, and send it to the senate in Noikinos for approval. They are unlikely to refuse it."

They would travel through Evaryanos on the way to Noikinos. It was their first comfortable stop, since the House of Horn owned an estate there. And currently there were only two members of the House of Horn—her and Jan. But the paperwork could still go missing between their signatures and the senate, and they senate could refuse.

"What if something happens between when the paperwork is filed, and when it's approved?"

"He's out of luck in that case," Grandfather said. "But of course, there's a simpler way to get him Anvarrid legal status once the adoption is final."

That was what she'd been thinking. "Will the adoption paperwork show up soon?"

"I can make sure it does on a specific date."

"As in . . . before we get to Noikinos?"

"Yes. I want to hold off for a while, but I can promise that."

"If I had a contract, and he signs it, will that hold up?"

"You want that contract signed and dated before there's trouble, but that should hold up."

Amal let out a pent breath. She was very glad that Grandfather was on her side. "Then can you get me a contract?"

Grandfather smiled. "Jan already has one."

Dalyan's head had begun to ache, likely because he'd been squinting to make out the handwriting that overlay the words on the page. He sat back and pinched the bridge of his nose.

He felt better every day, but he knew better than to think he was back to normal. He still tired more easily than he liked, and the headaches came far too often. One advantage of being young was that he would heal better than the old man he'd been based on. *I just have to be patient.*

Mikks had moved to one of the sofas and sat reading there. When he saw Dalyan move, he said, "Amal didn't send for me, so she must have skipped lunch."

She did have a tendency to work without stop. But Dalyan had been so engrossed in his book that he'd skipped lunch as well.

The book was a basic primer on electricity. Dalyan struggled with the Anvarrid terminology for a time, trying to come up with a better description for the concept he had in his mind. He knew what electricity was . . . he simply couldn't find Anvarrid words to describe it. Amal was correct; Anvarrid was a terrible language for this sort of thing.

There was no other option than to teach himself Horn. So he'd spent the first quarter hour puzzling at the context for words . . . until he discovered a glossary in the back of the volume he was reading. Soon he had a few Horn words in his head, at least the spelling of them. The pronunciation would require someone's help. Once he had some context, though, he could read more of the book, looking past the Anvarrid words to the Horn ones.

"How much Horn can you speak?" he asked Mikks then.

Mikks shrugged. "Just a few words here and there."

But the pronunciation rules must be the same for given names as for the language, so that gave him a few clues to start with. "I haven't eaten lunch, either," Dalyan recalled. "Have you?"

Mikks leaned over to peer toward the main hallway. When Dalyan did likewise, he could see an older man standing there, his uniform marked with an engineer's trim. The man held a slender book in his hands.

"Come on in," Mikks called to him.

The man stepped over the guideline and came down the twenty-sevens hall to join them. "Mikks," he said, nodding. Then he turned to Dalyan. "I'm Theo, one of the Oathbreakers."

Dalyan introduced himself, aware it was probably unnecessary since the man had clearly come to meet him. He invited the newcomer to sit, and Mikks came back to the table to join them.

Once settled, Theo said, "Signe has gone on to bed, but she told me you wanted to read some of the early texts. She suggested I bring you this one, see if it might be easier to read."

He held out a book, opened to a page full of text. Dalyan took the slender volume and glanced at the content. It was an elementary text on thermodynamics, comparing the idea to the generation of heat via energy conversion at a cellular level throughout the human body, which was then either rejected as excess body heat or held in by the insulating action of clothing.

Dalyan blinked at the words, sensing a surreal shift in the world about him.

The words in front of him weren't Anvarrid.

They weren't Horn, either.

"This is my native language," he said—not too loud for fear the words would vanish. "I can *read* this."

Theo snorted. "Father Winter always laughs at us for our stupidity. We should have tried that a week ago."

"Where did you get this?" he asked without looking up.

"Signe asked the Fortress whether it held texts in the Salonen tongue. Turns out, the Fortress has access to the entire Salonen library, so we asked it to make a book for you."

Dalyan was afraid to look away from the page for fear it might disappear. "You mean . . . you can make books I can read?"

Theo sat back, crossed his arms over his chest, and exuded satisfaction. "The great machines can do things other than repair the Fortress, as you well know. It's simply a matter of diverting time and resources."

"Can you produce a set in Anvarrid?" Mikks asked, a sharp spike of concern rising in him.

"Unfortunately, no," Theo said. "Anvarrid isn't in the Fortress' memories."

"I have trouble believing that no one has ever tried to teach the Fortress Anvarrid," Mikks complained.

"I'm sure someone has," Theo said, "just not *here*. You can, however, ask the other Oathbreakers when you get to the capital. Perhaps they have something better than ours."

Mikks slid the book out of Dalyan's grasp. "What in Hel's name? What kind of language is this?"

"It's the Salonen language," Theo said. "Nothing like Horn."

Mikks passed the book back to Dalyan. "Can you read that aloud?"

Dalyan looked down at the passage, trying to figure out a way to translate the complex words. "It's talking about making heat. How you either keep it or lose it."

Mikks tapped the table with two fingers. "No, I meant can you read those words *aloud?* I wanted to know what *that* sounds like."

Dalyan stared at the first sentence in that section and . . . nothing came to mind. He was looking at letters, and he could try to pronounce those letters as the Anvarrid did. Or he could try to sound like Horn. He knew that at least the *j* sound was the same, because Jukka started with the same sound as Jan. But . . .

"I have no idea what it's supposed to sound like," he admitted.

Theo nodded. "Signe said that might be the case. Just because you recognize how the words look, that doesn't mean you know how they sound. Ears and eyes, not the same."

In fact, now that Dalyan thought about it, he couldn't even be sure that *Jukka* was pronounced the way Amal said it. She'd likely pronounced it as a Horn would, using Horn pronunciation rules for a name that looked similar. But Anvarrid showed that the same letters didn't always mean the same sounds.

Theo rose and patted Dalyan on the shoulder. "We'll try to get some books made up for you over the next few days. When we have time."

Mikks frowned across the table at Dalyan as Theo walked away. "I guess I won't be able to keep up after all."

Is that what he thinks? "I have no doubt you will," Dalyan said firmly. "I can't speak a word of Horn, and to be honest, translating this into Anvarrid would be very difficult. I think the best way to do this would be to bounce it back and forth between us."

"You'll be carrying me half the time," Mikks said with a shake of his head.

"That's the best way to learn. If I can't teach it to you, then I don't understand it well enough, either."

Mikks pushed down his anxiety. "If the other Families don't have any Anvarrid translations . . ."

Dalyan waited, wondering if Mikks was going to give up.

". . . then I might try my hand at making some," Mikks finished. "Why not have a simpler Anvarrid translation to start with, and then look at this mess if you need more detail?" He nodded toward the book he'd been reading with its scrawled, handwritten notes.

Dalyan smiled, relieved that Mikks was still willing to work with him. After a couple of minutes, the rumbling of his stomach reminded him of the topic they'd been on before Theo arrived, and Mikks offered to go fetch some lunch for both of them.

Once Mikks had left him alone in the commons room, Dalyan rubbed his hands over his face. Then he gazed up at the gyrfalcon patterns running along the upper walls, trying to sort out his reaction.

He'd had doubts.

He'd had doubts all along that he was truly what the Horn thought he was: a man recreated centuries after his death. Dalyan hadn't been sure of his link to the long-dead Jukka Salonen. It had seemed *plausible,* but not real.

Until now. He could read Jukka Salonen's language.

Now he had proof—irrefutable proof.

He *was* one of the Originals, just as old Signe believed.

CHAPTER 8

AMAL DIDN'T TAKE the puppy with her when she went down to Six Below to join the twenty-sevens after dinner. During the afternoon, Gyda had hinted that the elders were displeased—no one could keep something like a puppy secret in the Fortress—and Amal figured she needed as little ill will as possible for now. Coming down the central stair, she ran into Freja.

"Just in time for the big show," Freja told her. "I'm going to take his stitches out."

Freja had a satchel over her shoulder, so she must have stopped in the infirmary after eating in the mess on One Down. She continued jogging down the steps, making it difficult for Amal to respond. She waited until they reached Six Down instead, where she could walk abreast with Freja. "I talked with Laurits today," she said. "He *came* to talk to me."

Freja cast a glance at her. "Was he romantic?"

"No," Amal said. "We had a pleasant talk. He knows where I stand. I know where he stands. Everything is fine."

Freja stopped in the hallway. "Fine?"

"He badly wants to be an Oathbreaker. He's willing to leave me alone if I can talk you into cooperating with him."

Freja blew out a vexed breath and let Amal feel a sharp stab of annoyance. "I don't like him."

Freja started walking again, so Amal trotted along with her.

"I understand," Amal said. "But he thinks the two of you would complement each other if you worked together. He thinks he'd know when to be cautious and you'd know when to jump ahead." That wasn't what Laurits had said, but she didn't mind stretching the truth if it would sweeten Freja's disposition toward the young man.

"By cautious he means wait another few centuries before trying *anything*," Freja snapped.

"The Oathbreakers have always had to be cautious," Amal reminded her. "We've always known that anything . . ."

"I am not talking about the Cince," Freja said. "I don't care what they do. I'm thinking of my children, Amal."

"So are we," Amal inserted. "We have to think of the long-term ramifications of anything before we experiment with it."

"Don't tell me the Oathbreakers haven't done anything for convenience before," Freja said, jaw clenched. "Are the ice screws a *necessity*? Did the Oathbreaker who pulled the idea for those out of the Fortress' memories know for certain something bad wouldn't happen? That no Cince would ever get their hands on one? Because there are three sitting out on the glacier right now, waiting to be taken."

Amal held in her arguments. Freja was right; the last time they'd crossed the glacier, they'd left three of the explosive ice screws—items that shouldn't exist in Larossa— behind. "We used those to save Mikks. We had to."

Freja stepped closer. "Then why not *this*? Mikks is hearing things, his shadows again, just like his father. What if Hedda inherits that? What if the Fortress can create a medicine to get rid of those voices? Shouldn't we find it to save him? To save my daughter?"

That had always been the problem—the length that infirmarians would go to save a single life. The Oathbreakers had long been charged with not allowing the lives of individuals to take precedence over the safety of the Families as a whole.

"I understand," Amal said. "I do. I just want you to be appropriately cautious. If you can make a valid case to the Oathbreakers, don't you think they would listen to. . . ?"

Freja swept away that question. "Did they let your father die? Your brother and Anton? Was that influenza something that could have been stopped if the Fortress had helped them?"

"No," she said. "It was too fast. The Founders never defeated basic human frailties. We have to accept that they had *some* limitations."

Freja's lips thinned, but then she shook her head. "I have to try."

"I know," Amal said. "Just be willing to listen to him. Try to compromise." She was asking a lot of Freja. Laurits was far behind Freja in training, and she would constantly be slowing down to help him. Freja nodded once, even though she didn't let go of the irritation that she clutched around herself. "Thank you," Amal said.

Freja walked on. "If I change my mind, I'll let you know."

"Fair enough."

They reached the twenty-sevens' hall with its gyrfalcon motifs and stepped over the guideline. Amal spotted Dalyan immediately, sitting with Mikks at a large table, Jan and Magnus standing over them looking down at a book. Dalyan glanced up and caught her eye, a strange expression on his face.

"Mikks decided that he would train with Dalyan," Freja told her.

That was the first Amal had heard of that idea. "Has he been thinking about it?"

Freja headed toward the group of men. "Yes. He just didn't want to tell you until he made up his mind."

Just as Freja hadn't told her she was thinking of leaving the guard. She'd had to hear that from Magnus. Amal followed, worrying at that thought. *Have I lost touch with my yeargroup?*

"Well, clear a space for me," Freja told the men. "I want to take those stitches out."

Magnus obligingly moved out of her way, and she drew up a chair behind Dalyan's. For his part, Dalyan seemed startled by her declaration, but didn't argue.

Jan picked up the slender volume they'd all been staring at and handed it to Amal. "He can read this."

She looked down at familiar letters strung together into unfamiliar words, then raised her eyes to meet Dalyan's. "This is the Salonen language?"

"Yes," he said, and then flinched when Freja did something with her little scissors. "Theo brought it to me, and it appears that I can recognize it when I see it. Not speak it, though."

Freja pushed gently to get him to tilt his head to one side.

"Ask about the puppy," Mikks inserted with a sharp grin.

That was addressed to her. "The puppy?"

Dalyan's cheeks flushed, chagrin spilling about him now, not related to Freja's movement. "I . . . recognized the word *nimi* once I saw it written."

Amal sat on the couch across from their table so he could see her without twisting. "What does it mean?"

"Name," he said. "I was trying to think ... ow! I was trying to think of a name for the puppy and that was what I came up with."

Amal had to hold in her laughter. "You literally named your puppy *Name*?"

"I named her Nimi," he insisted, "which happens to mean *name*."

"Don't move," Freja said. "And you didn't recognize the word then?"

"No." Dalyan flinched again. "There was no context."

Freja sat back, plucked something out of her satchel, and dabbed at his scalp.

Mikks grinned at Amal. "So now you know not to let him name ..."

Amal felt her mouth drop open.

Mikks' eyes flicked toward Dalyan and—after a pause that went on a split-second too long—he finished, "... anything else."

How long has Mikks known? Does the whole yeargroup know?

Dalyan wondered if he'd missed something. Amal's shocked reaction—consternation?—told him that there was a greater significance behind Mikks' teasing.

Freja pressed something against his scalp. "Hold this pad there for a minute or two. There's a little blood, but as long as you treat your scalp with caution, you should be fine."

Freja moved away as if nothing had been said, cool and unemotional as always.

Dalyan glanced back at Amal, whose cheeks were still pinkish. *Why would I name anything else?*

Amal hesitated, and then asked, "Are you going to change the puppy's name?"

That was a diversion, but he wasn't going to press her for her true reaction in front of everyone else. "No. I'm used to it. She may even know it's her name by now."

Amal nodded. "You may be right."

He pulled the pad away from his scalp and was relieved only to see a few small spots of blood left from the removal of his stitches. He had a short fuzz of hair growing in, making him hopeful he'd return to looking normal soon.

The conversation had moved on past him, circling back to Mikks studying again to become an engineer and the interesting fact that the Fortress could make new books whenever they needed one. Amal hurried to clarify that diverting resources like that had to be kept to a minimum, but the speculation on what else *could* be produced quickly spun off into the realm of silliness, with other members of the yeargroup drifting over to join the conversation as it progressed. Soon they were all gathered around on the couches near the table while the children ran up and down the hallway. Juliane settled next to Amal to rock her baby, incidentally keeping Dalyan from sharing the couch with Amal.

He felt strangely outside their wild speculations, odd since he was sitting in the middle of them. He was one of those *things* a machine had produced. For the moment, at least, the others seemed to have completely forgotten that.

He suspected that Amal's yeargroup had learned more about their own Fortress in the last two weeks than they'd known their entire lives. That must be unnerving to Amal and the other Oathbreakers, and it all came down to his arrival here. He'd upset their world. It didn't surprise him that some of the elders didn't like him much.

He watched Amal as she launched into a discussion with Juliane. Her eyes stayed on Juliane's baby as the woman shifted the infant from her shoulder to her lap to swaddle her more tightly in her gray blanket. Dalyan had yet to hear that baby crying. Juliane asked whether it was feasible to have the machines produce fresh diapers and, to feed that effort, consume those already *used* along with their contents. That provoked a series of appalled reactions as the others started discussing where that waste in the Fortress went anyway. Apparently most of them didn't like contemplating sanitation engineering any more than he did.

Amal looked tired, as if she hadn't slept well despite having a bed to herself last night.

The ambient in the room was one of curiosity and . . . amusement. Most of the yeargroup was truly interested in the discussion, whether or not it ranged into foolishness at times. But underneath that curiosity, Dalyan could sense Amal's preoccupation. He wasn't completely sure it was her, but the strange dragging feel of it matched her expression.

"No, I think we should *all* learn it," Mikks said. "This will change things."

What did I miss? "Learn what?" Dalyan asked.

"Horn," Mikks said. "Wouldn't hurt for some of us to learn Salonen, either."

That dragged Amal back into the conversation. "It would put each one of us in violation of the treaty. It's one thing for me to do it, or Jan, but for someone else it's a potential prison sentence."

"How is it different for Signe, then?" Mikks asked. "She's pure Family."

"And she's willing to take the risk of arrest."

Mikks shook his head. "It's our language, Amal. Are the Anvarrid going to come here and take Horn from us? I think not."

Dalyan peered at Mikks across the table. "If I understand about the treaty, it's not illegal for you to learn the Salonen tongue, is it?"

"But you can't pronounce it," Mikks pointed out before turning to Amal. "Does the Fortress have records of how Salonen is pronounced?"

"I . . . don't know," she admitted. "I can always ask."

Dalyan thought he could see where Mikks was taking this.

"Because if there's going to be some decision made about Salonen Fortress," Mikks said, "then it will take more than one person. It will take teams of people, most of whom will need to speak Salonen."

Amal nodded. "The engineers were discussing that earlier. We'll actually have to send climbing teams first to assess whether any of the entries to that Fortress are even accessible."

"How many entries are there?" Jan asked.

Amal cast a disturbed glance at her brother, chagrin surrounding her. "The appropriate number, Jan."

Jan's dark brows drew together. "I only know of two entries to Horn."

"That's all you're supposed to know," Amal said. "Main entry and refuge exit."

Dalyan grasped at a flicker of knowledge stored in his head. Horn Fortress would have been designed with a section that could be completely sealed off from the main body of the Fortress—the refuge. It would have to be accessible at all levels, and have its own path of egress in case of emergencies. But there were sure to be half a dozen other ways in and out of the Fortress. The Fortress had to have access for engineers to get to the things they needed to repair. And vents, like the steam vent Amal had shown him. It wasn't part of the Fortress, but he would bet there was a connection between that vent and the Fortress itself.

"Are they kept secret because of the invasion?" Mikks asked.

Dalyan suspected that meant the *Anvarrid* invasion, since he couldn't think of any other.

"Yes," Amal said. "And that's all any of you need to know right now."

Jan opened his mouth to protest, but shut it. Mikks folded his arms over his chest and glared at Amal—not angrily, but with frustration all about him.

"The Oathbreakers are dedicated to keeping secrets," Freja said, reflecting no emotion at all. "I've always thought it was from the Anvarrid, but it's just as much from the rest of the Family."

Dalyan wanted to step into the argument, but this was Amal's fight. And he had very little idea what to say other than to beg Mikks and Freja not to be so hard on her.

Amal sniffled and her upper lip shook, but she lifted her chin. "Do you have any idea, Freja, what it's like to know these things and not be able to talk?"

Magnus rose. "Stop it, Freja. You're upsetting everyone."

Freja flushed. "I'm sorry, Magnus."

Amal regarded her hands in her lap. To Dalyan it felt like she was pushing her emotions back under control. "I'll head back upstairs," she said. "That will give everyone a chance to talk it out."

Without waiting for a response, she rose and walked past him, not even looking back. Dalyan glanced across at Mikks, who was rolling his eyes dramatically. Then Juliane rose and held the baby out toward Dalyan, "Take her," Juliane said. "I'll go talk to Amal."

I'm probably not the one Amal needs to talk to right now. Dalyan put one hand under the baby's head and cradled her with the other. Juliane jogged off after Amal, brushing a couple of playing children out of her way as she went.

Dalyan gazed down at the swaddled creature in his hands, wondering what Juliane intended to say. The baby's skin looked fragile and pink, and there was a faint smile on her face. He bounced her a couple of times, since that seemed like the appropriate thing to do. She was only a few weeks old, so smiles at this age weren't real smiles. But it *seemed* like a real smile.

"Pretty good at that," Mikks commented.

Dalyan laughed. "It's not that hard to hold a baby."

One of Mikks' eyebrows rose. "You knew to put a hand under her head. I didn't the first time I held Hedda."

"I've worked with puppies," Dalyan said. "They're fragile, so I figured this one would be the same."

Mikks' eyes narrowed, but not with distrust. Dalyan tried to grasp what he was sensing of Mikks emotions, but it eluded him. *Amusement?*

"I think that Juliane should take over as Second for now," Freja said to Magnus. "I'm not doing my job."

Magnus tilted his head, a hint that they should move to one side of the common room. Freja went with him. Mikks sighed heavily. "That's my fault. I'm sorry."

Jan reached over and clapped his shoulder. "No, this is about the infirmary, not about you."

"I made it worse," Mikks said.

Something had spoiled the friendly ambient in the common room, but it was likely a *combination* of Freja and Mikks and the situation the twenty-sevens were in now. And his arrival was at the base of that, too. "As did I," Dalyan said.

"I think we need to meet tomorrow," Jan said. "Perhaps discuss assignments."

"Tomorrow's Firstday," someone behind Dalyan said to Jan.

Dalyan twisted around to spot Philip, Juliane's tall husband, sitting behind him. *How long has he been there?* "This *is* yours," he said, lifting the baby.

"You're doing fine," Philip said, waving one hand vaguely. "You probably need the practice."

"You just want a nap," Jan said with a shake of his head.

"I do," Philip said wistfully.

"How about on Second?" Jan offered. "First thing after Amal reports to her office." When most of the others agreed to that time, Jan said he would discuss it with Magnus.

I'm not invited to that. Dalyan gazed down at the baby in his lap. *Neither is Amal.*

Juliane returned and sat on the sofa behind Dalyan, clearly not intending to reclaim the baby from him. "Amal has gone on up to her rooms."

"Do you want her back?" Dalyan asked, holding up the baby again.

"You seem to know what you're doing," Juliane answered. "I'll let you keep her for a while."

Dalyan sighed. This was *not* what he'd planned for the evening. The conversation flowed on about him, calming in nature as the yeargroup's children approached the couches and interspersed themselves among the adults sitting there. They'd apparently tired themselves out running along the hall.

Young Sara eventually took pity on Dalyan and stole the baby away from him. She bounced the infant expertly in her arms as she returned to sit next to Jan. "I'm good with babies," the girl told Dalyan in a grave voice. "I can watch her for a while."

"Thank you," he said.

"When you need me to look after your baby, I can," she offered.

Dalyan nodded, suddenly aware that the others about them had gone quiet. "I will keep that in mind."

He drew a slow breath, forcing his mind not to pick at the girl's statement.

None of them are particularly subtle, are they?

Amal bathed when she reached her room, letting the hot water beat on her skin for a time as she mentally sorted out what was happening in her yeargroup. Mikks and Freja might be the most vocal, but she was certain they *all* had concerns about the situation.

When she'd first told them about the great machines and Dalyan's creation, they had taken it well. Since then, however, they'd had time to tease out some of the ramifications of what they'd learned—not just the capacities of the Fortresses that they'd never known before, but how that information had been hidden from them by the engineers at the same time that their languages were stripped away by the treaty with the Anvarrid, all to hide them from the Cince. It wasn't an easy truth to face, that your understanding of the world and your people was incorrect. That your people's history and knowledge had been stolen.

Out of fear. When did we move from caution to fear? At the time of the invasion? Or even before that?

Since her people had been created here, they had lived in their Fortresses, most content to stay within those walls their entire lives. They had been alone in Larossa for centuries before the Larossans arrived, and only began trading with the newcomers when it was argued that the Families had a responsibility to provide seed and farming help. After all, that was the entire purpose of the seed vaults within the Fortresses—to safeguard seeds for the future. A few Family personnel left the Fortresses to live among the Larossans, forming enclaves of Family outside the Fortresses for the first time. They'd had a peaceful existence as benef-icent advisors to the Larossans ... until the Anvarrid invaded. The Families had closed back in on themselves then, but Amal wondered if they shouldn't have been more out in the world before that, doing more than advising. They had knowledge then that could have changed the world.

Amal dried herself off, dressed for bed, and settled in front of the fire to towel dry her hair.

She wanted to urge caution, like Laurits. It was ingrained into her, a part of her training as an engineer, and as the Oathbreaker. But what if all her predecessors had made the wrong decision?

Because the Cince are ahead of us. We've been hiding so long that we have no idea what they know.

Tomorrow was Firstday, and little would be done then, but when Second came, she would be meeting with Theo and Signe to decide exactly what to tell the Oathbreakers from the other Fortresses. They needed to find out how the pattern Dalyan was based on reached Cince hands. They needed to know which Anvarrid were actively working for the Cince, teaching infiltrators like Dalyan. And they needed a course of action.

A knock came at the door. Amal opened the door partway and peered around the edge.

Sofie stood there, a struggling puppy under one arm. "Amal, did you forget something?"

Amal groaned, but took Nimi into her own arms. "I am sorry. I was . . ."

"Upset," Sofie said. "I could tell. I took the beast outside just now, so you're probably good for a few hours." Sofie *had* been among the guards who witnessed Amal running across the main hall with a peeing puppy on the previous morning.

"Thanks. She's not . . . well trained."

Sofie laughed and reached across to scratch Nimi's head. "She's only a few weeks old."

Amal had no idea how well trained a puppy should be at this age. "I suppose."

Still chuckling, Sofie bid her a goodnight. Amal shut the door and considered the puppy. She carried her over to the basket and put her down there. "You need to stay here tonight."

When she returned to her chair by the fire, the puppy tumbled out of the basket and followed. Amal sighed, picked her up, and cradled the puppy in her lap so she could scratch her belly. She preferred this sort of problem to the question of deciding the future of her people.

The group in the common area thinned out as the evening progressed. Dalyan had fetched his pencils and sketchpad and had occupied himself with drawing, partially so that he'd have some distance between himself and the others. He needed to think.

Once most of the children were abed, the adults began retiring to their rooms as well. Freja left to return to the infirmary, and Dalyan went to his own quarters, stripped off his sweater and shirt, and lay on his bed. He ordered the lights down, intending to sleep, but his mind wouldn't settle. He needed to talk to Amal.

He'd thought at first that the others held a mistaken belief that he and Amal might have children together. She simply hadn't told them he was sterile, or Jan hadn't. Dalyan had told the two of them, but not any of the others.

The more he thought about it, though, the more uncertain he became. It wasn't so much the hint by Philip that he needed to practice holding a child, or even Sara's assumption that he would have one for her to watch. Instead, it was Amal's reaction when Mikks had joked that he shouldn't be allowed to name anything. That made him question whether he might be wrong.

He couldn't *prove* he'd been created sterile.

He only had the word of his instructors at the facility for that. They'd told him everyone at the facility was sterile, a consequence of the Memory Plague that had stolen his childhood memories. Only he'd known that plague was a lie. That made him question almost everything his masters told him.

But not that he was sterile. He'd never questioned that.

Never for a moment.

Why not? *Out of everything, why did I accept* that *as truth?*

He still believed it was true, a gut-level reaction.

He lay in his simple room, untangling that knot in his mind. He truly believed he was sterile. Jan would tell him to trust his instincts, that even a latent sensitive had *some* ability to sort truth from falsehood.

He didn't know how much time had passed, but he called up the lights. He shoved away his covers, put on his jacket and house shoes, and left his room. Fortunately, the common area was empty at the moment. He stopped at the guideline—but then stepped over.

He'd come to Six Down via an elevator. He had no idea where he was relative to the stairwell. He closed his eyes and tried to remember something about how to find his way in the Fortress.

If this were a facility he'd designed, he would be able to ask it, just like he asked it to raise the lights. If he did that, though, and Horn answered, it would answer him in Horn. That wouldn't help. He gazed down the hallway, trying to decide whether to go left or right. Left, he decided, as most of the twenty-sevens seemed to go left when they passed the guideline.

He turned that direction and began walking. He would surely see the main stairs when he reached them.

The Cince facility had directions painted on the walls. Here all the directions had been removed. He made it past several hallways undisturbed before he noticed a pair of raised rows of chevrons running along the wall at waist height. Both rows pointed in the direction that he was going.

But the upper one will tell me how to find the stairwells. It was a simple design, efficient. It would work even in pitch blackness.

And so he made his way up, crossing paths on occasion with a stranger—or rather, he was the stranger here. He nodded and climbed on, aware he was moving painfully slowly. By the time he'd climbed five sets of stairs to reach One Down, he wanted nothing more than to sit down for a while.

But he needed to talk to Amal.

He gazed at the chevrons on that level for a moment before deciding that the upper one led to the grand stair that would take him to the Keep. On One Down there was more traffic, others moving from place to place. Most were busy on their own tasks, their minds occupied with one concern or another. A couple regarded him with curiosity. They watched him for a moment, but chose not to comment as he passed. He tried not to let it worry him.

This was where the services that operated at all hours would be, he guessed: the infirmary, the mess, the chaplains . . . people who might be needed in the dead of night. Sentries would be based on this level, too. He walked along, his house shoes making soft sounds on the floor. No one seemed inclined to interfere with him. He reached the main commons, a wide and cavernous room, and recalled catching a glimpse of it from the other side.

That had been right before the Fortress struck him down. He felt an unexpected flash of horror in the pit of his stomach.

I'm going to have to pass through that same archway to get to Amal.

He'd never thought he'd react badly to going through here. There was no choice, though. He had to push himself through. Clenching his jaw, he walked into the commons and fixed his eyes on black and blue paintings of flowers that adorned the walls. He traced the vining pattern with his eyes as he walked until he'd come to the entryway. He laid one hand on the wall, closed his eyes, and stepped into the gray hallway that separated the arched opening from the grand stair.

The hallway remained silent, though, save for the sound of his house shoes. Dalyan ignored the squirming of his stomach and walked on until his hand felt the archway at the other side. He opened his eyes on the stairwell that led up to the Keep—the grand stair.

Two sentries stood there, both watching him with annoyance. The woman looked to be near Dalyan's age. The younger of the duo, a large young man with pale hair neatly braided and tied, held out his arm to block Dalyan's path. "Where do you think you're going?"

CHAPTER 9

D ALYAN STEPPED BACK, not seeking a confrontation with the two sentries in his path. "I'm only going up to the Keep."

The younger sentry glanced at the other, who seemed inclined not to interfere, as if questioning people leaving the Fortress was normal. The younger rounded on Dalyan again. "What business do you have up in the Keep at this time of night?"

Dalyan gestured down at his house shoes. "I have a bedroom up there. I would like to go collect my belongings."

"He's probably going to see Lady Horn," the other sentry supplied, making a calming gesture. "She came up a couple of hours ago."

The younger one folded his arms. "What business do you have with Lady Horn?"

"Am I under arrest?" Dalyan asked. "Lady Horn informed me that I wasn't."

"You're not," the elder sentry said to him. "Do you have a duty shift upstairs?"

"We should take him to the armory cells," the other protested.

The elder had a vexed look on her face, but she was annoyed with her partner, Dalyan decided, not him. She pointed to the podium to one side. "If you don't have a duty shift, you have to sign out so Magnus will know where you are."

Magnus? That told him a lot. She knew exactly who he was, what yeargroup he lived with, and thus, very probably, why he wanted to see Amal . . . or at least a part of his reasoning. "That's fine," he said quickly "I'll do that."

She gestured him over while the large young man loomed behind him, irritation flowing around him like a pond of blood. "How do we know he's not a spy?" the young man asked.

Is that what the elders think? Still?

The woman folded her arms over her chest, jaw firming. "Why would a spy be in the Fortress already? We're here to keep strangers out, not Family members in."

"He's not Family," the young man insisted.

Footsteps coming down the stairwell provoked Dalyan and then the sentries to look that way. Another man approached landing, eyebrows pinched together. He looked young enough to be the same age as the angry sentry. He paused several steps up when he saw his contemporary scowling at Dalyan.

"Don't you think we need to take him to the cells?" the angry sentry asked the newcomer.

The other young man came down to the last step. "Not tonight, Nils. I was supposed to escort him upstairs, but my instructions got crossed. I'll take him up now."

That was all subterfuge, but Dalyan didn't argue. Nor did the female sentry.

"He's already signed out," she said. "You can take him."

The younger man on the steps gestured for Dalyan to join him.

I'm not going to get a better offer. Dalyan had no idea what the man's motive was, but since Nils' reaction was proof that he was still seen as an interloper by some, he needed all the help he could get. "I'm not at my best," he admitted. "So I may need to stop partway up."

"Did you walk up from Six Below already?" his escort asked. "Elin would have you carted back to the infirmary if she knew."

Infirmarian, Dalyan guessed. He gave the young man a more thorough survey. He was blond, with a handsome face that Dalyan suspected got him his way more often than was good for him. "You're Laurits, aren't you?"

The young man glanced back as if to reassure himself they'd gone far enough not to be overheard. Dalyan had intentionally pitched his voice low, knowing the acoustics of this long stairwell meant voices would carry. "Yes. Was Nils threatening you?"

"Not much," Dalyan admitted. "But I'm not in any condition to fight him if he took it in his mind to physically drag me away."

Laurits made a scoffing sound. "You're lucky I'm not dragging you back to the infirmary myself. Elin left orders that you weren't to climb stairs for two weeks. You're going to get a stern lecture from her when she catches you."

He had only met the head infirmarian once, but she did seem excessively stern.

And he *was* tired. At least the fluttering of panic in his stomach had fled, making this damnably long stairwell easier to climb. Even so, Dalyan stopped talking to save his breath.

The puppy snored quietly, lying on her back with all three legs up in the air.

Amal considered the puppy on her quilt, ruing her weakness. If her father could have seen this, he would have been aghast. *Dogs sleep on the ground.*

But the puppy had kept getting out of her basket and coming over to the bed to yip at Amal. It wasn't that Nimi didn't want to sleep on the ground, Amal suspected, but that the pup didn't want to sleep alone. They had taken her away from her siblings and put her into the place where she was the only dog. That must be lonely.

Amal stroked the pup's tummy, earning a sleepy noise from the creature, and smiled.

A soft knock came at her door. Amal held in a groan. She was warm and comfortable, and didn't want to know what Sofie wanted this time. "Come on in, Sofie," she said anyway.

The door opened. "It's not Sofie," Dalyan said.

Amal turned over. Dalyan stood at the door, leaning against the door frame. Behind him, Amal saw another man—Laurits. Laurits clapped Dalyan on the shoulder and disappeared from Amal's sight.

"Can I come in?" Dalyan asked.

Amal threw back the bedding and went to draw him inside. She sensed nervousness from him, and a dragging tiredness. "You weren't supposed to come upstairs."

"Do you mind?" he asked.

"No, are you all right?"

He cleared his throat. "I may have been pretending that I wasn't as winded as I am. In front of Laurits, I mean."

Amal laughed. "Here, come sit down."

She led him over to the bed, and he sat on the edge.

"I needed to talk to you," he said. "By the time I reached One Down, I knew it was going to wear me out, but by then I had gone far enough that I didn't want to stop."

A squeak came from under the covers. Amal realized that, in her haste to get to the door, she'd thrown the quilt over the bed's other occupant. She reached past Dalyan to draw the quilt back, and Nimi's legs flailed in the air until she flipped over. Dalyan smiled broadly and dropped onto one side to pet her. The puppy began licking his face, her tail wagging.

Amal sighed and moved her pillow so she would have a spot to sit down. She brushed her fingers through Dalyan's uncut hair. "You missed her."

"I did," he said, "but I came up here to see you." He rolled onto his back, scooting the puppy out of his way as he did so, then levered himself up to a sitting position. He faced her, his expression worried. The puppy hopped between them to be petted, but Dalyan picked her up and carried her to the basket. "Bed," he told her firmly as he set her inside.

Amal watched the puppy fidget as Dalyan returned to sit on the bed next to her, but Nimi stayed in the basket. "How did you do that?"

He looked sheepish. "It's the only command I had time to teach her."

"Nohr kept telling her to *stay*, and she wouldn't."

"She knows Nohr doesn't mean it," he said. "Amal..."

"She wouldn't stay for me, either."

"She doesn't know that command yet. I needed to talk to you."

Amal braced herself. She wanted it all out at once, so there would be no doubt. "Yes, I think I'm pregnant. Yes, of course, it's your child. No, I'm not upset, and I hope you're not either."

For a moment, Dalyan sat with his mouth agape, as if she'd said too much for him to process at once. She probably had.

"I said I wasn't planning on having a child," she added. "I wasn't. That doesn't mean it's a bad thing, that I don't want this child."

"I'm not upset," he said. "Shocked, perhaps. But not upset."

She touched his cheek. "You thought you were sterile. I know."

"That's what I don't understand," he said. "Amal, I believed them. My instincts told me that was true, no matter what else they said that was wrong . . ."

"I know." She related what Freja had told her about the Originals being *temporarily* sterile. His lips pursed as he thought through that. "So, it was actually the truth," she said, "what they told you. While you were there."

His eyes lowered to the quilt, his emotions locked down where she couldn't sense them.

After a moment, Amal touched one finger to the flat spot on the bridge of his nose, provoking him to raise his eyes to hers. "If I asked, would you sign a contract with me?"

Dalyan pulled her hand away from his nose. *She's nervous.* He could sense that. He wasn't going to ruin the moment by equivocating. "Yes."

She licked her lips. "You're not going to argue?"

Whatever difficulties there might be ahead for them, his relationship with her was one thing he *didn't* have doubts about. A few days ago, she'd said she wouldn't consider anyone else, and if the elders objected to this, that would only make Amal more determined. "No."

She let out a laughing breath, relief surrounding her now. "There are some legal hurdles still to handle, so I'm not sure when yet."

"Whenever you want," he said. "Tell me what to do and I'll do it."

"You probably won't be able to go to Salonen," she said.

"I figured that out."

"And there will be people who don't approve. People who think an outsider took the place of their son."

"You mean Vibeka?"

"Yes . . . or that little contingent that still thinks you're a spy."

Despite being winded, he *had* managed to talk to Laurits more on the seemingly endless trek up the grand stair. Evidently, Nils at the sentry stand at the bottom of the stair had been one of those who thought he should have a chance at wooing Lady Horn instead of an outsider.

Laurits suggested that the idea that Dalyan was a spy was being put forth in those yeargroups as a justification for vilifying a man none of them had met. That was the downside of having yeargroups, Dalyan suspected. Members of a yeargroup could talk themselves into something illogical, and since there was no disagreement among them, they would believe they were right.

When he told Amal that, she shook her head. "Why do you think Mikks always argues about everything? That's what he's doing . . . taking the opposing side of an argument just to make sure it's considered. It's good for us to have someone who questions the group."

He hadn't thought of Mikks' usual argumentativeness in that way, but she had a good point. "Then you shouldn't mind that the yeargroup is meeting on Second to discuss everything."

Her shoulders slumped a little anyway. "I suppose they don't want me there."

"Me, either, I think."

Amal nodded slowly, her mind reflecting a pall of hurt now. What began as a wonderful conversation had gone woefully in the wrong direction. Dalyan pulled her into his arms, shifting to lean back against the headboard. She buried her head against his jacket and burst into tears.

He rubbed one hand over her back. "Are you all right?"

"I can't help it," she whispered after a time, a flush of embarrassment accompanying that statement. She drew back and wiped her eyes. "It's a pregnancy thing. I'm fine now."

Dalyan stroked her cheek. "We will be fine. The twenty-sevens will hash it out and come up with a response to all this. And then we'll all move on."

"I know," she said with a sniffle.

He quelled his urge to laugh.

She pinched his side anyway. "I felt that."

"It's very romantic," he said.

"Oh, yes, I'm at my most attractive when my eyes are red." Amal sighed and leaned against him again. "It was only one night, but I missed you."

He kissed the side of her neck. "I missed you, too."

For a moment, he felt her desire rising, but she ruthlessly forced it back down. "Would you mind staying here tonight?"

"I am too tired to walk anywhere else," he admitted. "I was rather hoping you would let me stay."

She drew back, stood up, and held out a hand to help him rise. Once he was on his feet by the bed, she started unbuttoning his jacket. "You have to stay. Apparently, you're the only one Nimi listens to."

The puppy's triangle ears pricked up at the sound of her name, but she stayed in the basket.

Dalyan let Amal pull the jacket from his shoulders and set it aside. He stepped out of his house shoes and a moment later they were comfortably lying in the bed, her head on his shoulder.

Amal sighed, but before he could ask why, he'd fallen asleep.

Dalyan woke disoriented, but his brain finally sorted out that he was back in the Keep in Amal's bed. She slept on, a faint smile tugging at her lips. He slipped out of the bed and rushed in the chill air to the bathroom. Then he picked up the sleeping puppy, carried her out into the main hall past the sentries, and out onto the grassy hillside next to the terrace. Nimi stumbled sleepily, but carried out her orders. Once he was convinced she was done, Dalyan carried her inside.

By the time he returned, Amal had woken.

She stretched her arms out and smiled sleepily at him. "Are you coming back to bed?"

That sounded like an excellent idea. He set the sleepy puppy back in her basket, kicked off his house shoes, and slid under the quilt.

It was the most wonderful feeling, the sense of belonging he had with Amal.

I am going to have a wife. I am going to be a father.

Those were strange thoughts. The Cince who'd created him could not have predicted this path for him. Amal was putting a frightening amount of faith in him. He intended to do everything possible to earn that faith.

"It's Firstday," she said.

"Since I'm already up here, I could go help with the animals in the sheds, I suppose," he said. "So Sidana can spend the time with her family."

"You are her family now," Amal reminded him with a chuckle. "You're supposed to spend the afternoon *with* them."

He'd forgotten that. The adoption made him part of Eldana's family, another place to belong. "Then who takes care of the sheds?"

"I'm sure she's arranged for some of the local lads to do it." Amal took a large breath. "You could . . . would you mind staying with me for a while, first?"

"I'm not in a hurry to move." The bed was comfortable, and he wanted to stay here with Amal all day.

"No, I meant . . . when I meet with Sander. I could ask him to come up here. I'd like him to meet you . . . if you don't mind."

He hadn't thought of that. Amal's son, Sander, was an abstract to him. He knew the child existed, but had never seen him. Sander was in a yeargroup, and thus only in his mother's presence on Firstday. So far, Dalyan hadn't wanted to intrude on Amal's time with him. "Do you think he would want to meet me?"

"He already knows about you and me. Things like that don't stay secret long here."

"That's not an answer to my question."

She turned on her side and propped herself up on her elbow. "We'll leave for the capital in a week or two, so I think there may not be much more time. This Firstday, next Firstday, perhaps the one after that? So now would probably be wise. Just an introduction. I don't expect you to spend all afternoon with us."

She was worried; he could sense that. And yet she still hadn't answered his question. "I'll do that."

She blew out a breath that tickled his ear. "Thank you."

He shifted to face her. "Do you know? I feel much better now."

Amal's dark lashes lowered, and a faint flush colored her cheeks. "You did walk up all those stairs, even though Freja told you not to."

He slid one hand up her side and cupped her breast. "I wonder what other forbidden activities I could manage."

She laid her hand over his. "You know that if this kills you, Freja will never *ever* let me forget that I disobeyed her orders."

"She keeps saying I'm healing faster than she expected."

"She did take out your stitches early," Amal agreed, and leaned closer to kiss him.

He could feel her arousal growing, an almost tangible force that he could push away. He wrapped it around him instead, his body responding immediately. Amid their shortened breaths, she promised to make it as easy on him as possible. She untied the drawstring of the trousers he'd slept him, her hands warm on his skin. Then she slid over him, their shared eagerness growing until they both came with surprising quickness.

Laughing, she dropped her head against his chest.

"It's a little more difficult now," he admitted into her hair. "Pushing your feelings away."

She pushed up to gaze down on him. "The two-sensitive problem. I trust you'll learn to control that. And if not, we'll still enjoy ourselves, just more quickly than before. Turn your head."

"What?" That last statement surprised him.

"I want to see if you're bleeding. Look toward the wall."

Dalyan turned his head so she could look at the spot on his scalp where Freja had removed his stitches. "Anything?"

"Not a spot. Freja will never know."

He laughed shortly. "She'll know."

Amal slumped down against him with a sigh. "You're right. We can just hide from her."

Dalyan was chuckling to himself as he fell asleep.

Amal had butterflies in her stomach. She wasn't often nervous about things. She'd faced down the other Oath-breakers, stood in front of the senate, and argued with trade delegations. And none of those things left her feeling like this, like her gut was full of tiny angry things that might escape her control and stab her internally until she was dead.

But she'd asked Nohr to send word down that she wanted Sander to come up to the Keep instead of meeting with her in the common area of Six Down. She waited in the inglenook, while Dalyan was outside on the terrace with Nimi. She'd had to admit to feeling a touch of guilt about that, but she was willing to use the puppy to soften any resistance Sander might have to Dalyan's abrupt inclusion in their family. She wanted this to go smoothly.

"Mama?" Sander peered around the edge of the ingle-nook. "Why did you want me to come up here?"

"Come sit with me," she said, reaching out one hand.

He sighed heavily, but complied.

She asked after his week, and the other children in his yeargroup—which included Jan's eldest daughter, Astrid, and Eldana and Magnus' twins—and listened while he chattered on about his friends and learning to wrestle, the highlight of any week for Sander.

His brown uniform made him look older than he was in her mind. By Family standards, he would be a child for years to come, but the step from his mother's control to his yeargroup was a huge one. She still thought of him as her little boy, and missed him terribly most days. Other days, she barely thought of him, days when she was too busy, or too preoccupied with other things in her life . . . like Dalyan.

She reached up to touch his dark hair, but pulled back. He hated that. Even when there was no one to see her do so.

His coloration came from her—light brown skin and near-black hair. Other than that, he was Anton's child, with a stockier build, firm ideas about everything, and no desire to question the world around him. He would be a terrible choice for her heir. Currently she was leaning toward choosing one of Jan's daughters instead, either Astrid or Sara. Fortunately, Sander didn't care; he preferred the Family to Anvarrid ways. Then again, a great deal could change before her son turned twenty-five.

When he launched into a tirade about something Astrid had done—apparently asking questions that made a class run longer than he liked—she hugged him. "Don't let it bother you," she told him. "Members of a yeargroup have different needs at different times, but they all need to support each other."

He mouthed the last words along with her, evidently having heard that mantra more than he liked. "Fine," he said, in a petulant tone.

She took advantage of his sulk to jump in. "I wanted to talk to you up here because there are some things I need to tell you."

That increased his sullenness. "I already heard."

Better not to assume he's heard anything accurate. "What did you hear?"

"You have a new friend," he said, flushing just a bit. "You know, a friend in your bed."

Amal didn't laugh at the clumsy euphemism. Yeargroups developed their own terminology and slang along the way, so that was probably what all his yearmates called it—a friend in one's bed. "I'd like you to meet him today."

Sander shifted his bottom on the inglenook's bench, then slumped against the stone wall. "Do I have to?"

"I'd like you to," she repeated. "Just to say hello." She waited, expecting him to turn mulish on her. She wouldn't force him to meet Dalyan.

Sander's mouth twisted, his emotions still feeling sulky to her. But it was guarded, and she felt him trying to force it down, as if he was looking for something good in the situation. "I heard he has a puppy. Is that true?"

There it is. "He does have a puppy, although she sleeps in my room now because she can't live Below."

"Why are we not allowed to have puppies Below?"

"Because they make a mess everywhere," she said, surprised he'd gone that direction. "Poop, I mean."

"Babies do that, too," he observed, "but we have *them* Below."

Perhaps he'll study law one day. "True. But they grow out of it. Dogs don't."

"Hmmm." After a moment, he sat up straighter. "I'll do it."

"Why don't we go out on the terrace, then." She rose and held out her hand to him.

Sander took it after an instant's hesitation. "Can I see the puppy, too?"

Amal hid her smile. "I think she's out there already."

She opened the door to the terrace, where Dalyan sat cross-legged on the stone, hand-feeding Nimi. The puppy still drank milk when offered, but Dalyan had soaked tiny bits of meat and bread for her to eat. Sander immediately went to join them, sitting on the terrace across from Dalyan as if they were old friends. He raised a hesitant hand to stroke the puppy's white fur, and Nimi spun around to see him better and promptly fell over on her side.

"It's hurt!" Sander exclaimed.

"No, she was born that way," Dalyan said. "Do you want to try to feed her?"

Sander's eyes flicked back and forth between the food and the puppy's wagging tail. "What do I do?"

So Dalyan had him pick up a bit of the food with his fingers, warned him of the puppy's very sharp little teeth, and let Nimi mouth the food off Sander's hand. Sander's face glowed when Nimi nibbled at his fingers.

Amal let out a breath, relieved that the puppy gambit had worked as expected. *Perhaps he'll work with the live-stock one day.*

After rescuing Nimi from Amal's excited son, Dalyan walked her out to the sheds to join Sidana's family there. It had been an interesting compromise, having them all get together outside the Keep instead of Below, but it was a beautiful day. He got to meet Eldana and Magnus' sons for the first time—August and Arthur—who were apparently agemates with Sander. They weren't as impressed with Nimi, likely since they'd grown up visiting the sheds with their mother. And he had a friendly talk with the Milas, Sidana's husband. Legally *his* father now as well, Dalyan recalled. Milas was tall, and as fair as Sidana was dark. The two of them made a striking pair.

They all shared a friendly meal at the large table on one side of the sheds. Dalyan spent some time trying to get Ponyo—Nimi's mother—to accept her back, but she more or less ignored the puppy now. Nimi's siblings were rambunctious, so he let her play with them for a time, but removed her when one nipped her hard enough to make her yelp. Nimi was only half their size, still the smallest of the litter by far.

"We're having a meeting tomorrow," Eldana told him when they were sitting in the hay with the litter. "You're not supposed to come, but ... we may send for you to come down to clarify some things. Or send for Amal. Can you tell her that?"

He sighed. The exclusive meeting bothered Amal, but there wasn't anything he could do about that. "I'll let her know. I guess I'll come out to the sheds to work. She'll be in her office tomorrow, I suppose."

"She's easier to find than you are," Eldana said with a nod of her head.

That didn't stop Freja from finding him later that afternoon. She tracked him out to the sheds and took him aside to look at his scalp and ankle. She inspected his injuries with an annoyed expression on her petite features. That matched what he could sense of her irritation, her emotions sharply breaking out and then tucking away again in the manner he'd come to expect from her.

"I suppose you have no intention of following instructions any longer," she said when she had him put his boot back on.

"About the stairs . . ."

She folded her arms over her chest. "You climbed the grand stair when specifically told not to."

"I needed to talk . . ."

"I assume you've had sex as well."

Dalyan felt his cheeks go warm. Freja was nothing if not blunt. "Yes, I . . ."

"Fine." She snapped. "Try to exercise a modicum of caution. The twenty-sevens have a lot riding on your brain. You drop dead on us, our risks don't pay off."

And with that baffling pronouncement, she walked away in the direction of the Keep. Dalyan stared after her. *What risks?*

CHAPTER 10

S ANDER HAD STAYED with Amal longer than usual, mostly out of excitement over getting to play with an actual puppy. But he went back down to the Fortress to spend the afternoon with his friends, leaving her alone for a time. With time on her hands, she went down to her office and started working on her statements for the upcoming meeting with the other Oathbreakers.

There was also the matter that they needed to forward to the Daujom—about the Anvarrid men who had instructed Dalyan at the facility where he'd been created. She pulled out the sketches that Dalyan had made of their faces. A dozen men of unknown House affiliation.

All they could do was hand the sketches over to the Daujom. The true question was how much to tell the Daujom about the men's work in the Cince Empire. How much could she say without crossing into Oathbreaker territory? How could she explain Dalyan to them?

When do we tell the king?

Telling the Daujom was tantamount to telling the king; after all, the Daujom was run by the king's brother. Surely anything they told the Daujom would be referred to the king. But perhaps they could request that the information be held confidential. Finding someone within the Daujom who could do so was another matter.

In any case, they had to report it. If these men *were* Anvarrid citizens, then working with the Cince government to send agents back to infiltrate Larossa was clearly treason. They had already sat on the information for a few months because of its problematic Oathbreaker connections, but the time to inform the government was now.

Amal rubbed at a tense shoulder. One of the Oathbreakers in Lucas Fortress was the king's niece—Rachel— and the daughter of the man who ran the Daujom. Rachel Lucas might be able to connect Amal with the right member of the Daujom, one willing to be flexible about the treaty.

It had to be someone senior enough that when the time came they would command the respect of the king and the king's brother. Someone conversant enough with all the Anvarrid Houses that they'd know where to start looking for the traitors.

The Fortresses could communicate with each other, an advantage that allowed them to set up these face-to-face meetings in the capital when necessary. The Six Families used that ability sparingly to avoid drawing notice, but it gave the Oathbreakers a way to pass information. Amal made a note to contact Rachel ahead of the meeting.

When Amal finally went back up to the Keep, she found Dalyan in her bedroom, sitting on her bed and sketching. Nimi was curled up contentedly next to him. As Dalyan had already eaten dinner with Sidana's family, Amal asked the kitchens to send her a tray of food.

He set aside his sketchbook to talk with her, his fingers absently scratching Nimi's belly. "I didn't think I should go back downstairs tonight," he said. "Since they're meeting tomorrow."

He and Eldana had apparently talked about the proposed meeting of the twenty-sevens, including the request that the two of them remain available to go down to Six Down to answer questions. He then related Freja's interesting comment about the twenty-sevens having something riding on his brain. Amal suspected that referred to his training as a new engineer, but Freja could be frustratingly cryptic at times. She *could* go down and talk to Freja to find out what was happening, but decided to trust her friend.

They spent much of the evening talking instead. Dalyan worked with Nimi on a few commands—with mostly comical results—as Amal surveyed the drawings in his sketchbook. Afterwards, they made love, managing to keep their responses under control enough that they lasted more than a few minutes, but not much.

Amal laughed as she eased away from him onto the covers. "You know that this takes practice, right? Slowing down?"

Dalyan, lying on his back still, sighed, already drowsy. "I know. I just . . ."

And he fell asleep between one word and another.

She peered at his profile, letting herself worry now that he wouldn't be able to sense it. This was all unfolding far faster than she liked. She wished he could have had months to rest and heal, but events were moving forward at an alarming pace. She only hoped he could keep up.

The next morning, Amal sat at her desk, her mind spinning along useless paths. It wasn't Dalyan this time that had her worried, but what the twenty-sevens were doing. When Gyda appeared in her office, shaking her head,

Amal didn't know what to expect, but she could tell the older woman was perplexed. "What did they ask you?"

Gyda shook her head. "They asked me not to discuss it with you. Not until they've talked to you. Johan was going in to talk to them as I left."

Between them, Grandfather Johan and Gyda essentially ran the province whenever Amal and Jan were absent. They would have to do so again when they went to the capital to meet with the other Oathbreakers. "I see."

Gyda shrugged and turned to the paperwork that Amal had already worked on that morning. "I'll take this to Records."

"Gyda, do you know anything about the adoption papers going missing in transit to Records?" Her secretary had been the one handling those papers, so Amal felt it was fair to ask.

"I put them on the counter in the proper basket," she said, a hint of irritation flaring about her. "The papers *did* get to Records, although Johan wasn't there when I put them down."

She hoped Gyda's annoyance wasn't due to her asking. "I'm not questioning your integrity, Gyda. I trust you."

"I should hope so," Gyda said. "I am just peeved that someone moved paperwork they weren't supposed to touch."

The word *peeved* came out forcefully enough to leave no doubt that she could have used a stronger term. Gyda didn't like things out of their place. That was why she was so good at this job—she had a passion for logistics and was meticulous in her work. It infuriated her when others weren't.

"The point being," Gyda added, "that your friend cannot sign a contract until the adoption paperwork is filed. Once it is, though, I'm sure some of the elders will move to annul any contract before it matures."

A contract could be annulled within ten days of the initial signing, either by the parties involved, or by the elders of the Family. Amal wasn't sure that Vibeka and Viktor—and possibly Elin—had enough allies among the elders to stop the contract from maturing. That particular Family law, based on older Anvarrid law, had originally been intended to terminate any contract that was unsuitable. Over the years, *unsuitable* had evolved to include a vast array of complaints, including illegality, consanguinity, or coercion. Amal suspected Vibeka intended to mark Dalyan unsuitable because of his Cince masters even though he didn't serve them, and other elders might find that worrisome enough to act.

"You worked with Sebastian," Amal said, naming the Family's head legal counsel. "Do you have any idea which way he would lean?"

"Your chances are good, but ... I can't promise he'll agree with you."

Amal looked down at her desk and sighed. "I've made up my mind."

Gyda cleared her throat. "If Dalyan's what they think he is, then they should be trying to keep him happy, not interfering."

"He ... embodies change," Amal said. "There's a large contingent that doesn't want change to come here."

"Even though it already is?" Gyda shook her head. "Hiding our heads under our wings isn't going to make the Cince go away."

Gyda rarely volunteered her opinion on things, so Amal was surprised—and gratified—to know that Gyda supported enacting the contract. "How do I convince the elders of that?"

Gyda leaned back and folded her hands over her stomach. "That is the real question, isn't it?"

An hour later when the twenty-sevens asked her to come talk to them, Amal still didn't have an answer. She accompanied Sofie down the main stairwell, headed for the twenty-sevens' hall.

"No one's upset with you," Sofie volunteered.

Amal glanced at her. Sofie wasn't a sensitive, but knew Amal well enough to know she was tense. "Thank you."

"We all like Dalyan," Sofie added as she took the turning and went down the next well.

Amal trotted after her. "That's good to know."

"And the dog." Sofie stepped out on the landing and waited for Amal. "But we have a mountain of things to discuss."

Amal nodded and followed. When they reached their hallway, she saw her yearmates gathered in the common room. None had dressed for duty save Sofie, who must be the one who'd agreed to act as runner to fetch everyone they wanted to talk with. It was a relief, in one way, that they were making wide inquiries before making any decision.

The ambient in the room was tense, as if they'd been arguing.

Sofie directed her to one of the sofas, where she ended up sitting facing Magnus and Juliane. Magnus told her first that Juliane had taken over as Second, explaining why Freja sat on one of the couches farther back with Mikks, Jan sitting on the arm of their couch with them.

"We've made some decisions," Magnus said. "but we need guarantees from you, as Lady Horn, before we talk about them."

Amal knew better than to promise without knowing what. "What do you need?"

"We want you to file a line of succession with your House attorneys in Evaryanos."

Amal blinked. That was a strange first request, but it was something she should have done two years ago when she'd come of age. "I'll do so en route to the capital."

"We need a guarantee from you that should the elders decide, for any reason, to exile one of us from the Fortress, you will provide funding for us to live in the Keep or, if needed, set up additional housing beyond that."

"Is this a contingency plan?" she asked, her stomach cold.

"Yes," Magnus said. "There is a possibility the elders will react badly to our actions."

"What actions?"

"We haven't made a firm decision yet."

"Yes, I'll guarantee that the group will have room and board somewhere." Amal waited, wondering what would be next.

"That's all we needed from you," Magnus said. "Sofie, we need Signe again."

She was being dismissed. Amal rose. Juliane pressed her hand, a feeling of reassurance accompanying that gesture, but let her go.

Dalyan had spent the day in the sheds, helping out with some of his old duties under Sidana's watchful eyes. She didn't want him to tire himself out, so he spent most of his day watching the litters of puppies and trying to keep Nimi out of trouble. The puppy wanted to play with her siblings, but they were much larger than her and didn't seem to recognize that. She was butted over several times before Dalyan picked her up and set her in his lap. She seemed content enough with that, so he kept her with him for the remainder of the day, carrying her between different chores.

He *could* come up with a sling to carry her about. But she couldn't live her entire life in a sling, so he needed to find a way for her to be around the other pups yet still be safe. He made a mental note to discuss that with Sidana later.

Mikks caught up with him as he was raking out one of the dog's sleeping bays. He picked up the puppy first, and then addressed Dalyan. "What are you willing to do?"

Dalyan set the rake aside and wiped his hands on his trouser legs. "A lot of things, obviously."

"Of what the twenty-sevens ask you," Mikks clarified. "What are you willing to do?"

"Am I not supposed to go downstairs to answer questions?"

Mikks stroked Nimi's head while her tongue lolled out. "We decided sending me up would be easier on your health than making you come down and then up again."

"Thanks." He considered the question for a time. "I'll do what the twenty-sevens ask, so long as Amal isn't hurt by it."

Mikks handed Nimi over. "That's what I told them you'd say."

"I don't want any of you hurt, so if you need me to leave or to turn myself over, I understand."

Mikks clapped a hand on Dalyan's shoulder. "That's not the way we're leaning, brother."

Dalyan watched as Mikks headed out of the shed. He had no idea what that question meant, but Mikks' calm demeanor suggested that things on Six Down were going peaceably, at least.

He finished up his work shift and, after chattering with Sidana for a time, took Nimi back toward the Keep. He bathed, dressed in a pair of loose trousers and a sweater, and settled on his bed to wait for Amal. Nimi slept in her basket, worn out after her long day in the sheds.

At some point, someone had brought some of his clothing up from Six Below, along with the book that Theo had made for him, so Dalyan read that. When Amal finally knocked on his door, he'd almost reached the end of that volume. He would have to ask Theo to produce the remainder of the book for him soon. He let Amal in, and immediately wished he could ease her worry, so he told her what Mikks had said to him.

She shook her head. "I'm worried they'll end up getting in trouble."

"They need to make that decision, though," he said. "Not you."

She sighed and sat on the bed, putting her back against the headboard. "What are you reading?"

He sat next to her and tilted the book so she could see the words. "The text Theo made for me. I'm almost finished with this."

"Ah. I wish I knew how it was pronounced." That was accompanied with a sense of wistfulness.

"Me, too." Not only was he unsure of how the letters were pronounced, he had no idea where the accent fell in those words either. Even if he could sound them out, he wouldn't know they were correct.

She pointed at the word for *thermodynamics*. "That word means . . . studying the relationship between heat and energy, right?"

"It does. What is it in Horn?"

"Termodynamik," she said. "Yours has a couple of extra letters, but . . . if they're . . ."

"They have to come from an outside language—well, that or one from the other. It would be like using a Horn word when you don't have an equivalent in Anvarrid."

"We do that sometimes," she admitted, "even though we're not supposed to."

A knock came at his door, and Dalyan went to answer it. Magnus stood and waited outside, his demeanor suggesting that he'd had a very long day. He carried a couple of uniform jackets over his arm. "May I come in?"

He didn't want to step over the threshold unasked, Dalyan realized. "Yes, come in."

Magnus stepped inside and shut the door behind him. "Glad to do all this at once."

Dalyan shot a glance at Amal, who'd risen. He could sense her nervousness, not hidden since Magnus wasn't a sensitive and wouldn't feel it. "Do what?"

"Let you know what we've decided," Magnus said. "And ask whether you're going to join with us."

Amal stood very straight. "Tell me."

Magnus licked his lips. "We have decided that we will be the Horn Family's point team on Salonen. We will coordinate the climbing teams, the debris removal, the entry, and if possible the rehabilitation of Salonen."

"Who is we?" Amal asked quietly.

"The twenty-sevens. We've all chosen to do this together. We will need you here most of the time, but if Salonen is raised, then we'll need to inhabit it. We'll need engineers there, so we need you and Dalyan, but if not, Mikks and Sofie will just have to do their best."

"I don't . . . did you say Sofie?"

"Yes. We knew it would take more than one," Magnus said, "so she volunteered to train with Dalyan and Mikks."

Dalyan hadn't had any idea Sofie was interested.

"You're talking about taking engineers away from Horn," Amal said. "You can't do that. We're already short-handed."

"We've talked extensively with the engineers. They say it could be as many as ten years to clear the way into Salonen, at least an opening large enough for practical use."

"I don't know," Dalyan said. "I think some of the possible openings are accessible."

"We've sent a message to the team in Melyrep, hoping they'll join the effort. Plus we plan to ask the Oathbreakers if they could transfer additional personnel from the other Families who might want to join us."

Amal pressed a hand to her chest. "You're talking about a joint effort between the Families?"

"Yes," Magnus said. "We don't have enough personnel to do this on our own. But I suspect there are young people out there who would give their teeth to join in."

Dalyan had no doubt of that. "And if we have to kill Salonen?"

Magnus let out a hearty sigh. "We'll still learn from the experience."

Amal swallowed. "What about the treaty?"

"If the king's people object to Family being involved in this, we'll leave rather than put the Horn Family in danger of violation. That will have to be addressed with someone in power in the capital, I'm not sure whom. But we're all aware of the possible repercussions."

"That means ... leaving your children behind."

Magnus nodded grimly. "Signe has given us an idea of what Salonen might be hiding. The weapons of war the Cince might find in the Fortress' memories, the terrible things that could ruin this earth. And that needs to be protected. We're willing to take the chance, knowing that our children will be safe in Horn, even if we're separated from them. We're hoping it won't come to that. We're hoping that the throne will grant permission for the expedition."

Sensing Amal's worry, Dalyan glanced over at her. She laid one hand over her mouth, and then said, "You mean that I need to convince them. *The king.*"

"You will," Magnus said, "but even if you don't, we intend to go forward with this. And we hope that you'll join with us."

Dalyan nearly laughed at the idea that he'd refuse. They were joining him, rather than the other way around. "I'm with you," he said. "This is all my fault to begin with."

Magnus shook his head, but took one of the coats over his arm and held it out to Dalyan.

It was his own uniform jacket, Dalyan realized, but someone had painstakingly stitched on the soutache trim that represented the engineers, a set of stylized stair steps across the chest that folded back on themselves. "I thought I was supposed to do this with my own hands," he protested.

Amal laughed. "That's one of those things everyone says, but . . . no one actually does. Do you even know how to sew?"

"A bit." He could mend a rip in his clothes or a tear in his tent, but had no more experience than that. He'd dreaded the sloppy job he'd do on the trim.

She took the jacket and held it out for him to try on. Dalyan pulled his sweater off over his head and let her put the jacket on him. A chill ran through him. *I'm wearing a real Family uniform now, trim and all.*

"Who did the sewing?" he asked as he buttoned it, fumbling a bit with the buttons in the hidden placket.

"On yours, Freja," Magnus said. "She's good with a needle."

Amal surveyed his jacket. "It looks good. Um . . . what's the design on the shoulder?"

Dalyan twisted to see his right shoulder. *I'll have to take the jacket off to view it properly.*

Magnus displayed his own sleeve for Amal to see. The design looped back on itself several times and then came to a point halfway to the elbow. Magnus already had the First pattern on his cuff, and the horizontal bars of the military across his chest. "We're currently calling the new pattern *For Salonen*. Lousy name, but that's not my specialty." He held out the other jacket. "Amal?"

She took it from him. "Are you still my First?"

"Yes," Magnus said. "No one's abandoning you. There have been a few posting changes, but that's to free up people."

"Good." She gazed at the jacket. The right sleeve now possessed a design like Dalyan's. "Who did mine?"

"Mikks did," Magnus said. "I think he and Freja were racing to see who would finish first. We'll meet with the elders in the morning. I expect you both to be there."

"They won't like this," she said.

"Yes, they will. They get the advantage of taking action on a threat with no risks to themselves." He gave them a grim smile. "We know what we're doing, Amal. Have faith."

She set one hand on his shoulder. "Thank you, Magnus."

"It's a simple enough proposition," Magnus repeated. "We take on the task, we take the responsibility."

Amal couldn't remember having been in an elder's meeting like this before. Not a meeting that droned on and on for hours while they quibbled over the wording of every statement Magnus made. She had to admit that she would have given up in frustration and walked out long ago if not for his dogged determination to get them to agree.

The division among the elders was clearer now than before. After a couple of hours she could tell which ones were acting on Vibeka's behalf. Surprisingly, it was mostly among the older elders. Or perhaps that wasn't surprising, as they tended to be more conservative. But they weren't a majority, and Amal had the feeling Magnus had forced them into a decision on this before they had all their partisans lined up. She would thank him later.

They bickered a while longer, but were interrupted when Villads slipped into the room and gestured for Signe to join him by the door. She rose and went to talk to him quietly, the air of concern about her growing. She let him leave and returned to her seat, but held up one hand. "We have a new concern," she said. "Villads says this morning he sent out messages to the other Fortresses. As usual, they all responded to let us know they'd received the message. Salonen did as well."

The other elders erupted into a flurry of discussion. Amal put a hand over her mouth, not trusting herself to keep quiet. Dalyan glanced at her as if asking for clarification. "What does that mean?" he whispered.

She leaned closer to whisper. "It means Salonen *is* alive."

CHAPTER 11

T HE ROAD TO the capital was not a terrible one. It wasn't good, either. Maintaining the road during the icy Horn winters was impossible, and the summers were short.

Amal had to admit that they also left it that way to discourage people from coming to Horn. The first day of the journey, therefore, was wretched, with the heavy traveling coaches rattling and bouncing slowly along the dreadful road until she wanted to get out and simply walk to their first night's stop.

But she couldn't. Dalyan sat next to her, looking a touch green. It wasn't travel sickness, he promised her, just tiredness. He held Nimi in his lap, stroking the puppy as if that motion was the only thing keeping him from losing control.

"The road will be better tomorrow," Amal promised him.

Mikks laughed, and Sofie chimed in. "It will be *a little* better tomorrow. After we get to Evaryanos the roads are maintained by the throne, and they have more money to throw at it."

Amal didn't argue that assertion. The king did have more money. "We'll stay at the inn tonight in Calanos. You can get a good night's sleep there."

Mikks held his book up and began reading again. It was a text on electricity, and Sophie stopped him periodically to ask for an explanation. They were good questions, Amal noted, and since they were elementary, Mikks recalled enough from his earlier training that he could answer himself. Occasionally he asked Amal for a word in Horn, and they would all repeat it a few times, trying to get it fixed in their heads.

That lead to a discussion on resistance and capacitance. Most of that information was never used in day-to-day work as an engineer—after all, the Fortress generally assembled all the parts for them—but it was still good to understand the basics before working on the Fortress' systems. And even if Mikks and Sofie merely replaced prefabricated parts all day long, that was a necessary part of the job and would free up others to do more involved work.

On the other hand, Mikks was already speeding ahead of Sofie and Dalyan in learning the Horn language. He seemed to have an instinctive grasp of how the language worked, particularly when he compared it to Anvarrid. He viewed the two languages as systems, as structures for encompassing ideas, and that skill would make him a viable replacement for Villads one day. He wanted to work on Salonen, too, but currently all he had was the books Theo had created for Dalyan to study. Even so, Amal suspected Mikks would soon be the leading speaker of that language in Horn.

When the coaches bumped and stumbled into Calanos, the cobbles of the roads there made a new racket, higher pitched and more regular. To everyone's amusement, Nimi began howling along with it, as if it sang to her.

"Do you think she'll do that the whole time we're in the capital?" Sofie asked.

"I hope not," Amal said laughingly.

The inn in Calanos was a large one, accustomed to serving large groups. The innkeeper, a tall older man with some Family blood in his background, arranged for them to have their customary rooms, adding one more for Sofie. They had the inn to themselves, so they sat about the fire in a private dining room for some time after dinner, the occupants of each coach apprising the others of what had been discussed. They tried to carry on a short conversation in Horn, but Amal had to provide words through most of it, so they let it drop after half an hour or so.

After Dalyan carried Nimi outside and brought her back in, he went up to their room to settle the pup in for the night. Amal took a moment to draw Jan to one side to discuss their meeting in Evaryanos tomorrow. The innkeeper had agreed to send a rider ahead to warn the House law firm that they might have to stay late to handle some Horn paperwork. Since they were the firm's primary client, Amal had no doubt they would wait for her.

Then she finally dragged herself back up the stairs, leaving Magnus on duty for the night. She had no doubt that the inn was safe, but she would have said that about the Keep as well. Since an assassin had attacked them not far from the Keep, Jan preferred to err on the side of caution and keep someone on guard at all times.

When Amal stepped inside the room, Dalyan had already undressed for bed. "How are you feeling?" she asked.

"Like I'm still bouncing and rattling on the road," he admitted.

She stripped off her uniform jacket. "That will go away with a good night's sleep, I promise."

"I keep wondering if I'll never get better," he said with a sigh.

"Go to sleep." She stroked his hair back from his forehead, wishing she had an answer. "I'm going down to the bathroom, and I'll be back in a moment."

When she returned, he'd followed her suggestion and fallen asleep. She snuggled into the bed next to him and wrapped an arm around him.

For his sake, Freja and Elin had both wanted them to wait longer before heading to the capital. Even though he'd managed to climb the grand stair between the Fortress and the Keep a few times, even though his stitches were out and his burn was looking better, they still thought he needed more time to recover. But given Signe's announcement that Salonen was responding to Horn's messages, the level of urgency had risen starkly. There was simply no other choice.

And they could have left Dalyan behind, but the other Oathbreakers needed to see him. She needed them to speak with Dalyan, to witness that he was a person, not a thing. And they needed to understand that he might not be the only one. So he'd come with them.

She wrapped an arm about his waist and shifted closer to him, praying that their gambit would work.

The second day of travel *was* better. Dalyan was grateful Sofie had been correct about that. The roads were less bumpy, and he was feeling more himself. When they made one of their stops so everyone could get out of the coaches and stretch their legs, Jan and Freja switched with Mikks and Sofie to spend the last portion of the drive with Amal.

The discussion, Dalyan realized, circled around whom they would select as the Horn heir. The age of adulthood for Anvarrid was twenty-five, so it was a long way away for any of their children, but they spent time discussing the merits of the three eldest: Sander, Astrid, and Sara. While Sander was Amal's son, none of them thought he would be the best choice for Lord Horn. The eldest of Jan's daughters by Freja, Astrid was apparently precocious but combative enough to make Freja question whether she would be able to be diplomatic. It was their middle child—Sara, who'd petted Nimi the week before—whom they all seemed to think would do the best if forced to take the seat of the House of Horn if something should happen to both Amal and Jan.

Apparently both of them had put off filing the recommended line of succession for some time now, hence Magnus' forcing them to it. Dalyan carefully stayed out of that conversation. He and Amal might be having a child together, but he wasn't going to assume that child would figure in any official inheritance.

Amal and I are having a child together.

Every once in a while, the idea struck him again, unfolding in his mind as if he hadn't known it before. Or he hadn't grasped the meaning. Sometimes it was accompanied by a flare of panic that he wasn't prepared to be a father. But that always faded into a sense of pleased wonder.

So he sat quiet throughout the discussion, ignoring the pointed glances that Freja cast his way at times. He listened, scratching Nimi's back contentedly as Freja picked white hairs off her trouser legs. Her motions weren't accompanied by true irritation, at least not as far as he could sense, so he didn't let it worry him too much.

When they reached the city of Evaryanos, the other coach went on to the house Amal's family owned, stopping only so Dalyan could hand Nimi over to Sofie, and Nohr could take position on the roof of the vehicle. Their coach went farther, coming to a stop in the middle of a city that was far more cosmopolitan than Dalyan expected. The buildings were an unusual combination of the light and airy buildings one saw in the capital—large arched windows in buildings of pale stone with arcades and courtyards inside— and the steep roofs and conical towers he'd seen in the Horn. The roads were finely cobbled, with uniform pieces of stone carefully fitted in a softer bed that must need regular maintenance. Prayer flags were strung across the streets, their bright colors and golden sigils hinting that there had recently been a Larossan religious festival—or one was about to take place. Dalyan could hear wind chimes, so they must be near a temple. The streets were busy, with carriages and coaches and wagons all making neat lines, as if they wanted to get there in the most efficient manner.

Dalyan dropped the shade back down. Freja and Jan were checking their pistols, resuming their role as Amal's guards, he realized. "Should I have a pistol?"

"No," Amal said. "You're here to sign paperwork, not guard me."

The paperwork for his adoption had been formalized as one of Magnus' requirements from the elders, so this was something else. "A contract?"

"Yes," Jan told him with a chuckle.

Amal had asked, and he'd agreed. He simply hadn't known it would be today. Dalyan nodded and shut his mouth. He didn't want to say anything wrong and jinx his good fortune.

Jan stepped down from the coach first, waved to Nohr up top, and surveyed the surroundings. Only then did he signal for Amal to emerge. The coach had stopped directly in front of an elegant building of pinkish stone that glowed in the late afternoon sunlight. Amal stepped down, and Jan quickly swept her off the sidewalk and through the building's front door.

"Let me go first," Freja told Dalyan.

"Are you guarding *me*?"

"Actually, I am," she said with her first smile of the afternoon. She stepped down from the coach and gestured for him to join her.

Dalyan stepped down and they crossed to the building, leaving Nohr with the coach.

A finely garbed Anvarrid gentleman opened the door for him, so Dalyan went inside, far enough that Freja wouldn't be stuck on the sidewalk. She shut the door, and told the young gentleman to lock it. Then she gently shoved Dalyan down the hallway ahead of her.

It was clearly an Anvarrid building. Fine carpets in subdued shades of gray lined the halls, but the tapestries were far more colorful. Dalyan almost paused to stare at what looked to be a battle scene with horses, but Freja pushed the small of his back to move him along.

Amal already sat stiffly before the wide desk of a self-important looking man with thinning hair. The man gestured for Dalyan to sit in the only other empty chair.

In his guise as her guard, Jan stood behind Amal's chair, arms folded over his broad chest. Freja went to stand behind the offered chair, leaving Dalyan little choice but to comply. He sat down in the chair, trying to evaluate the unknown man now sitting behind the desk. He wore Anvarrid dress as well, a tight-fitting olive jacket heavily embroidered in silver along with full black skirts over black trousers. If he was a lawyer, he was an Anvarrid one. His bent nose and darker skin looked much like that of the young man at the door, so perhaps that hadn't been a doorman, but his son.

"I was most pleased to hear from you, Amalandrian," the lawyer began. "As always, I look forward to seeing you."

Dalyan's sense of the man was of a sincere desire to serve, a reassuring thing. His use of *Amalandrian* startled him until he recalled that was Amal's Anvarrid name, the suffix *-ian* meaning lady. Addressing her as *Lady* Amalandrian would be redundant.

Amal inclined her head. "Cousin Oradion, it is a pleasure. I've come to file a line of succession."

Amal glanced over her shoulder at Jan, who produced a large envelope from inside his jacket and handed it to her. She passed it along to the lawyer. "In case of my death."

The lawyer glanced at the closed envelope. "I trust that Johan has everything in good order."

"He always does," Amal said placidly. "I'd like a stamped copy before we leave."

"I'll have Idan file that for you, Lady Horn." He rang the bell on his desk and the young man from the front door came into the room, bowed, and took the envelope away to stamp it. "We can have everything ready for you tomorrow."

"I'm certain there's a great deal of paperwork for Jan and I to sign," she said. "Can we arrange that for the morning?"

"Of course, Lady Horn," the lawyer said. "You also had a contract for me to witness?"

Jan drew out a second envelope and gave it to Amal. "I'll need you to witness our signatures and file the paperwork."

"With the senate?" the man asked, glancing quickly at Dalyan. Surprise flared around him.

"Yes," Amal said. "I am of age."

"Of course, Lady Horn," he repeated, settling back into his chair with returning equanimity.

Amal opened the envelope, unfolded the paper, and laid it out on his desk. She leaned forward to pick up a pen and dabbed it in the ink. Then she signed the first sheet of paperwork, adding a flourish underneath her signature. She passed that sheet to Dalyan. "Will you sign?"

He glanced at the document. She had signed as Amalandrian, House of Horn. "What surname should I use?" he asked. "Horn or . . ."

Jan's hand came down on his shoulder. "Horn."

Dalyan paused, but signed as Dalyan Horn, his adopted name. He could feel the lawyer's curiosity about that exchange, but clearly they didn't want him to say who he was beyond being a member of the Horn Family.

"I'll witness." Jan took the pen from Dalyan, dipped it, and wrote *Jan, House of Horn* on one of the lower lines. He put the pen back in its stand and handed the document to the lawyer, who perused it and then signed it himself. Amal handed over the second sheet—a copy—and they repeated the process.

"I will file with the senate," he said. "Is there anything else for today?"

Amal rose. "Not today, cousin. I'll come back in the morning and we can work through any documents left."

Dalyan had risen when Amal did, and the lawyer did the same. The lawyer bowed to Amal, and then to him, a gesture that Dalyan almost returned, but stopped when Freja's grip on the back of his jacket prevented him. He barely managed not to stumble back into her.

"Shall we go?" Amal asked blandly.

Dalyan went, tracing back the direction they'd come. The young man held open the door for them, and Freja slipped out ahead of him to check the street between them and the coach. She gestured for them to come out, and Amal went, setting a hand on Dalyan's elbow to draw him along as well. Once they were all in the coach and underway again, Dalyan turned to Amal. "What just happened?"

"You're now her consort," Jan said, patting Dalyan's knee. "Congratulations."

"Consort?" He could tell that they were all amused, as if they'd played a prank on him, but if so, he had no idea what it was. "Is there a significance to that? Beyond being her husband?"

Amal leaned her head against his shoulder as the coach rattled on. "The difference is that I signed it as Lady Horn."

"For a standard Family contract," Jan explained, "she doesn't even have to sign it. Father never bothered to sign my mother's."

"And if she signs it?"

"If you have a signed contract with Lady Horn, you are not merely her husband, you are her consort," Jan said. "And among other things, that means you are technically Anvarrid now and cannot be arrested by the Daujom without them taking Amal to court."

"It protects you," Amal said, "even from the king."

"Your elders won't like that," Dalyan said.

"No, a handful of them won't like it. The majority are perfectly willing to accept you in that role."

Role? "Wait ... does that mean I'm not Family any longer?"

Freja laughed. "No, you're both, like Jan and Amal. Now you have to make two cultures happy."

Amal had wanted to see Dalyan's reaction to his first sight of the estate. It was still amazing to her that she and Jan owned this place. To keep it in good condition, the House of Horn had tried to keep someone living in it year-round, but with the size of the House dwindling, her grandfather had finally rented it out. Fortunately for Amal, they had gone the last few years without a tenant, so when she and her guard traveled to the capital, they could stop here and relax for a day before moving on. Otherwise, save for a smattering of servants and a small contingent of guards, the place stood empty.

I should do something about that.

That had been a low priority for her and Jan. Now it offered a potential location for the twenty-sevens to inhabit should they be forced out of the Horn Family. After all, she'd guaranteed that they would have a place to go. It wasn't ideal, being two days' travel from the Keep, but it was large and well-maintained. The rents collected over the years had paid for upkeep and the ridiculous amount of work that went into maintaining the roof.

Dalyan had spent most of the trip from the city to the estate talking with Jan about the duties of a consort.

She should have discussed this with him before. She *should* have. But she hadn't wanted word to get around that she was taking this step. The elders had known she intended to give him a contract. She hadn't said she would sign it, and enough of them had assumed that, like her father, she wouldn't bother to formalize the marriage by filing it with the senate. She hadn't done so with Anton, after all. But Anton had died before she became Lady Horn.

Amal suspected he wouldn't have wanted to partake of the duties of a consort anyway, even rare as they were. She sighed, feeling traitorous for thinking such a thing of Anton.

"What's wrong?" Dalyan whispered.

"Guilty memories, that's all," she returned. Since they'd passed the gate onto the estate some time ago, she leaned past him and lifted the shade. "Look."

He paused, but peered out the coach's window. "What . . . what is that?"

"Our estate." She half-stood and banged on the wall to get the driver to stop. After a moment the coach was still, and she prodded Dalyan to climb down to get a better look at the monstrosity on the hill. "It's called Evaryenist."

He stood next to the carriage and gazed at the distant building, mouth agape. "You mean this is your *house*?"

Amal laughed at the idea of calling the thing a house. The building on the hill was three stories and housed approximately three hundred bedrooms. More than that number of chimneys—many with fanciful twists and masonry work—jutted up all over the roofline, along with a number of small onion-dome-topped guard towers in addition to the main tower in the center. The beige stone was not the granite so common in the capital, but a much softer limestone that grew harder with age and exposure. "That . . . is not a house. Not exactly a palace, either. More a small town, or a medium sized one. The central part is called a keep because it's four-sided, but it's not very defensible. It's generally considered a very large *manor*."

"What is the purpose. . . ?"

Freja had closed the coach door, but leaned out the window. "It's a huge waste of money. That's its purpose."

"She's right," Amal admitted. "No one wants to pay for the upkeep, and I haven't had time recently to find anyone to rent the place."

Dalyan licked his lips. "It's bigger than the royal palace."

Amal took his hand. "There are a frightening number of palaces in this country that are bigger than the king's palace. Jan and I happen to own one."

Dalyan stared at the manor a moment longer. "Well, shall we go see it?"

If she walked with Dalyan toward the manor, it wouldn't take long to reach it, but that would force Nohr to walk as well, so she decided not to. She gestured for Dalyan to climb back into the coach and they moved on. The coach stopped on the drive and they stepped down before the manor's main door. When they went inside, Dalyan was surprised by the empty and echoing stone halls. "Are there no furnishings?"

"Not in most of it," Amal admitted. "Maintaining that much furniture, not to mention the carpets and hangings, was ridiculously expensive. In the past, when it was rented, the renter would bring their own. We've decided to leave the unused wings empty. Easier to keep them clean and maintained this way."

Dalyan shook his head. "Amazing."

She laughed. "We have a residential hall, I promise. It's furnished."

They walked in that direction and Amal spotted Indaris Coatine walking quickly toward them. The Larossan woman and her family maintained the manor, a position that had been in that family for six generations now. She hurried forward to greet them, not quite running, and stepped forward to embrace Amal.

Amal hugged her back. She'd first met Indaris when she was a child of five and her father left her in Indaris' care when he took the rest of his family to the capital. Amal had taken sick on the road, and he didn't want her sneezing and coughing in the coach with them the rest of the way. She'd spent a couple of days in bed, but the remainder of the month, she was teenaged Indaris' shadow. She had learned more about running a household in those few weeks than in all the years since. "Indaris, I've brought my husband. This is Dalyan."

Unlike Family women, most Larossan women wouldn't touch men who weren't family, and Indaris was no exception to that rule. Indaris stepped back and bowed to him instead, her near-black eyes twinkling. "I am pleased to meet you."

Dalyan almost returned the bow, but Jan stopped him with a hand to his shoulder. "I am pleased as well," Dalyan said instead.

Indaris turned to Amal. "Iladin can serve as valet for him, if you like," she said. "And I will dress you."

"That would be fine," Amal said, wondering how Dalyan would adapt to being dressed by a valet. He was apparently going to have to work on not bowing to others. She wrapped a hand around Indaris' arm. "Jan, can you show Dalyan the rooms while I talk to Indaris?"

"Of course," Jan said. "You two go catch up."

Amal winked at Dalyan and headed down the hall with Indaris, hoping to get all the local news.

Dalyan followed Jan along the ornate, echoing halls. There were guards, he saw now, men and women in Family uniforms who must live here all the time. They nodded to Jan—surely they knew him—and didn't interfere. And since Jan didn't mention them, Dalyan decided not to, either. Eventually they reached a guarded door. The older man who stood on duty there opened the door for them after only a perfunctory glance at Dalyan.

Behind that door lay a hall far wider than the Keep's residential hall, with white painted walls and ornate carvings along the ceiling. The carpet underfoot was the same as the Keep's, though—variations of black wool. The wall hangings were lighter, more finely woven, but they still showed off the excellent wools of the province. "Does Amal host trade delegations here, too?"

Jan laughed as they walked along. "Not recently. When the House was larger, in our grandfather's day, there was a permanent presence here and a lot of the trade negotiations were handled here. Our father met people here occasionally as well, but Amal and I prefer to stay at the Keep. If someone needs something signed, they have to come north to the Keep. Or leave it with the law firm. That works, too."

"Ah." Dalyan clasped his hands behind his back. "And do you trust them? The law firm?"

"That's why it's good to have Indaris here. The guards don't get the same reception in town. Indaris is local, though. She always has plenty of information for Amal, including whether anyone thinks the law firm is misrepresenting us. She keeps an ear to the ground and has dozens of friends in the city. Plus she helps run the distribution of tithe excess to the poor."

That the excess tithe was distributed to the poor was news, but Amal had long ago told him that the Horn didn't need the tithe the other houses sent to them. That sounded like a wise choice.

Jan opened a white-painted door. "This is Amal's room, which I assume you intend to share."

Dalyan could sense Jan's amusement with those words. "Yes, I do."

"Good." He stepped aside so Dalyan could go inside.

Dalyan stopped on the threshold, startled. Amal's room at the Keep was no finer than the one they'd given him. The bed was comfortable, the fire warm, and the desk well-made. But this...

"Don't stand on the threshold," Jan said, and pushed him into the room.

Dalyan complied, walking around for a moment before returning to Jan. The vast room in front of him did belong in a palace. The bed was draped with fine white fabric with blue-embroidered pillows and bed-hangings. The carpet was a deep blue, and it looked thick enough that he wanted to take off his boots and sink his bare feet into it. The curtains were white and black, and every surface seemed to bear some form of gyrfalcon motif. The pale stone mantel had a falcon head carved in stone on each end. A door opened off to the left into what he thought might be a sitting room or library, and to the right there was a dressing or bathing room.

"Bigger than you expected?" Jan asked.

"Ah, yes." Dalyan laughed. They must enjoy springing this on visitors, this opulent living arrangement. "Is your room this large?"

"Yes, it is," Jan noted. "Uncomfortably so. I never have felt easy here."

Given that Jan had grown up in the Fortress where quarters were small, that didn't surprise him. "When Magnus asked Amal to guarantee that the yeargroup would have a place to live, did he mean this?"

"More or less," Jan said. "It's a place to fall back to, should something happen to the Fortress. That's why we don't sell it. We could literally move the entire Horn Family here, rather than seeing them scatter as happened to the Salonen."

My people. That reminded him of another topic. "Amal didn't want me to say I'm a Salonen, did she?"

"No," Jan said. "We want to keep that secret—as much as we can—until we're in front of the other Oathbreakers."

"Fine." Dalyan sighed, feeling tired now that it was all over. "Do you have any idea where Nohr took my dog?"

"Your dog is currently in the kitchens, sir." A Larossan man walked into the bedroom, his hands folded politely in front of him. "The cook is preparing a meal for it."

"Her," Dalyan said.

"Her," the man allowed. "I am Iladin Coatine, and I will be serving as your valet while you're here." He surveyed

Dalyan from head to toe, dark eyes critical. His own garb was immaculate and tastefully embroidered, making Dalyan embarrassed by the state of his travel-weary uniform. "I understand you are now the consort, so I am currently locating appropriate garments for you, and . . ."

Hearing that pause, Dalyan worried.

". . . we need to do something about your hair," Iladin finished. "Yes, that needs work."

"Don't worry," Jan murmured, one reassuring hand on Dalyan's shoulder. "He cuts Mikks' hair every time we stop here. He knows what he's doing."

Dalyan swallowed. Given that he hadn't had his hair cut in months and now had a patch that had been shaven, that was probably a good idea.

CHAPTER 12

AFTER A LONG discussion with Indaris about the town and the local news, Amal returned to her own quarters in the residential wing of the manor. When she opened the door, she saw Iladin helping a man lace up his sleeves. For a split second, she didn't recognize him, but he turned halfway at the sound of the door.

It was Dalyan, but a Dalyan who looked very much like an Anvarrid lord.

His dark hair was cut in a very Anvarrid short crop—knowing Iladin, it was likely the current style in the capital—that brought Dalyan's eyebrows and cheekbones back into prominence. Iladin had dressed him in one of Samedrion's old outfits, white trousers overlaid with a layer of stiff-pleated white skirts, the hems embroidered in black. His white jacket was laced tight about his chest and arms, but Amal suspected they would have been tight to begin with. Her eldest brother had been leaner than Dalyan.

Dalyan turned to face her. "What do you think? Will it do?"

She wasn't close enough to sense his emotions, so she went to his side. He reflected nervousness, along with a strong desire to please her. And she thought she could feel weariness under all that. "You look . . . magnificent. Good enough to meet the king."

He flushed as he did whenever she complimented him. "Thank you. I don't want to embarrass you. Jan said he could work with me tomorrow on proper manners. While you're gone, I mean."

She'd intended to take Jan with her, but she could make do with Magnus. "That would be . . . a good thing. I . . ." She glanced at Iladin, who held his eyes averted.

"I will return later," Iladin said, "to help you unlace that, sir."

"No need," Amal told him. "I can do that."

She would swear that one corner of Iladin's mouth turned up in a smile, but otherwise the man remained stone faced.

"And thank you," she added. "You've done an excellent job, Iladin."

He bowed and walked out of the room, closing the door behind him.

"There has to be some compromise," Dalyan said, "where this is laced but I can still move without splitting a seam."

She smiled at him. "This sort of attire is made to show that you don't need to work. That you can afford to linger about all day while a servant laces and unlaces you."

"I understand that, but this is unreasonable, Amal." He flexed one arm slowly.

"Did he have you flex your arm before he laced it? That helps."

"I see. And how does one keep this white clean?" His jaw clenched. "I'm not sure . . ."

"If you get it dirty," she told him, "someone can clean it. If they can't, you give it away and have something new made. This is an Anvarrid *lord's* attire, not a stable hand's."

He sighed heavily, eyes closing.

He hated this. She could see that without needing to sense it.

The white of the high-necked jacket made Dalyan's hair and skin look darker, and highlighted the fineness of his skin. If he'd been one of those men with ruddy cheeks or blotchy skin, it would have shown, but he had no such flaws. He looked shockingly handsome.

Amal took his left wrist and began unlacing his sleeve. "I'll get you out of this."

He let loose a pent breath. "I may not be cut out for this. Being displayed like a prize, I mean."

Amal laughed, ducking down to loosen the laces under his upper arm. "Believe me, I wasn't either. If it's any comfort to you, I will be equally uncomfortable in what I'm wearing when we go to the palace." The first sleeve unlaced, she went to his other side to undo the other. "Do you swim?"

He lifted his arm higher and tried to look at her under it. "Swim?"

"Do you know how to swim?"

"I . . ." He went still, as though the question required great thought. "I know how to swim."

Amal touched a hand to his back to warn him before she started the laces at his waist. "Is that something you remember, or something you've actually done?"

He considered for a moment. "I think I know how to swim, although I've never done so."

Then it was a talent that had come with him into this life, a relic of the man he was based on. "This wing has one other surprise. There's a hot spring feeding the water here, and there's a pool just outside the house."

She drew the last round cord out of the jacket's back. Dalyan held out his arms and she carefully tugged the jacket off, leaving him in several other layers, but far more comfortable. She folded the jacket. "Better?"

Dalyan exhaled. "Yes. How often do you have to wear these?"

"Only at the palace," she promised him. "You've seen the blacks I wear back at the Keep. They're not nearly as tight as the whites."

He shook his head. "A hot spring that close to the house? That must cause mildew."

She laid the jacket over a chair back. "I never said this house was easy to maintain. There's a reason this monstrosity is built of stone rather than wood. Furniture doesn't like the damp, either."

"Perhaps not," he said.

Amal laughed as she unhooked the back of his skirts.

Dalyan dropped the straps and carefully stepped out of them. That left him in his long, loose shirt and white trousers. "Are you supposed to be acting the part of my valet?" he asked.

Amal laid one hand on either of his cheeks. "I'm currently acting the part of your wife. Sometimes I forget how handsome you are. There's something about men all dressed up in their finery that reminds me that you are the peacocks of our kind."

He flushed again, dark lashes dropping to hide his eyes. "I shall have to wait to see you in the white to see if it flatters you like the black does."

Amal shook her head. Most of the whites had been her mother's, and were cut for her instead. Amal hadn't had much desire to have new garb made for only a few appearances per year. Dalyan would find out when he saw them that they were not her style. Perhaps when they were in the capital, they could both be fitted for new garb. It wasn't as if she couldn't afford it. "Why don't you come with me down to the pool and try swimming. I promise you'll sleep sounder afterward."

He gave her a smile that was only a little weary. "That sounds nice."

The manor continued to surprise Dalyan with its opulence.

Only fifty feet from the walls of the house, the pool was connected to the doors by a smooth flagstone walkway. The pool itself was shaded by a planting of trees and awnings that would keep the sun off it in the hottest part of the year. The builder had put in a rectangular basin made with stone walls, large enough for a few dozen people to enjoy the steaming water at once. It was only waist deep, but ledges around the sides allowed people to sit there. The others had come ahead of them and sat around the corner of the pool closest to the manor.

When he glanced up, Dalyan saw a handful of sentries on the many-chimneyed roof, watching Amal even on her own territory. He shouldn't have been surprised.

He managed to undress and settle in water without displaying too much embarrassment, he hoped. It was one thing to know that it didn't meant the same thing to the others—after all, nudity was common within a yeargroup—but he still wasn't comfortable with it himself. Once he was in the water, though, he settled on the ledge next to Amal in the liquid heat and contemplated whether he might fall asleep there. The others chatted about what they planned to do the next day, where they wanted to go into town, and what awaited in the capital, all things that concerned him less than where his puppy was.

He woke when Amal shook his shoulder. "We're going back inside."

Dalyan glanced up and saw that the sun had set some time ago, the skies around them dark. The others were already halfway up the walk to the manor doors. "How long was I asleep?"

"Not long, I promise." Amal climbed out of the pool and wrapped a huge white towel about herself. Then she held one out for him.

Dalyan rose obediently and climbed up into the chill night air. Amal swathed him in the towel, and he shivered. "Where are my clothes?"

"Nohr has them," Amal said. "Don't worry, you'll get them back. Let's go get something to eat, find Nimi, and then you can go to bed."

Dalyan went willingly. They ate a light dinner and then collected Nimi. The puppy, worn out by attention from a dozen admirers in the kitchen, promptly fell asleep in her basket. Dalyan was nodding off himself, so Amal coaxed him into the oversized bed with her. She would have liked to spend the evening in bed with him, but as soon as his head hit the pillow, he was asleep.

She watched him for a time. She hadn't expected a simple haircut would alter his appearance so much, but it changed what he seemed to be. He looked more Anvarrid, more confident, more sophisticated. She sniffled, and realized that she'd begun to cry. *How vexing.*

She couldn't keep him completely safe. It wasn't possible, and every leg of the journey would take him closer to the capital. Legally, the contract he'd signed should protect him. Legally, they wouldn't be able to seize him. But she couldn't actually stop anyone.

She hadn't been as blunt about that as she should have.

The city's streets were not unlike the capital's, Dalyan decided, only it was smaller. The roads were neatly cobbled and traffic moved along quickly. He'd gotten glimpses of them the evening before, but he'd not seen much of the city center itself.

"It's actually the financial capital of the province," Freja said, pointing out another building of the pale stone so common here. "Banks everywhere."

"I see." Dalyan had spent most of the morning sitting with Jan, learning how he should behave in front of the king. Actually, it was the king's guards that concerned Jan more. They were quarterguards, which meant they were charged with judging the intentions of anyone who came into the king's presence. They were required to be sensitives. That had set off a long discussion of the guards back at the Keep. Those who guarded Amal's person did not have the requirement, while those who guarded the main hall—and residential hall when she was present there—did, an odd contrast. Jan said that guards like him were to use their eyes to watch, whereas the quarterguards, who held stationary posts, were there to use their *talents* instead. They complimented each other.

So every sentry Dalyan had passed in the residential hall was aware of his feelings at all times, even when he and Amal were in a closed room. Dalyan wasn't sure he liked that. It implied a lack of privacy that would never change.

"It's just around the corner," Freja said.

She'd wanted to come into town after luncheon to shop for supplies. Jan permitted it, so Dalyan accompanied her on the streets now as she led him toward a favored store. Shopping wasn't one of his skills. Having only visited stores on his journey to the capital, a few while there, and the ones in Melyrep, he didn't have a great deal of experience. He did, however, know that most storekeepers expected him to haggle, an activity for which he felt a deep-seated dread. He intended to let Freja do all of that.

The store to which she led him was an old one that stocked winter expedition supplies. The Larossan owner took one look at Freja and simply waved her past, leaving them unsupervised with his merchandise. "He knows us," Freja explained.

Dalyan had guessed that already. Judging by his white hair, the man wasn't much younger than Grandfather Johan, his dark face lined and serious. He certainly kept a tidy store. Tents, snowshoes, foodstuffs, and all manner of gear crowded the store's shelves and hung from the ceiling. The store smelled of old leather and musty wood.

Freja seemed to know what she wanted and exactly where to find it. Dalyan ended up with several boxes of shortbread, a large quantity of jerked meat—beef and reindeer—and a quantity of sewing items—fine needles and black thread. When she was done, he carried them to the front for her, where the shop owner busily tallied up a column of numbers.

"Freja," the man said without looking up. "Is this all?"

She laughed. "Yes, Mr. Rijan. Can you deliver it to the manor?"

He did look up at her this time. "Tonight?"

"Yes." Freja plucked out one small paper bag and showed it to the owner. "I'm going to take this with me, though."

He leaned forward to peer at the bag. "Fine, I'll add it to the tab."

She tucked the bag in one pocket. "We're heading to the capital, so you should expect some extra deliveries."

The man nodded sagely. "Not a problem. Bear my greetings to Amal and Jan, please, and Gyda when you see her."

Freja smiled at him and inclined her head. "I will certainly do so."

He turned dark eyes on Dalyan. "And who is this? A new guard?"

Freja made an ironic little flourish with one hand. "This is Amal's husband, Dalyan."

"Ah, the new husband," he said, his white brows drawing together. He leaned forward to give Dalyan a more thorough perusal. "People are curious. Asking around. Shall I admit that I've met him?"

Dalyan licked his lips, unsure whether anyone was supposed to know about the contract yet.

Freja grinned, something Dalyan rarely saw her do, but her hand gripped his arm tightly. "Of course, Mr. Rijan."

He inclined his head toward Dalyan. "Then I will tell all how pleasantly silent you are, sir. Unlike the pushy child with you."

Dalyan felt his cheeks flush, but Freja dragged him toward the door before he could answer. "We need to get out of here," she said quietly, anxiety rising about her.

He let her guide him back onto the sidewalk. "What's happening?"

"Rijan said people have been asking about you," she said, her eyes surveying the traffic about them, a quick glance at each pedestrian.

"Have the lawyers. . . ?"

"No, they wouldn't peep. That means someone else did. Someone back at the Horn."

"Does he. . . ?"

"No, he meant customers," Freja snapped. "If he'd meant the manor staff, he would have told me so. So someone who's shopped there is trying to pry out information. I didn't think this would actually happen."

The manor's carriage was a couple of blocks away, if it was even still there. "Are you going to drag me all the way back?"

Freja stopped and let go of his arm. "No. Of course not. What was I thinking? Go ahead of me."

Dalyan was unsure what she meant now. A young man walked past, stepping into the street to avoid him and casting an annoyed glance his way. "What do you want me. . .?"

"Walk on," Freja said. She withdrew a pistol from a jacket pocket and, after checking to see that it was loaded, slid it into her sash. "Go to where we left the carriage. I'll follow."

Like a guard. Freja was worried for his safety. Dalyan walked on, Freja behind him, turning when he thought it was proper. He spotted the carriage waiting near a stable yard and headed that direction. He'd just set one hand on the carriage's door handle when a man walked around from the rear of the vehicle, pistol drawn.

He was Larossan, Dalyan guessed from his darker skin, but taller than most Larossans. His blue tunic was unadorned and he wore the brown trousers of a servant, yet he didn't walk like one. He held that pistol like he was comfortable with it and radiated an air of satisfaction that Dalyan could almost taste in his mouth. "Dalyan Horn?" the man asked, one brow lifting.

Dalyan resisted the desire to glance back for Freja. *I don't want to get her in trouble.* "Yes?"

"You'll need to come with me," the man said.

Dalyan fought to remain calm. There was no point in letting this man know he was alarmed. The truth was, if they separated him from the Horn, there was no guarantee he would ever get back. Amal might have legal recourse, but he was sure he would sit in a prison cell throughout the legal proceedings. He had no idea how long that would take.

"By whose authority?" he finally remembered to ask. Jan had stressed that was important—if someone was going to arrest him, he should find out who it was.

"I'm with the Daujom," the man said, gesturing with his pistol toward the side of the carriage. "Put your hands there."

"I'm sorry, sir," the driver called down in a rueful tone. "I didn't see him."

The Daujom had stayed behind the carriage, out of the driver's line of sight.

"Don't worry," Dalyan called up. He laid his hands against the side of the carriage, wondering what the unknown man meant to do. The Daujom patted the pockets of Dalyan's uniform jacket, the back of his sash, then his ankles. He'd come to town without any weapon, so this search was pointless. "I'm unarmed," he said anyway.

"Put your hands behind your back," the man ordered.

Behind his back? "Why?"

"I'm going to tie your hands together." The Daujom jerked one of his arms down and behind him.

He wasn't well trained enough to defeat this man. The Daujom, even if they looked Larossan, were often children raised by the Lucas Family, and thus knew how to fight. Dalyan didn't see a point in fighting. So he lowered his other arm. A rope tightened around his wrists.

CHAPTER 13

D ALYAN WAS RELIEVED when he saw movement from behind the carriage, Freja following the same path his captor had.

"I would let that man loose." Freja held her hands wide to show she had no weapon. "This is going to be peaceful, Daujom, unless you make it otherwise."

The man's hand clamped down Dalyan's shoulder, pressing him forward so that his cheek rested against the wall of the carriage. "This man is a foreign agent," he said. "I can do as I wish with him."

"He's a member of the Horn Family," Freja protested.

Dalyan wasn't sure that would make a difference.

"Not my problem," the man said. "I was told to take him in to the capital."

Freja crossed her arms over her chest and glared at the man like she had at Amal when she'd brought Nimi to Six Down. "We are taking him to the capital."

"He's wanted *in custody*, Infirmarian." The man's voice took on a derisive tone, as if Freja couldn't fight because she was an infirmarian.

That was likely a mistake.

Freja dropped her arms, took a step closer, and set one hand on the pistol at her waist. "Let me be very clear, Daujom. You . . . are holding the Horn *Consort*. Our *consort*. Now, you can tangle with me, the Rifle on the roof of the stables, or the other guard who's coming around behind you right now . . ."

Dalyan swallowed. *Who?*

". . . or you can recall that, legally, you cannot touch an Anvarrid citizen without proper legal documentation. And a consort has Anvarrid status, no matter what he held before the contract."

"Move away," Nohr said from behind them.

The man stepped back, his hand leaving Dalyan's shoulder. Dalyan turned and saw that Nohr was indeed a few feet away, rifle in his hands. He'd fluffed up his braids, looking his most savage. With the carriage between himself and the stables, Dalyan couldn't see if Eldana—the other Rifle among the guards—was actually on the roof, but he wasn't going to question Freja's word.

Freja hadn't taken her eyes off the Daujom. "This is simple. You can let the Daujom know that he's the consort, so if they want him, they're going to have to go through the courts. Or fight us, your choice."

Jaw clenched, the man held his hands wide, as if in surrender. Feeling the rope go slack, Dalyan shook it off.

"I'll forward that message, Infirmarian," the Daujom said.

"Good," Freja said. "Sir, if you'll get in the carriage, we'll get going."

It took Dalyan a second to realize she meant him when she'd said *sir*. He dutifully opened the door and climbed into the carriage. Freja followed, closing the door behind her and leaving Nohr behind to watch their retreat. The driver released the brake when she pounded on the front wall, and the carriage rolled forward. Dalyan didn't say anything until they were some distance from the stables.

"Hel's tits," Freja said under her breath, irritation flaring around her briefly.

"Did you know that was going to happen?" Dalyan asked.

"Yes and no. No, not actually." Freja's head tilted as she peered at him. "We knew there was a chance that someone back at the Horn had notified the local Daujom representatives here. I just didn't believe anyone would be that idiotic. I thought Jan was being overly protective when he had Mikks and Nohr follow in the other carriage. They've been ghosting us since we entered the town." She let out a vexed huff, but he could tell she was calming now, packing away her frustration.

"Jan suspected someone would try to grab me?"

"Yes, and he'll remind me of that for the next month."

She was more irritated by that, he guessed, than she was by the threat to him.

"Then again," she added, "now the local Daujom personnel know that you're a consort, and that will keep them from trying again."

"I suppose that's better," he said, still not feeling too sanguine about the whole thing.

"It was more frightening for you than me," Freja allowed.

He chuckled. "Why was Mikks on the roof, not Nohr?"

"They must have decided Norh was more intimidating," Freja said with a half-shrug. She dug into her jacket pockets. "I honestly didn't think the Daujom would have someone in the city, especially this far from the capital. Fortunately, he was willing to see reason. You get the ones who don't know the law and think that they're above it. If it was one of those, we might have had to kill him."

The carriage had reached the edge of the city, signaling relative safety. "Kill him? You wouldn't actually...?"

"Found it!" Freja held up the paper bag from the store. "I owe you these."

When she offered it to him, he took the bag. He hadn't been paying attention that closely in the store, so he hadn't caught what it was. He peered at the paper label on the bottom and then grinned. *Roasted cashews.* The day he'd met the Horn, Freja had confiscated his bag of cashews. They were a treat he'd been saving, since they were imported from overseas and quite expensive. She'd eaten them all. "Thank you."

"You *could* share," she pointed out.

Conversations with Freja often jumped about, so he wasn't too surprised she'd gone off on a strange tangent. He opened the bag, poured a few of the nuts onto his hand, and handed the bag back to Freja. "Would you have killed someone for my sake?"

She popped a cashew into her mouth and peered at him from the other side of the bench. "I think I like you enough that I might have."

He gazed at her, worried. He often couldn't read Freja's emotions. She held them tight to herself.

"I don't know," she said after a moment. "I've never killed anyone."

He licked his lips and sat back. He *had* killed someone, an assassin who'd come after *him*, but threatened Amal as well. While other assassins had died in pursuit of him, he hadn't actually killed one before that day. "You're pragmatic. I think..."

"You never know how you'll react to something until you get there, Dalyan." She shook her head, a hint of ruefulness surrounding her before she tucked it away. "When I was younger, I thought I would be a wonderful mother. I love my children, but I am not as good with them as I expected to be."

He'd known that about Freja, even if no one had said it aloud. It was the sort of thing one didn't say about others.

"The point being," she added, "it was a shock to me when I realized that. I never thought I would be . . . cool to my children."

That was terribly personal. If it had been Amal, he would have told her that some people were likely better with older children than younger ones. Freja wouldn't appreciate that effort to comfort her.

"The man I killed," he confessed instead. "I have trouble thinking of him as human. Every time I think about it, something in my mind says that I killed something else, something inferior."

"And that bothers you?" she asked.

They were passing a bright green field now, a plant he didn't recognize. "Yes. Think of how your people have treated me—like I'm no different than you. But I'm more like that assassin, aren't I? He was probably made in a machine like me, sent on a mission like me. For me to think of him as less important than me is hypocritical."

She peered at him. "Are you telling yourself that to excuse your actions?"

"I don't know," he admitted. "I just . . ."

"You want to be fair and honest. To everyone, even a man who's tried to kill both you and Amal." She shook more cashews out of the bag onto her palm and then handed it back to him. "You haven't justified your existence to yourself, Dalyan."

He wasn't sure what to make of that. He tucked the bag into a jacket pocket as the carriage rattled on.

"Thank you," she said after a silent moment. "For not questioning whether I *could* kill him. I've been lax about practice lately, and I'm not sure I wouldn't have accidentally shot you, instead."

Now *that* was truly frightening.

As soon as they reached the estate, Amal went in search of Dalyan. The guards told her he was sitting out in the pool, so she went there and found him sitting there by himself, staring out at the fields. She knelt next to the pool, hoping she didn't overbalance and fall in. She was still in full uniform.

She could sense his mood, a low ebb of his spirits. He wasn't despondent, but he wasn't happy either. "What's wrong?"

He sighed. "I sometimes forget what an abysmally poor choice I am for your husband."

She'd already heard that a Daujom had tried to arrest him. She would have expected something closer to outrage or fear as a reaction to that occurrence. His self-doubt was a surprise. "Why do you say that, Dalyan?"

"I'd forgotten I'm not one of you. Just when I was feeling comfortable among you, like I had a place here, he comes in and tries to arrest me as a foreign agent. Which *I am,* Amal."

She touched his hair, short enough now that she could see the newly scarred spot behind his ear. In a way, she felt like his foreignness had been cut out of him with that device, but that wouldn't do for the Daujom. Or the king. "Dalyan, we *want* you to think of yourself as one of us."

"That doesn't change what I am, Amal. I'm a foreigner."

And yet he looked Anvarrid, *sounded* Anvarrid. Her mind kept insisting to her that he couldn't be foreign.

"You've chosen to stay with us," she reminded him. "You *are* one of us now."

"Freja could have been hurt today," he said.

"Stop." She pinched the tip of his ear. "Don't try to take responsibility for Freja's actions. If she didn't want to protect you, she wouldn't have."

Amal waited. He didn't agree, but he didn't argue that point, either. "Come. Let's eat dinner, and then we can make plans for the rest of the journey."

He rose from the pool, wrapping one of the large towels around himself before he followed her back inside. Once he'd dressed, they made their way back to the dining hall where the others already sat around a large table, discussing events back at the Horn with the resident guards.

Since each residence must be guarded by the Horn Family, that meant there were always guards assigned here. Usually they rotated off after a few months and returned to the Horn, but a few always opted to stay at the estates. Discussions about home were, however, always welcome. The resident guardsmen even introduced themselves to Dalyan, all seemingly pleased to meet him, so perhaps none were in Vibeka's faction. That had worried Amal somewhat, since Vibeka held control of all guard postings, even the postings to the estates.

Dalyan slept fitfully that night, and woke with a cry long after midnight. It was the same dream he'd had before—the one where he ran down strange hallways searching for someone named Katja. And as before it left him shaken and upset. His heart raced, and Amal could feel the anguish all about him even as he tried to conceal it. He hated talking about the dream. He lay there, stricken for some time, the emotions of the dream slowly leaking out of him.

It was the one memory he had from those Jukka Salonen had left behind, a moment of such pain and loss that it had become indelibly stamped on the pattern the Cince used to create Dalyan. Unfortunately, Dalyan had no actual memory to go with it, no context. He rose after a time and carried Nimi outside to take care of her needs and came back to bed less agitated.

"Do you think it would help if you knew?" Amal whispered. They could ask the Fortress who Katja was. If she'd been his wife or lover, there might be some mention of her in the records that Signe had found on the man.

"No, I don't want to know. I want to stop having this dream." Dalyan turned onto his side, away from her, still trying to calm himself.

Amal understood. It wasn't *his* dream or *his* pain. It was unfair that he had to live with it.

CHAPTER 14

THE REMAINDER OF the journey passed without incident. Dalyan simply stayed close. He spent each evening with the group, making another set of sketches of his instructors back at the facility. Since Dalyan had rarely spoken to anyone else during those six years, those faces were burned into his mind's eye. It was simple to recreate them.

In the carriage, he and Mikks and Sofie discussed the texts they were reading, trying to match Horn words to Salonen ones, guessing at the pronunciation. They were, at least, getting the proper words into their heads. Amal helped straighten out a few misconceptions, but for the most part allowed the three of them to haggle out their studies themselves. They would learn more, she claimed, if they did it themselves.

They alternated between inns that were clearly familiar to the group and estates of friends of Amal's. Both of the estates they visited were far smaller than hers, but still larger than the Keep. Neither was occupied by the owner at the time, a strange waste of land. According to Mikks, the summer was the time for the Anvarrid to be in Noikinos, leaving the crops to tenant farmers and managers. They didn't dirty their hands with soil. Given that Mikks' parents had been farmers, Dalyan chose not to comment on that.

Amal didn't actually dirty her hands, nor did Jan, but they did involve themselves in the province's farming interests. Since he might be expected to help with those duties at times, Dalyan paid attention to everything Amal said on the topic.

A broken axle stalled them on the road near the capital, so they arrived at their destination past dark that night. Fortunately, there was enough moon to get them to the plateau where the estate was located. Even in the relative darkness, Dalyan could tell that it was a smaller estate, and the manor was far plainer than the palaces he'd seen in Noikinos before.

"It's stark," Amal said, "but it's warm in winter."

That was a virtue to the Horn, he knew. Having overwintered in the mountains near the Horn Glacier, he concurred.

The house had a single guard tower, with a conical roof, and steep rooftops on wings that formed a square around a courtyard. He wasn't sure of the colors in the evening's darkness. There were stables to one side where a contingent of stable hands and a half-dozen Horn sentries waited. Amal introduced Dalyan to the sentries, most of whom were older men, all apparently pleased that Amal had remarried. None were obviously partisans of Vibeka's, but he wouldn't be able to tell that just by looking.

Dalyan followed Amal inside the manor. It was well lit, and furnished. The white granite walls bore the same type of tapestries he was beginning to consider as essential for Anvarrid residences. There were old battle scenes, depicting the invasion, he guessed. The pale tile floors were covered with figured woolen rugs in blues and dark gray, and black-painted light fixtures glowed and hissed on the walls. It was an elegant place, but lacked hominess.

"I'm getting homesick for the Keep," he whispered to Amal as they made their way down one of the first-floor halls.

Amal laughed. "I am all the time. I should love to travel—after all, most Larossans are never able to leave their home towns—but I don't."

A servant approached them, a woman far older than Indaris. Her dark skin and mostly gray hair identified her as Larossan, and her shrewd eyes took in Amal's weary-looking state, Dalyan's presence, and Nimi on his arm. The other guards passed her with fond greetings and headed on down a hallway they clearly knew. Amal stayed behind to introduce him yet again. Her butler, as she called the woman, was named Enala Hansine and had worked for Amal's father before her. They discussed Amal's plans for the evening, and agreed that other details could be worked out while Amal was dressing the next morning.

Once introduced, Dalyan inclined his head and made a half-bow to the woman, remembering to keep his distance.

"And I will take that," she said, gesturing with an underhanded motion toward Nimi. She carefully plucked the puppy off Dalyan's arm, managing to do so without touching him. Then she bowed again and headed off in a different direction than the guards had. So Amal led Dalyan down the halls to the residence of the manor.

Her bedroom was far smaller than the one at the other estate, but he liked it better. It was similar to hers—and his—back at the Keep. The bed was draped with a quilt in shades of gray, and the bed curtains were the familiar black wool. Even the carpet underfoot must have come from the Horn. Dalyan sat on the edge of the bed and sighed with contentment.

"If I have to spend time here, I might as well be comfortable," she said, amusement wrapping around her. "We can pretend we're back home."

He liked that idea. Perhaps he could get a decent night's sleep. They waited for the servants to bring in the baggage, and then went to join the others for dinner. The illusion of being back at the Keep faded as soon as they left the bedroom, though. The kitchen staff seemed intent on impressing Amal and her guard and thus served a meal of five courses.

The table was small, though, not the long banquet table meant for a hundred. The nine of them sat around the table, all relieved to have the travel over with.

"They don't know," Mikks said after the second course of a spicy soup of root vegetables and greens, "that you have to appear at the palace—I mean, in very tight-fitting clothes."

"Oh Hel," Amal said. "I wonder if I can convince the king to forego formal dress someday."

"Clothing is what separates the Anvarrid from the Larossans," Jan inserted smoothly. "If you can't wear a workman's entire year's salary on your back, then you're not Anvarrid enough to be called Anvarrid."

Dalyan didn't argue, but he knew Iladin had carefully packed those white robes for him to wear. "I should skip the rest of the dinner."

"My cook would be mortally offended," Amal said, which earned laughter from the others and kept the tone in the room light. They all knew what would happen in the morning, and Dalyan wished he could get this over with.

The meeting with the Oathbreakers was scheduled for later the next day, after the meeting with the king, but could be conducted in Family uniforms. If he was going to be questioned endlessly—he expected more questions from the

Oathbreakers than from the king—at least he would be comfortable if they decided to torture him.

Her butler entered the dining room between courses, her mien serious, and walked to Amal's side. "Lady Amal, you have a visitor. She says it's urgent."

Amal gazed up at her. "Enala, would you ask her if she'd be willing to join us here?"

The woman inclined her head gracefully and swept back out of the room.

"Who do you think it is?" Jan asked.

Amal's lips pressed together. Excitement coiled around her now, accompanied with a surge of hope. "I think it's Rachel."

That set the others to nodding, which told Dalyan they all knew who this Rachel was.

"Rachel Lucas, the king's niece," Amal told him when he asked. "I've asked for her to be present when we meet with him, so I'm sure she wants to know why."

"I didn't know."

"I wasn't sure she would do it," Amal admitted. "I *hoped* she would come."

Amal still omitted things when she talked with him. He tried to be understanding about that. Sometimes she said things, assuming he would simply know about the things that she didn't include. It wasn't always intentional. Sometimes it was, though, like this.

The door opened again, the servant this time accompanied by a young woman in Family uniform, the trim for *engineer* across her chest—the Lucas pattern was slightly different from the Horn's, but close enough that Dalyan couldn't mistake it. A pretty woman with delicate features, she was younger than the rest of them, likely in her early twenties. Her coloration was a mixture of Family and Anvarrid, with dark hair worn in the thirteen braids that the

Lucas Family favored, but her skin was much fairer than Amal's. More like Jan's. She had the many-hued green eyes that sometimes showed up in Anvarrid families.

The servant introduced her and then slipped out. Rachel moved toward the table where Jan was pulling out a chair for her. At her first step, Dalyan noted the dip of her shoulder. She limped, rather profoundly. Since Jan was already there, Dalyan quelled the urge to get up and help her to the offered seat. Once she was sitting, Jan pushed in her chair. "Have you eaten yet?" he asked.

Rachel hesitated. "Uh . . . no. It's my . . ."

Dalyan watched as she blinked. He could sense her frustration building as she sought a word in her mind, yet that didn't show on her face other than a faint trembling of her chin.

"Early time to eat," she finally said.

"Ah," Jan said. "I'll see if the kitchens have something suitable for breakfast."

Her shoulders slumped, as if relieved to hear that word. Jan left, hunting a servant, and Amal turned in her seat to face Rachel.

"You want to know why I've asked for you to join us when we meet the king tomorrow," Amal stated.

Rachel nodded and gestured at the guards sitting around the table.

"They all know," Amal said. "We're going to make changes at the Horn, and among other things, we'll need many more Oathbreakers. My guard have all agreed to the liability of breaking the treaty. Of becoming Oathbreakers, in various capacities."

Rachel shook her head. "Why?"

"Because of the man sitting next to me," Amal said. "Or rather, what he represents. The Cince *are* coming for Salonen."

This time the young woman showed a visible reaction. She swallowed, her jaw clenching again. "How is this . . . different?"

"Because Dalyan represents a new tactic. A new way of getting into Salonen Fortress. He *is* a Salonen."

The young woman's eyes flicked up and down his face. "No."

"You recall, don't you, that when the Cince made the Desida, they altered their patterns to give them special abilities?"

Rachel nodded again.

Amal continued. "They altered Dalyan's pattern to make him look more Anvarrid, but he is almost pure Salonen."

The young woman gazed at him. "No."

"Yes," Amal said, leaning forward. "He was *created*. We need to talk more about that later."

The corner of Rachel's lips tilted up, her reaction skeptical.

"I don't expect you to believe me," Amal said. "Would you believe your Fortress?"

Rachel sat back. "How?"

"A drop of blood will tell your Fortress what you need to know."

Rachel studied Dalyan for a moment, her emotions held close now. "Fine."

"We can do that before you go back," Amal said.

The servants showed up with the next course then, causing a halt in the discussion. They brought Rachel a plate that held flatbread, spiced potatoes, and what appeared to be chicken. A better size of meal in Dalyan's eyes, but he ate his curried fish instead. The group returned to discussing the morning plans in general terms while they

ate, but once the servants cleared out of the room and shut
the door, Amal turned back to Rachel.

"The question we'll be posing to the Oathbreakers
tomorrow," Amal said, "is how the Cince got a Salonen
pattern. And his *is* a Salonen pattern. Our Fortress told us
it's the pattern of a Salonen Original."

Rachel's eyes went distant, her face showing nothing.
But Dalyan could almost feel the tight spiraling of her mind
as she began to chase down the ramifications of that. Now
he knew why Amal had invited her . . . Rachel was intelligent
enough to grasp the possibilities his existence implied. After
a few minutes of ignoring her breakfast—as she was an
engineer, she might have just woken, after all—Rachel sat
up straighter. "How long?"

"We can't know," Amal said. "At least eight years."

Rachel's eyes flicked toward him again. "As a . . . not
an infant?"

Amal answered. "Yes, he was created as an eighteen,
we think. The Fortress' records support that."

She considered that for a moment before speaking
again. "Any others?"

"We have no way to know. He wasn't aware of any, but
why create only one?"

Now they were talking about him like he was a *thing*—a
watch or a steam engine. Dalyan tucked away his discomfort. His feelings weren't relevant to their discussion. They
weren't helpful. When he glanced up from his plate, Rachel
was watching him.

"The truth is," Amal summed up, "they could have
stolen one pattern . . . or a thousand. They could have the
patterns for every Family Original. Given his instructions
and how they chose to alter him, we believe their goal is to
gain entry to Salonen to steal its memories."

She went on to tell Rachel about the device in his head, about the incident at the entryway to Horn Fortress, and the subsequent removal of that device once the Fortress disabled it.

They talked on for a time, Rachel in her halting sentences and Amal eloquently insistent on the Horn's planned course. When Rachel finished her meal, she said she needed to return to Lucas Fortress. Dalyan took his napkin and, after getting a nod from Amal, used his dinner knife to make a small cut on his left palm. He let blood drip from there onto the napkin, then folded it closed and passed it to Rachel. She tucked it into a jacket pocket and, after the appropriate courtesies, left them to finish their meal. Jan walked out with her, intending to see her safely to her carriage.

"Now we pray that Rachel reaches the same conclusions we have," Amal said. "If she does, our chances with the king improve substantially."

It wasn't until they were back in their room, Nimi chewing happily on a knotted piece of rope in her basket, that Amal had time to talk to Dalyan privately. "I didn't offend you, did I?"

Already stripped down to the loose trousers he slept in, Dalyan paused as he tied the draw string. Not looking at her, just contemplating how he intended to answer. "You didn't say anything that was untrue," he said. "The truth bothers me more than your saying it."

She licked her lips. He'd clutched his emotions close. He was a far stronger sensitive than she was now, and could evade her senses. "That was a very diplomatic answer."

He sat on the edge of the bed, eyes on the puppy. "I get comfortable and forget that I'm controversial. That my very existence is controversial. Then it feels like a rebuke when someone reminds me."

He'd felt that way back in Evaryanos, like an outsider. Amal took off her coat and laid it over the chair. "Dalyan, we are all a problem to someone else. There are still members of the senate who object to me as Lady Horn. I have to ignore that."

His eyes lifted and a quizzical look crossed his features. "Why would they object to you?"

"Because I was raised in the Family. Some would have preferred that we elevate one of my cousins in Evaryanos to the seat of Lord Horn since *they* know how to behave properly."

His eyes narrowed. "That's why you wear the Anvarrid robes. So people will think you're behaving properly."

She felt her cheeks warm. "True. We give people what they want to see of us. Tomorrow, you need to be harmless, a man who never meant any harm."

"I never did," he protested.

"I know that." She sat next to him. "You need to show that to the king and his guards."

"He can still have me arrested, can't he? Even if you've made me your consort."

"Yes," Amal admitted. "He's the king. But if I can convince him to acknowledge you, then you're safe. That's why we're going to see him first."

"And you think his niece can make the difference?"

"He'll think I'm biased. But Rachel? If she comes to our defense, he'll be likely to believe her. I just hope that she does."

He glanced down at the small cut on the ball of his palm, which had scabbed over now. "She has proof, though."

"If she knows the right questions to ask," Amal said. "Rachel's brilliant. Don't let her halting speech fool you; that's left over from a childhood injury. Of any of the Oathbreakers, I suspect she'll be the first to come down on our side." She took Dalyan's hand in hers. "We can't have come this far only to have the king rip us apart."

He laughed softly. "I think Fate is more capricious than that."

Dalyan didn't believe in Father Winter, nor any god at all, but he had some faith in Fate, that there was a comprehensible order to the universe. Amal wavered in her faith, still not sure how she felt about her family's death. She was still going to pray for Father Winter's protection for Dalyan. It couldn't hurt, could it?

She had done everything she could to smooth the way for tomorrow's meetings. Amal leaned her head against Dalyan's shoulder. "We have to be strong tomorrow. We have to be sure of ourselves. This isn't just for us, but the twenty-sevens. All six Families, and all the country for that matter. We have to win."

He laid one hand on her stomach. "If the king has me arrested, executed, I know you'll take care of her. But I will do anything I can to stay with you."

Amal smiled, unable to help herself. "Her?"

"Well, she's a dau . . ." Dalyan pulled away, his mouth open in surprised. His sense of confusion swirled around her before he brought it under control.

She leaned forward to look at his face. "What makes you think that?"

"I don't know," he said, wetting his lower lip with his tongue. "But I feel very sure of it."

She wasn't sure what to think of that.

"The old man," Dalyan added. "I think Katja was his daughter."

Since the night he'd discovered she was pregnant, the other twenty-sevens had made light of his ease in handling Juliane's baby. Amal *had* wondered then if that was knowledge that had come with him into this life, a relic of Jukka Salonen's memories. Dalyan had said he had no experience with children, but he handled them well. Perhaps he'd inherited a skill-set needed for child rearing.

But if he was correct about Katja, it changed the meaning of that dream that plagued him at times. It wasn't something horrible happening to a wife or lover. *Something horrible happening to a child would be much worse.*

The very thought of something happening to Sander made Amal's stomach clench. "Maybe when we get back to the Horn, we could ask the Fortress if there are records . . ."

"No," he said. "I . . . it's not *my* life, Amal. It was his. I am not him, and I don't need to know."

She could understand that. He wasn't just a flawed copy of Jukka Salonen. His separate identity was important to him, and if she pushed for more information about the long-dead Founder, it would seem like she was devaluing Dalyan's unique identity. "I understand."

"Thank you." He gazed at her, his eyes falling to the buttons of her vest. "You said you would like to pretend we're back at the Keep. If we were, what would you be doing right now."

Amal laughed and let him carry her down to the bedding, his fingers busy at her vest's buttons. She ran her fingers through his very short hair as best she could. She was not going to be afraid tonight. *I am going to pretend that everything will be fine.*

CHAPTER 15

As HE DRESSED to meet with the king of Larossa, Dalyan had no idea whether he was coming back to this estate tonight.

After a light breakfast, he'd dressed as far as he could on his own. It was Jan who showed up to help him into the tight-fitting jacket. "How are you feeling?" Jan asked.

Dalyan paused in drawing on his skirts. They still hadn't heard from Rachel, but a visit with the king, once arranged, could not be put off. "Lost," he admitted. "I have no idea how to feel. Scared."

Jan critically surveyed the lay of the white skirts, and adjusted a couple of pleats so the black embroidery showed to its greatest advantage. "That sounds about right. The king has authority to have you arrested, consort or not, so be respectful. Be truthful. Jason will know if you're lying."

Jason was the name of the king's personal guard, the king's version of Jan.

"I understand," Dalyan said.

Jan helped him draw on the jacket, and once it was settled on Dalyan's shoulders, he carefully did up the buttons in their hidden placket. Dalyan felt silly having Jan do this, but it would keep him from wrinkling the jacket unnecessarily. "Goal one is to get the king to acknowledge you," Jan went on. "Getting his cooperation *before* we go to the Oathbreakers is secondary. We can do without that. Keep that in mind."

He was reiterating things Dalyan knew, more to keep him focused than anything else. "Yes."

Jan had tightened the laces under the arms, and was tugging on the ones that tightened the back of the jacket when Amal walked back into the bedroom.

If he'd thought he was wearing finery, he was speechless at the sight of hers. Amal's garments were black and white, like his. Her hair was braided and twisted into a coronet atop her head with white feathers wrapping it. Her jacket had enough embroidery for two, but it was embroidered to look like white feathers tipped in black. Unlike his high-collared one, her jacket's neckline dipped low, and the bodice under the jacket pressed her breasts upward. He had never noticed her breasts before . . . not like he did now. He swallowed. "Um."

"Don't breathe," Jan snapped just then, and yanked hard on one of the laces.

Dalyan held his breath.

Jan tied off the laces, tucked the ends inside, and patted Dalyan's back. "Fine, you can breathe now."

He let out his breath. "Thanks, Jan."

"Better you than me," Jan said, coming around in front of Dalyan to survey his appearance. "I hate House robes."

If they felt tight on him, he could only image how uncomfortable they would be on Jan.

Amal walked toward them regally, her mouth pursed. She probably *had* to walk regally, given the tightness of her jacket. "I wore this earlier this year," she said, "but I wasn't pregnant, then."

"Ah, that explains the . . ." He failed to find the correct word and made a gesture with his hands instead, trying to indicate the way her breasts were pushed up by the jacket's lacing. ". . . excessiveness."

She glanced down. "Excessiveness? I have exactly the proper amount."

Jan snorted. "If you're going to discuss this, I'll leave you two alone."

Amal made a gesture for him to leave, but Jan was already heading for the door. She came to Dalyan and laid her hands on his cheek. "I . . . I prayed over this. I know you don't believe in Father Winter, and I'm not sure how much I do, but . . . if it makes any difference, I'll ask for his help."

"What did you ask for?"

Her eyes lowered. "That we would say the right things, and that the king would be generous."

If he had someone to ask, he would have done so, too. "Good. I need all the help I can get."

Amal tried hard not to touch her clothing while in the carriage. The pregnancy had made the jacket tighter than before, but Freja had been careful not to lace it too close. Even so, Amal felt like her chest was about to spill out of the thing. She was definitely going to purchase something new, and soon. She wasn't going to spend the next several months squeezed into her mother's jackets if she had to come to the capital again.

She and Dalyan sat across from Mikks and Nohr, who were trying to work themselves up into the appearance they liked to present in the capital. Nohr had teased out his hair with a comb and tied the rest of it back in wild braids. Given his close-cropped hair, Mikks couldn't do much more than go without shaving, but it had been a couple of days, so a blonde stubble was forming on his jaw.

Since the estate was outside the capital city itself, the two carriages had a long way to go. That gave Amal more time to fret than she liked. Mikks kept the conversation light, and she had to fight not to laugh for fear of busting a lace. But eventually the quality of the roads told her they'd entered Noikinos itself. Occasionally Nohr would lift the shade to peer outside, but eventually he gave up and relaxed to wait out the journey. Amal had seen the city before. Even Dalyan had. So it wasn't until they reached the sentry line of the palace itself that the driver came to a full stop.

Amal waited, accustomed to this. The carriage door was opened from outside and a sentry stepped up onto the carriage's runner to peer inside at them. A youngish Lucas man with pale blond braids and a bulky shape surveyed them each slowly before turning to her. His face showed no expression, his emotions too suppressed for her to sense. "Lady Horn?"

She *had* seen this one before, likely one of a dozen or so who handled all the carriages that came through this gate. She couldn't recall his name, though. "I am."

"Are these men your guards?" he asked.

"The two in uniform are. The third is my consort."

She thought she saw a brief flicker of emotion—perhaps surprise—cross his features, but that was gone in an instant. "Are you willing to vouch for their intentions here?"

It was a traditional question, but they still meant it. "Yes, I am."

The sentry went still as he apparently considered her words, and the emotions behind them. "They're expecting you, Lady Horn."

He stepped down and shut the door, and the carriage moved forward again, heading around to the back steps of the palace, the true entrance. Almost no one entered through the front.

The carriage rolled around onto cobbles, coming to a halt again a moment later. Mikks opened the door from inside, jumped down, and then surveyed the area. It wasn't as if it could be unsafe there, not on palace grounds, but he did it as a statement that he wasn't going to take Amal's safety for granted. Nohr climbed down next, then turned back to lift Amal down. He put his hands around her waist and then turned and set her on the ground. It looked impressive, she knew, a display of his strength, but it also eliminated the chance of her getting her slippers tangled in her skirts and making an idiot of herself.

He turned back to regard Dalyan.

"I'll get down by myself," Dalyan said. He climbed carefully down the carriage steps, mindful of his skirts. Once he'd reached the cobbles, he gazed almost straight up.

Unlike Horn Keep, the royal palace was an airy creation of near-white arches and domes. Large windows faced out onto the back courtyard. The granite walls surrounded a courtyard, and atop those walls, sentries in black waited, unmoving. Those were the Rifles, like Eldana and Nohr, who could kill them before they made it inside the palace.

Fortunately, it was warm enough today that they wouldn't be uncomfortable inside. In winter, the place was chilly. This palace was designed like those in the homeland the Anvarrid had left behind. If they hadn't killed off so many Family engineers, perhaps the Anvarrid would have snugger palaces to live in.

The carriage rattled on the flagstones, moving on toward the stables. Amal tilted her head toward the stairs, and Dalyan followed her. Nohr and Mikks moved behind them. The stairwell doubled back on itself before leading up to the first floor of the palace. She stopped at the top landing, partly to let the sentries inspect her and partly to catch her breath.

The sentries at the palace door—an older man and woman this time—looked them all over carefully before letting them pass inside. One big difference between the Horn and the royal palace was that here there were sentries everywhere. At the Horn, they simply didn't have that much to guard. The Keep was small, and Amal was the only member of the House of Horn who lived outside Horn Fortress.

Here there was the king and his consort and his brother, as well as a far more opulent building to protect, along with the grounds. State functions took place in the receiving halls, and careful negotiations in the back rooms. The Lucas Family took their responsibilities very seriously. They had perfected their conformity, so that each sentry looked the same. Each sentry, male or female, wore identical uniforms, braided their hair in the same style, away from their faces and falling to the middle of their backs. The tactic was meant to confuse and intimidate. Amal thought they did *that* quite well.

Dalyan was holding his own, though, managing not to look intimidated. Nohr and Mikks had done this before, so she hadn't worried about them, but she was relieved that Dalyan was taking all the scrutiny in stride.

The two sentries opened the door for them and one of them accompanied them inside. The back entry hall of the palace wasn't its most impressive hall—more of an intersection point for the wide stone stairwells coming from the upper floors—but light from a series of stained glass windows spangled the white marble floor in a rainbow of colors. The runners in the halls were thick wool and silk, muted shades of brown so as not to distract from the brilliant tapestries on the walls—battle scenes wrought in jewel tones and highlighted with gold threads. The Valaren House colors were burgundy and brown, and those were present everywhere. Many of the outer windows were thrown open to allow the summer wind to sweep along the hallways.

The palace made Horn Keep look plain and dour.

"I am to take you to the Blue Receiving Room, Lady Horn," the sentry said as they walked.

Amal nodded. She knew the way, but he guided her along the hallways, while Dalyan trailed a few steps behind, with Mikks and Nohr farther back. They reached one of the stairwells and climbed up, heading for the third floor where the Royal House of Valaren had their residential wing. The bells in the palace's western dome began to ring as she stepped out onto the landing.

The guards on this floor were the king's quarterguards, all sensitives. A tall woman with an expressionless face stepped forward and nodded to the sentry who'd accompanied them, taking responsibility for them. She walked to a closed double door not far away and opened both doors wide so they could walk inside.

The Blue Receiving Room had finely painted blue walls, and the furnishings were all embroidered in blues and golds. It was a very non-Valaren room, but as Amal recalled, it had been decorated by the king's consort, Amdirian.

"We will wait here," the female quarterguard announced.

Amal obeyed, gesturing for Dalyan to stay where he was, between Mikks and Nohr. A short wait wouldn't kill them.

The quarterguard resumed being a silent post, displaying no emotion and merely waiting. It was a very Lucas skill. Amal had never understood their desire to disappear into the fabric of the hallways, which likely made it a good thing she was a Horn, not a Lucas. She wouldn't have fit in here.

She admired the embroidery on a silk throw over the back of one of the sofas. That might even be Lady Amdiria's handiwork. Then the inner door opened, and King Khaderion stepped into the room. "Lady Horn, welcome."

Amal gave him a half-bow, grateful she didn't have to go any farther. She wouldn't have been able to breath. The king came to where she stood and offered one hand. Amal took it and bent to touch her forehead to the back of his hand. Then she released it and stepped back.

The king was a tall man, possibly only a few years short of Grandfather Johan's age, his hair mostly gray. He had a lean form, and his stern features always reminded Amal of a blade, a man carefully honed to serve his purpose—to keep the country on a reasonable path in peace and relative prosperity. His burgundy House robes were heavily embroidered with black, a nod to the Lucas Family that had, for centuries, been closely tied to the Anvarrid House of Valaren. "I understand you have come to present your new consort to me."

Ah, the Daujom had gotten word back here faster than they'd traveled. "Yes, sire. May I present Dalyan Horn to you?" The king inclined his head, so she gestured for Dalyan to step forward. Dalyan executed his obeisance without flaw, releasing the king's hand and taking a couple of steps back to stand slightly behind Amal.

"Now, Amal," the king said, "tell me why the Daujom think they need to arrest this man."

Amal hadn't expected to veer into this territory so quickly. She'd hoped there would be a little social chatter. And she'd hoped for help. "First, sire, has your niece Rachel spoken with you about my consort?"

The king's hazel eyes slid toward Dalyan. "Only that she believes your claims, no matter how far-fetched they seem, she said."

Amal felt her lips tremble, she was so relieved. It wasn't a glowing recommendation, and she would rather have had Rachel here to corroborate her words, but Rachel had given her a foundation on which to start. "What I have come to tell you, sire, will seem far-fetched."

The king gestured toward the sofas. "Shall we sit, then? Your guards can wait outside if you'd prefer."

"That's not necessary." She sank down on one of the sofas and waited for Dalyan to sit on the other end. The king took the chair nearest her. One of the quarterguards slipped out of the room, only to return with glasses of wine. Amal took a sip and set her glass aside on one of the tables. She didn't want to drink too much and have to rush off to find a water closet. "Dalyan came here from the Cince Empire."

That announcement caused a stiffening among the remaining quarterguards.

"Is he a spy?" the king asked.

"No, sire," Amal said. "Although he was trained by them to infiltrate our country."

The king leaned back a bit. "I believe that makes him, by definition, a spy."

"Not exactly," she said. "He wasn't sent here to gather information about the Anvarrid or the Six Families or the Larossans. He was sent specifically to find a Fortress, one that was abandoned long before the Anvarrid arrived. It has stood empty ever since and never has been noted by the throne."

The king took a sip of wine and gazed at her with narrowed eyes. "You mean Salonen Fortress, which is full of water, if I recall my lore correctly."

"I do, sire. It's within Horn Province, though, which makes it my responsibility."

"And why would the Cince want an uninhabitable Fortress?"

"It is always difficult to guess another people's motive, sire, but we believe they wish to communicate with the Fortress. We cannot allow that to happen." She swallowed. "Sire, the Fortress of Salonen holds far too many secrets, and it *is* vulnerable. That is why the Horn are putting together a force to open Salonen ourselves. We intend to get there before the Cince, and either make the Fortress defensible again . . . or kill it."

The king's head tilted. "Can you kill a Fortress?"

"I don't know how much you know about my people's lore, but there was once a Family called the Sorenson, who killed their own Fortress and everyone inside."

Amal could tell that the quarterguards were perturbed. Most of them had likely never heard of the Sorenson Family. Their elders could ask their Fortress later if they weren't aware of the incident. Most, she was sure, would rather deny it had happened.

"That seems a drastic measure," the king said after a moment.

"I assure you, sire, it was not done lightly. They sacrificed themselves to end a sickness that had become rampant in their Fortress. It was done to protect the other seven Families."

"And what part does your new consort play in this?"

"He has the skills to determine whether Salonen can be saved."

The king's eyes fixed on Dalyan, and for a time he was silent as he considered her words. "And the Cince simply gave him to you?"

Dalyan opened his mouth to answer, but snapped it shut before anything slipped out.

"Again, sire, we don't know their motives, but he was sent to the province to *find* Salonen. If he had found it, if he had entered it, he would have died there. He wasn't told *why* he was supposed to find it, only that he must."

"And assassins were sent after him," the king said, proving that someone from the Horn *had* talked to the Daujom. "They nearly killed you, instead."

She wasn't going to deny that. Freja had questioned the actions of the assassins, and they never had come up with a satisfying answer for why they'd been unable to kill Dalyan. "Yes, sire. But his actions didn't endanger me, only their actions."

"And even though you knew that the Cince trained this man, you took him to your bed."

Ah, they'd reached the *Lady Horn is rash* portion of the discussion. For his part, Dalyan didn't seem inclined to argue with the king over that dismissive statement. "I did, sire," she answered. "I have not for a moment regretted trusting him."

"And you want me to trust him as well?"

"Yes, sire, I do."

"I am aware there was division among your elders," the king said. "I believe they wanted more control over your choice of your consort."

"Selecting a consort is my choice, not the Horn Family's."

"When elders of a Family lodge concerns with the Daujom without their House's knowledge, it concerns me, Lady Horn," he said in a harsh tone. "Some of your elders felt threatened enough by this man to try to have him arrested, using my Daujom to do it. And I do not believe that is merely a matter of unfortunate marriage choices. They were concerned enough to try to circumvent your plans. Have you weighed their objections adequately?"

That was a rhetorical question. "Sire, there are a handful of people within Horn who are spoiling for a fight. They don't like this business with Salonen Fortress, and feel it's not our place to protect it. That our resources should not be used to save a Fortress uninhabitable for centuries. That we should simply stay in our own Fortress and let the Cince do what they want outside our walls. They know taking action will bring change, and they don't want that. When enough of the other elders didn't agree, they tried to involve the Daujom instead to get their way. As for actual concerns about my consort, the only crime he committed was trespassing on Horn Glacier. He was unaware that was illegal. Yes, he's from the Cince Empire. Yes, they trained him. But not to spy on us and return information. They set him up to die in their service."

"Amal, walk with me," the king said, rising.

Amal didn't dare disobey. It was an unusual thing to be completely private with the king, and showed a great deal of trust on his part, so she rose and followed.

Dalyan stood in the middle of the Blue Receiving Room, unsure what to do. Two of the quarterguards had left with the king and Amal, but there were still two in this room, along with Mikks and Nohr. If Mikks or Nohr had followed Amal out, it would have implied that she didn't trust the king. And she couldn't win the king's trust if she didn't give her own.

Jan's instructions in the case of uncertainty were to call Mikks over and ask his opinion, so Dalyan did that. When Mikks joined him where he stood next to the sofa, he whispered, "Do I sit down and wait? Or would that be offensive?"

"Part of being an Anvarrid lordling," Mikks said, "is assuming the world waits on you, even the king, so do what you want."

He wasn't sure whether Mikks was joking. What he wanted to do was inspect the tapestries in the hallway, but leaving the Receiving Room was likely an unwise choice. He drew as deep a breath as his jacket would allow. The door opened without warning, and a woman stepped inside.

She was a short woman of older years, with a round and friendly face and steel gray hair in a simple braid that dropped almost to her waist. She wore the clothing of a servant, a brown tunic with black trousers and no petticoats, but nothing about her carriage suggested that. Given her dark skin, Dalyan guessed she was part Larossan. Her near-black eyes fixed on him. "Dalyan Horn," she said, "you will come with me."

Her voice held no doubt that he would comply. Dalyan regarded her for a moment, wondering if the king had set this up, if he'd led Amal away just to get Dalyan alone for this cheery little woman to pounce on him. His stomach twisted, partly because he knew Amal would be angry. Partly because he had no good option.

He inclined his head toward the woman—no point in not admitting she had greater power within these walls. "Of course."

"Sir," Mikks began.

Dalyan held up one hand to stop him. "I am in the royal palace. What harm could come to me? Stay here and wait for Lady Amal."

In truth, he didn't want to drag Mikks into this, or Nohr. Nohr stood near the door, anger on his face. He was letting the quarterguards feel that, an intentional display. Ignoring him, the woman opened the door, and Dalyan joined her. "May I ask where we're going?"

She peered up at him with her little birdlike eyes. "The second office of the Daujom. First floor, east wing of the palace."

She said that loudly enough for Nohr to hear, so it was meant to be repeated to Amal when she returned. Of course, Amal couldn't force herself into those rooms, but it felt to Dalyan like a promise that he would be safe for now, at least. "Thank you."

She walked down the hallway without watching to see whether he would follow. For a small woman, she moved briskly, so Dalyan had to hurry to catch her. She went down the same stair they'd come up, and then headed across the entrance through which they'd come to the opposite side of the palace. Sentries marked their passing with unresponsive faces, as if everyday someone dressed in ridiculous House robes hurried after the servants. Dalyan did his best to ignore them.

The woman stopped at a door and fished a key from about her neck. "Let's go inside."

Dalyan didn't argue. He stepped through the guarded door into an office space apparently comprised of a long, narrow hallway. Since this hall couldn't be accessed by the main hallway without passing a guard, Dalyan suspected that few people knew where this was.

"This isn't where the Daujom does most of its work," the woman said in a conversational voice, "but this will do for now." She opened a door to a smallish office with a large table and three chairs. "Come inside, and take a seat on the left."

This felt a great deal like being quizzed by his instructors back at the facility, and sent a prickle of nervousness down his spine. But he complied.

The woman sat in the seat across from him. "We'll wait a moment for the others. My name is Anna, and I'm senior here."

"Senior what?" Dalyan asked.

"Senior," she said. "And while you are not under arrest at this moment, that status would be very easy to change."

Amal walked along the hallway of the king's private residence, one hand on her stomach to keep her latest meal down. The king himself was not a sensitive—not that she knew—but his quarterguards all were and would be able to feel her anxiety. The king had split her away from Dalyan, and she had no idea what was happening to him. *This can't be good.*

The king led her up another stairwell to the west dome, under the great clock that chimed hourly. It overlooked the flagstone courtyard, and she had to hope that he didn't give in to an urge to push her through one of the open arches. But it was a place where no one could overhear them. Only his personal guard, Jason, accompanied them now, a stern-looking man in his thirties. He was bulky like Jan and could overpower her without trying should the king require that.

The king leaned on the waist-high ledge of one of the arched openings, gazing out over his gardens. The weather was beautiful and, since the wind came from behind the palace, not from the city, the air was clear. "What were you thinking, Amal?"

She stepped closer. "Sire, what are you asking me?"

"I know why you made him your consort. A legal consideration that protects him. But why marry him at all? You knew quite well that some of your elders didn't approve, and despite your reputation for rashness . . ."

Amal forced down a smile at that.

". . . you do have a good brain. So why marry him? Just keep bedding him until you tire of him. Or keep him as a guard."

"I love him, sire."

He put his back against the stone of the arch. "It doesn't answer my concern."

"But it does," she insisted. "How many times, sire, have others urged you to take a different wife? To put Amdirian aside and marry a woman who can give you more children? And yet you don't. I believe that is because you love her, sire. You don't wish to cause her pain."

His consort had only borne him one daughter before she was injured in an accident that left her without control of the lower half of her body. He had never taken another wife. Amal didn't think he had a Family lover, either, as her own father had. From what she'd heard, the king remained faithful to his wife.

"Amdirian is not of questionable origin," the king said.

Amal took as deep a breath as she could. "Sire, what do you know of the Oathbreakers?"

"That they violate their oaths on a regular basis." He frowned.

This was dangerous. She had just forced the king to acknowledge that his Six Families broke the treaty and that he *knew* of it. Amal stepped closer. "Do you know why?"

"The Fortresses must be repaired and maintained," he said. "For that reason, we have overlooked that minor violation of the treaty for the last two hundred years."

We meant the succession of kings that had led up to him. She doubted all of them had known of it, but some must have. "Yes, sire," she said. "And your forbearance has allowed the Families to continue to serve you as required. We are careful, sire, not to abuse that tolerance. We try not to offend."

"So my niece assures me." The king's jaw squared with determination.

"But the time has come where we can no longer let the Fortresses function at a minimal level, not even for the sake of the treaty," she said. "The Cince are a threat now, for reasons that I cannot explain without telling secrets you do not want to hear."

His brows drew together. "You presume to know what I wish to hear?"

"I will tell you everything, sire, if that's what you wish. Or you can continue trusting your Families not to betray you. But if you want our Fortresses to be safe, changes must be made. And Salonen must be protected, as it has never been during the time of the Anvarrid throne."

"So you've said, but how does this relate to your consort?"

"He is a Salonen. By blood, sire. That Fortress is his birthright. The Fortresses have ways of knowing those who are their children. It will open for him as it would not for any of us. Your niece tested his blood in the Fortress below us, so she can confirm that."

"The Salonen, such as they are, are spread across northern Kithria," the king said. "I suspect a man with Salonen blood is not hard to find. They wear silly scarves and talk about seceding from that country."

There were those within that geographical area who had dreams of seceding from the neighboring country of Kithria. And those in that movement *did* wear brightly striped scarves, one of the sillier affectations she'd heard of. Of course, a striped scarf would be more comfortable than the garb she was wearing now, so who was the fool? "Sire, you're talking of people who bear a bit of Salonen blood, a small percentage, diluted through generations. Dalyan is nearly pure-blooded. I cannot easily explain how, but he is."

"And that is your reasoning for making him your consort? Protecting him because he's a Salonen?"

"In a way, sire. Of all the Fortresses of Larossa, Salonen is the most vulnerable, and he may be the key to protecting that flank. He may be vital."

The king gazed at her, his gray brows rumpled. "Do I want to know all those things you're holding back from me?"

"I think that you should hear them from your own Family, sire. Not from the Horn. I am to meet with the Oathbreakers this afternoon. If you wish, I can suggest that they find a way to instruct you in as much as you wish to know."

He pressed his lips together and gazed at his bodyguard, as if mentally asking the man for his opinion. Amal
didn't look at the guard, not wanting to show weakness.

"I will acknowledge your consort," the king said, "with
one reservation."

Amal wanted to hold her breath, but answered, "And
what is that, sire?"

"He will remain here, subject to the questioning of the
Daujom. Not under arrest—*voluntarily*. If we deem at any
point that his actions cross the line into treason, he will be
placed under arrest. But he stays here until the Daujom is
done with him."

Now she couldn't breathe. Amal finally managed to
take in a breath after what seemed an hour, even though it
was only seconds. "Sire, I need him to meet with the
Oathbreakers this afternoon. They need to see him, to speak
with him. He is living proof."

"Then in the morning, he will return here," the king
said, face stern. "If I am satisfied he's not a threat, I will
protect him."

Tears began to slip down her face. Amal fought to hold
on to her calm. "Sire, I . . ."

"It's the only offer I will make, Amal," the king said.
"Let him prove himself to the Daujom."

CHAPTER 16

THAT THE KING was offering to give Dalyan a *chance* was something to hang on to. Amal had hoped for more. She'd prayed for more. But she would take this one advantage. "We will stay as long as the Daujom requires, sire."

"The question in my mind is, why did you not bring him here earlier?"

Amal gazed out over the royal gardens. This wouldn't reflect well on her. She'd made a mistake, and couldn't even explain the depth of that mistake to the king. "Sire, we thought he was little more than an adventurer at first. He cooperated with our questioning and even protected the life of a member of my guard. He protected me, as well. As far as we could tell, he was harmless. We trust him."

"We?"

"My yeargroup, sire. And most of the Horn elders. He has been . . . benign."

"One says that of tumors, Amal," he said in a dry voice.

She held in her laughter. "It is the truth, sire. He would never hurt one of us."

"How do you know that it's not an act, Amal? You have only known this man a few months."

She had an excellent answer for that. "Jan has questioned him extensively, and there are several strong sensitives among my guard who would spot any falsehood. And then there's Nimi."

"Nimi?"

"His dog, sire. A puppy, actually. He had been withholding something from Jan. I knew what it was, but Dalyan didn't know that. But when Nimi was born, the woman in charge of the livestock wanted to separate her out, to let her die. She has only three legs, you see. But Dalyan begged me for her life. When I asked it of him, he told me his last secret, the one he feared would lead to his death. All so that I would spare a newborn puppy—a three-legged one."

The king laughed softly. "He believes in protecting the vulnerable, does he?"

"Yes, sire." She turned back to him, her tears past. "It's what won me over, that he was willing to risk his life for her."

"I can understand that."

"It was one of our other Oathbreakers who figured out the import of who he was, sire. Not me. I missed it," she admitted ruefully. "I knew the facts, but didn't look deeply enough. That is my fault, sire. But we know now the seriousness of the threat and have brought him here as soon as he was well enough to travel to begin addressing it."

"You brought him to meet your Oathbreakers, not me."

"Yes, sire. Although we crave your blessing, it is the Oathbreakers who must act. They need to see him to understand what the Cince have achieved, and the depth of the treason behind it. Those two things I cannot explain to you without your having greater knowledge of the Fortresses. When they know, I believe they'll agree Salonen needs to be opened. If you ask them why, I believe the Lucas Oathbreakers will explain to you, sire."

His lips thinned. "And if I do learn what my Oathbreakers have to tell me?"

"The world will never look the same to you again, sire."

Amal descended from the royal household with Nohr and Mikks at her back, both simmering with anger. Dalyan was waiting for her at the stair's first-floor landing, a grim expression on his face, but he had his emotions under control. Amal couldn't feel fear from him. She suspected that was only by sheer will.

Or perhaps I'm the one who's afraid.

They didn't speak as they waited for their carriage to be brought up from the stables. There were too many sentries who could overhear every word, see every action. When it did come, Nohr checked it, helped her up, and then nearly tossed Dalyan back up into the carriage. Once they were all inside, he scowled across at Dalyan, "Why in Hel's name did you just go with her?"

Dalyan leaned back against the leather seat as the carriage began to move, looking exhausted. "I had no intention of running away from this. Ever. I don't want to be imprisoned again, but I *am* in Larossa without sanction. I was trained by the Cince, and the king's people have the right to question me."

"We have been trying to put you beyond their reach," Nohr snapped. "What do they think they're doing, arresting the Horn Consort?"

"I'm not under arrest," Dalyan said softly. He didn't think he'd ever seen Nohr angry before. "I am submitting to questioning."

"The king has said," Amal jumped in, "that when the Daujom is satisfied, he will recognize Dalyan as my consort." Dalyan cast a startled glance her way. Evidently whoever held him hadn't told him that part. Or perhaps the woman didn't know of the king's promise. Not yet. "What did she ask you?"

Dalyan closed his eyes. "Nothing yet. That was all preparatory to being questioned. They explained what would happen ... for all that time."

"Tell me."

He sighed. "I will be questioned in the presence of a pair of scribes, one of whom will be a sensitive, plus an Oathbreaker, and Anna herself. She told me to expect it to take days. *Several* days, she said."

"I hope it's Rachel," Amal said. "She'll understand you better than most Oathbreakers, and she can influence the king."

"I'm not to come here," Dalyan said. "I'm to stay at the estate, and they will come there. It is not precisely house arrest, but they did request that I keep my movements to a minimum."

"That's house arrest," Nohr said, his tone merely annoyed now.

Mikks had remained silent throughout, but spoke up now. "Will they allow any of us to stay with you through the questioning?"

"I didn't think to ask," Dalyan admitted. "I think ... I'm not sure I want anyone to hear this."

Amal took Dalyan's hand in her own. "We'll all be close. If you decide you want one of us there, ask her. It can't hurt to ask."

"What did the king say about Salonen?" Dalyan asked, diverting the topic away from himself.

"I think he intends to speak with Rachel or others among the Lucas Oathbreakers. He didn't commit to anything." Partially, she suspected, because he wanted to know more about Dalyan before he made any judgment.

They had come here hoping to get two things from the king, and had achieved neither.

It all depended on Dalyan now.

Dalyan was relieved to change out of the tight formal attire and get back into his black uniform. Once he'd mostly dressed, he lay on his stomach on Amal's bed and tickled Nimi's belly as she wriggled and squeaked. She was a spot of joy in an otherwise bleak day.

He hadn't told Amal, but Anna had made clear that she would happily place him under arrest whenever she felt like it, consort or not. He didn't want Amal to see that. Not Mikks or Nohr, either. They would feel compelled to interfere, and he didn't want trouble for them. So he wasn't going to ask to have anyone present.

"You're getting white hair on your vest," Amal observed as she walked in. She'd also changed into Family uniform, looking normal again to his eyes—the Amal he knew, not Lady Horn. She sat next to him and began massaging his neck with one hand. "I'm sorry."

Nimi struggled to get up and toppled over. She nearly rolled off the bed, but Amal caught her in time. Nimi rewarded her with an enthusiastic yip.

"I'm glad we brought her," Amal said. "She makes you happy."

He hadn't said so, but he'd worried about leaving Nimi behind. He'd feared someone might hurt her, someone like Nils. He rolled onto his back to gaze up at Amal. "Do you remember that night when we hid in a venting shaft?"

She put the puppy on the other side of him and lay down next to him. "Yes. Things were less complicated then."

"I miss that. I miss being no one."

She leaned her head back against his shoulder. "I understand. I miss being Amal of the twenties. But we don't have a choice anymore."

True. He couldn't turn back time, no matter how much he wanted to. "When we get back, we should spend a night down there."

Amal laughed. "I think we should. We could play cards all night."

"Exactly what I had in mind." Amal had shown incredible trust that night, leaving her guard behind and spending time with him instead. It had been the first night in a long time that had brought him hope. And she had kissed him, rather thoroughly, leaving him no doubt that she intended more between them. "Perhaps more."

"I see," she said, apparently content to let the implication of sex alone.

But now that he thought about it, the yeargroup hadn't played at tiles since he'd been injured, weeks now. Everything had been too serious. "We should just play tiles tonight. The yeargroup that's here. Not worry about the other Oathbreakers, the Cince. Just us."

"We'll do that," she said. "We missed Firstday, so we need a break."

He'd lost track of the days, but she was right. They'd been traveling and had missed it. "Today is Fifth, isn't it?"

"Yes, it's Fifth," Amal said.

A knock at the door preceded Freja's yell that the others were waiting on them to eat lunch, so Amal rose and then held out a hand for him. "Come on."

CHAPTER 17

THE OATHBREAKERS had come to the estate, some from each Family, Amal told him. That was good news, as they'd been doubtful any of the Jannsen would come. But three pale men with intricately braided hair sat at one end of the table, eyeing the others—and each other—suspiciously, and then quickly hiding their emotions, faces still.

Dalyan stood near the back of Amal's contingent while she argued with the group over the inclusion of her *entire* guard in their meeting. Converting a full yeargroup into Oathbreakers was shocking, but Amal answered their concerns firmly and calmly, playing the role of Lady Horn even though she wore her Family uniform. She'd managed so far not to delve too deeply into the subject of Salonen, so these were merely preliminaries.

"The Jannsen," Dalyan whispered to Mikks. "What's wrong with them?"

Mikks smirked. "Two of those are from Lady Montaris' guard, and one is an Oathbreaker, so they're from different sides of their civil war."

"Guards?" Amal had explained the Jannsen issue to Dalyan, which hinged more on a flawed perception of racial purity than reason. The elders of Jannsen had decided that all sensitives must have a taint of Anvarrid blood and had, for the last few years, done everything possible to boot their sensitives out of the Fortress, even the children.

"Those two guards used to be Oathbreakers before their elders kicked them out," Mikks said, pointing his chin that way. "They've asked to be included in all meetings, even if they no longer have access to their Fortress."

And that meant the lone Oathbreaker who worked *inside* the Fortress wasn't a sensitive. Or was successfully hiding it. The Jannsen were nearly as obsessed with perfection as the Lucas Family, Dalyan noted, their faces cool and distant. Rachel Lucas was the sole representative of the Lucas Family present, and there were two each from the other Families: Lee, Andersen, and Halvdan. Like the Horn, the Lee representatives seemed to be more mixed. One had sandy blond hair and fair skin, but the other, a dark-haired woman, sat near the Jannsen Oathbreaker. He occasionally cast a scornful glance her way when he thought no one was watching him.

I would have loved to believe that the Six Families were more united. Then again, given that even the Horn elders were split over his presence, Dalyan decided human nature simply overrode mutual interest at times.

After another exchange between Amal and the ancient man who was the Andersen's senior Oathbreaker, the group finally agreed to let all eight of them sit in on the meeting, although they were given places farther from Amal, which meant straining to hear everything. Dalyan went with the others, going where Amal pointed, and ended up sitting between Mikks and Sofie. That would give the three of them a chance to confer during the meeting. Mikks had his notebook out, pencil ready.

"What I haven't introduced is the problem that pro-voked me to ask for a gathering," Amal said. "Rachel Lucas knows much of this because I needed her help with the royal family, and she can corroborate some of what I say."

Amal went on to tell the Oathbreakers about finding Dalyan on the glacier, the subsequent interrogation by Jan, and the information that he'd been trained by the Cince to find Salonen, but had refused to report back to them. She spoke of the assassins who tried to kill him, both near the glacier and at the Horn. The Lee representatives seemed unsurprised by this information, as if they already knew, which was interesting.

"Dalyan, will you stand up so they can all get a good look at you?" Amal said.

He rose. He wasn't the consort right now, he was merely an engineer-in-training, so he did his best to project respect. He licked his lips, uncomfortable having so many eyes on him.

"Dalyan has voluntarily turned himself over to the Daujom," Amal said, "and they'll question him as long as they feel appropriate over the matter of treason by some Anvarrid Houses. But that's where their concern over him ends. It does not lie where ours does, because his presence here indicates a far *deeper* treason, one that had to be carried out by an Oathbreaker."

That set off whispering among the different groups.

Amal began talking again, telling them this time of their return to Horn Keep, and sending Freja down to the infirmary in the Fortress to check a sample of his blood for possible sicknesses. "When I spoke to the Fortress later, it told me that Dalyan is, without doubt, almost pure Salonen. He was not born, he was *created*."

Another wave of chatter built between the groups, and Dalyan was aware of the distrustful glances being thrust his way. They had just changed their opinion of him from person to *thing*. A tremor of fear ran through him. Sophie's hand patted his arm beneath the table and she shot him a reassuring look. "Give them time," she whispered. "They're reasonable people."

Since this was her first time attending one of these meetings, that was likely wild speculation. But that was another reason for having the whole guard here—to protect *him.*

Amal waited patiently for the discussion to die down. "Last night I asked Rachel Lucas to test Dalyan's blood in Lucas Fortress. Rachel, did it verify what I just claimed?"

"Yes," Rachel said loudly. "It did."

A few of the Oathbreakers looked skeptical, and Dalyan suspected they wanted to come peer at his skin and check his teeth. Those were the most visible indicators that he'd been created as an adult—his skin didn't show enough aging, and there wasn't enough wear on his teeth.

Amal went on. "It wasn't until almost two months later that our senior Oathbreaker cracked the mystery of how the Cince managed that. The Fortress searched its memories for her and verified that Dalyan is a Salonen Original."

He swallowed. They had been working up to this moment since he woke after the Fortress killed him. This was, literally, the moment of truth. He kept his chin up, aware he was being stared at once more.

Rachel nodded, backing Amal's claims again.

"I've heard," the dark-haired Lee woman said, "that he actually can read the old Salonen tongue, and recognizes technology he's never seen before. Is that true?"

"Somewhat," Amal said. "He can read Salonen, Vigdis, but he's not sure of the pronunciation. The head infirmarian tells us that the verbal part of language uses a different portion of the brain than the written part."

The Lee woman—Vigdis—tugged something out of one jacket pocket, laid it on the table, and shoved it across toward Dalyan. It slid to a stop a few feet in front of him. A black item not much larger than a deck of cards but flatter, he could tell that it was meant to be held in his hand. He picked it up, and it began to glow faintly.

"What does that do?" Vigdis asked him.

Dalyan went with his first instinct, the best way to access his hidden knowledge. "It shows you things, information."

He touched the surface with one finger and spoke a word . . . one that meant for it to come alive. The little thing didn't respond; it just continued to glow. "I think it needs the Lee word."

"Po," she supplied, head tilting.

He touched it again, said her word, and the little item glowed more fiercely. An interlaced set of designs appeared on its surface. He tapped one, and lights sprang up from the thing in his hand. They resolved a few feet above him into a floating representation of the world and its moon. There were gasps, and the younger Andersen jumped to his feet as if he was considering fleeing.

Dalyan tapped the device and the world and moon shrank smaller, now including the sun and the other planets. "This one apparently shows us the solar system," he said. "I can try all these others, but I think you've made your point."

"I have," Vigdis said, holding out her hand.

Dalyan leaned closer and handed the device back to her.

"Have you ever seen one of those?" she asked.

"No," Dalyan said. "It makes sense, though. It draws power from my hand, translates what I want to see into light, and shows it to me. It has memories in it, like memories of a Fortress."

"A limited version," she said. "But yes. When I'm hanging upside-down in a maintenance shaft, it's useful to have a diagram of the panels loaded into it."

Dalyan turned to Amal. "That's what they used. One of those. That's how they got a Salonen pattern out of a Fortress. Had the device record it into its own memories and then handed that device over to the Cince."

He sat down, pleased that he'd figured that out. It felt like a breakthrough, the first time he'd made connections to his hidden memories intentionally.

"I don't have time for this chicanery," the Jannsen Oathbreaker said, not bothering to hide his annoyance. "I don't know how you did that, but it's sleight-of-hand."

The Lee woman laughed. "Willem, you're an idiot. Do you not even know how your own Fortress functions? We all have access to these."

Some of the other Oathbreakers exchanged surreptitious glances. The Jannsen puffed up like he was close to exploding, but Vigdis ignored him. She spoke to the little device, going through a series of commands that caused it to display the stars above her, followed by a body of neatly printed text, and then a diagram of the human body.

Freja nearly leapt across the table to see that better, but settled for fixing an accusing look on Amal. Jan put a hand on Freja's arm. Amal made a *calm down* gesture, and Freja settled back, a scowl on her face and her arms crossed over her chest. Annoyance flared briefly around her but she quickly dampened it.

"That's why we don't show infirmarians these devices," Vigdis said, one dark brow lifting as she gazed at Freja. "It's why we don't make them Oathbreakers, Amal. They sulk when they realize they don't have the best toys. And then we have to remind them that when they are given toys, they break the world."

Freja didn't respond, keeping her temper in check, but Dalyan suspected that was by will alone. Dalyan hadn't missed the veiled reference to Sorenson.

"Our infirmarians are studying the Fortress' records," Amal said, "including the incident at Sorenson. We have decided to trust them to make wiser decisions in the future. We need their knowledge, because they, more than any of us, understand what the Cince achieved in creating Dalyan. The Cince knew enough about human patterns to alter his appearance, making him look more Anvarrid so he could travel through Larossa without drawing notice."

"They can't have," the younger Andersen objected. "You can't just alter patterns."

"They did," Amal repeated. "And they also created him with a device in his head that tried to do what the card device does. Only . . . much smaller. It tried to gather the Fortress' memories. Fortunately for the Horn, our Fortress is self-aware, so it retaliated and destroyed the device, greatly injuring Dalyan in the process."

"If the Cince have done this once," Vigdis said, "acquiring an Original's pattern and altering it so it's more to their liking, what's to say they haven't done this fifty times? A hundred? If this man is a Cince plant, even an unwilling one, there could be many more already in Larossa, perhaps ones who are not reluctant to aid their masters."

"True," Amal said. "They seemed focused on Salonen, else they wouldn't have made such an effort to find Dalyan's pattern. They wanted very specific knowledge. The Salonen Founder on whom Dalyan is based was a Disaster Recovery Specialist. That was what they wanted him for—to raise Salonen and hand it over to them."

"And what would they do with Salonen?" Vigdis asked. "Why do they want one of our Fortresses so badly? Do they not clearly have at least one of their own?"

"That's the question none of us can answer," Amal said. "But given what secrets the Fortresses hold, we cannot let them get their hands on it. And Salonen *has* resumed responding to communications between the Fortresses—the very reason we rushed this meeting—so we know that it is, in some part, still alive."

That was greeted with uncomfortable murmurs.

"I think that our first course is to secure the six Fortresses," Amal pressed on. "I have approached the king about this, and hope he understands that some allowances in the treaty must be made to protect our homes. We cannot protect him if we can't protect ourselves. Once we do so, we then need to find the source of Dalyan's pattern. It had to be an Oathbreaker who stole it and handed it over to the Cince. That means it's someone we know. It could be someone sitting in the room at this moment. We need to find out who."

Rachel Lucas patted one hand on the long table to get Amal's attention. She kept going until all the other Oathbreakers were silent. Then she rose, a piece of paper in her hand—a prepared statement. "I spent this morning talking to my Fortress. I asked it to hunt for a theft. It happened twenty-seven years ago. Only one pattern taken. By an Oathbreaker, Stian Lucas, who died two days after that. He was found murdered in an inn in Noikinos. No solution to his murder."

That explained why Rachel hadn't been present this morning when they'd met with the king.

"That's very convenient," the Andersen man protested.

"Rachel," Amal asked, "was it the pattern of Jukka Salonen?"

"Yes," Rachel said, sitting down again. "It was."

"We all still need to check our own Fortresses." The Lee Oathbreaker stuffed her device back into her pocket.

"Lucas found one pattern that was missing. That doesn't mean we haven't all had thefts. Rachel, do you have any idea of his motive? Why give something to the Cince?"

Rachel shook her head. Apparently once she was past her prepared speech, she reverted to short answers, or nonverbal ones.

"Again, we don't know why they're doing this," Amal said. "But we must take steps to protect ourselves, and Salonen. To that end, the Horn are putting together a team to excavate and open Salonen. We only have the most preliminary timeline at this point, as even clearing a path into Salonen could take a decade."

"That mountain range crosses into Lee, so we'll send a team as well," Vigdis said. "We'd prefer to work under Horn's lead, not separately. A unified effort."

Dalyan glanced at Mikks, who looked surprised.

"Does Lee have Oathbreakers to spare?"

"Not many," she said, "but we'll train more. Climbers we can provide now."

"We'll talk," Amal said to her.

Dalyan felt some of his discomfort fade. The talk had veered away from him, and over to planning and coordination. The Jannsen Oathbreakers didn't seem inclined to participate. The Halvdan didn't talk at all, but paid close attention. The others worked out steps they could take to secure their own Fortresses, bringing the Fortresses back to self-awareness. Mostly small steps until they knew whether the king would prosecute the treaty violation or not, but it was progress.

It went on for another couple of hours, Dalyan guessed, with the discussion becoming more technical as they moved into territory that only engineers could understand. He did his best to follow and *most* of it made sense, but he suspected some of the others were lost. They were all here more as a show of strength for Amal than for their technical knowledge.

After that, the group broke up, each Family's representatives saying their goodbyes to Amal. Most were civil, although the Jannsen Oathbreaker was stiff and unfriendly. The two Lee representatives were the last to leave. Vigdis took Amal's hand between her own. "Tell Theo that I say hello."

Amal nodded. "I will. And thank you for your support."

"Thank Theo," the woman insisted with a sly smile.

Jan escorted them toward the main door, the last of their guests to leave.

Freja immediately turned to Amal. "When can I get one of those . . . things?"

Amal laughed, relief spilling about her now that the others had gone. "I didn't even know that existed, Freja. I'll check with Vigdis for details, but if she's got one . . ."

"Then we should," Freja finished.

"The Lee have clearly been using their Fortress at higher capacity than we knew," Amal said. "Surely that means they'll be on our side."

"They're also at threat if the Cince do anything in their mountains," Mikks said. "Evidently our Theo knows Vigdis Lee, huh?"

Amal just shook her head, smiling.

"So, did we win this one?" Dalyan asked.

Amal lifted her eyes to meet his. "It's not over. It won't be over until all the Families agree to act. But for now, it looks like we're winning."

The evening had been a pleasant one, all nine of them determined not to mention Dalyan's upcoming interrogation. Joined by a handful of the guards stationed at the estate, they ate, played tiles until Dalyan looked to be half asleep, and drank whiskey from the local Noikinos distilleries. Nimi lolled on one of the couches like she was the lady of the province.

Later, Amal walked with Dalyan to their bedroom. She shouldn't have tried the whiskey, even just one glass. Dalyan, for his part, seemed remarkably unaffected by the whiskey despite having had more. That was probably some other improvement the Founders made to their Originals. She could ask the Fortress later. If she remembered.

When they got to her room, Dalyan carried Nimi to her basket and set her inside so she could rake the blanket around how she liked it. Amal watched, bemused, as she leaned against the bed-poster. Once Nimi was settled, Dalyan laughed as he helped Amal undress. Not mocking, she could tell. He was *relieved*. He was content for now, and far more hopeful about the upcoming trials. She was pleased they could give him that, the pretense that everything was normal.

She turned to toss her sweater over the rack near the door and felt his contentment change to worry. She could almost feel sleepiness dragging at him, and the anxiety that accompanied that now—the fear that he would never get back to what he considered normal strength. "What is it?" she asked.

"You could have had them all look at me like I'm a horse for sale," he said. "It would have helped your case. I am grateful that you didn't."

She sat down on the edge of the bed and tugged her shirt off over her head. "Dalyan, I never want other people to see you that way, as some . . . creation of the Cince. You aren't. You are yourself. Unique."

He sat down next to her and started unraveling one of her braids. "Thank you."

Amal let him work on her braids since he was the one who liked her hair loose. She concentrated on the buttons of his shirt instead. "It's just the truth. No need to thank me for saying it."

He grasped her hair and leaned close to kiss her. Then he drew back enough to rest his forehead against hers. "I would love to do more than that, but I am so tired."

She touched his cheek. "And so am I. Just sleep for now, Dalyan."

To prove her point, she pulled away and crawled under the covers. Dalyan finished undressing and tugged on a pair of sleeping trousers. Then he turned down the lights and settled next to her in the bed. He fell asleep almost instantly, his body relaxing against hers.

Amal stared at his profile in the moonlight. The moon was near full, although she couldn't recall if it was waxing or waning. Travel always confused her sense of the days passing.

She could have done that. She could have had the other Oathbreakers look at Dalyan's fine skin, at his perfect teeth. She probably should have pointed out the spot behind his ear that was now scarring, just so they would know where to look for a device in an invader's scalp.

But he was her husband, not merely evidence to lay before them.

She was terrified what waited for him tomorrow, so she wanted to spare him today.

As Lady Horn, she should have been more ruthless.

As Amal, she simply couldn't.

CHAPTER 18

DALYAN WOKE IN Amal's bed. She'd slept heavily, likely the consequence of those few sips of whiskey she'd had the night before. But the sun would come up soon, and hazy pink light filtered through the sheers that were drawn over the windows.

He gazed up at the black canopy overhead and tried to force away his dread. Sometime soon, that small birdlike woman would come here to question him. Given his short discussion with her the previous day, Anna's interrogation would make Jan's relentless questioning over the course of a month seem feeble in comparison.

He'd been questioned over and over at the facility, something he'd never told Amal. He'd only hinted at it with Jan. His masters had deprived him of sleep, starved him, and withheld water. They'd never done anything that left a mark on him, but they had made him miserable for weeks. Perhaps it had been months. His grasp of time had flowed away. It had all been in an attempt to get him to admit to memories he didn't have. It had been terrifying and baffling, and he'd endured it. He'd survived it, but that was all. He never wanted to talk about that time again.

But he'd agreed to this. He'd agreed to answer Anna's questions as honestly as he could and for as long as it took. He was going to bare his soul to them. He was grateful that they wanted to do it here, in Amal's territory, so to speak. That reassured him. He had to hope the king's people would be kinder to him than his masters ever had been.

He reached over and ran a finger along Amal's straight nose. Her eyes fluttered in response, and she sighed and stretched. "It's still early," he said. "Not quite dawn."

"Mmm." She turned on her side to face him and laid her arm over his waist. Her fingers touched the small of his back as she eased closer.

"Does your head hurt?" he whispered in her ear.

"Hmmm, no." Her fingers wandered farther, under his sleep trousers to cup his backside, her favorite place for her hands, it seemed. "I'm awake now if you are."

If I am? "I woke you up," he protested.

She kissed him, suddenly serious. Her arousal blossomed around him, dragging him into a sudden fire of need. He pushed her back onto the bedding, coming halfway atop her so he could kiss her as deeply as he wished. Her hands continued to roam his back, clutching him close.

Someone knocked on the bedroom door. "Amal!"

Amal whimpered and refused to give up her hold on him, and Dalyan grimaced against her lips. "We have to answer."

"No we don't," she whispered.

But Dalyan drew back when the knocking became persistent. He threw off the covers and rose just as Jan yelled through the door, "Amal, we need to talk. Now!"

Fortunately, the cool morning air was enough to quench any remainder of his arousal. Amal was sitting by then, her slender back bent. Dalyan grabbed his sweater off the chair's back and pointed his chin toward the bath-room. "I'll stall him."

Amal went, and he checked to make sure he was somewhat presentable as she went. Then he opened the door and slipped outside. "She'll be here in a minute," he told a visibly upset Jan. "What's wrong?"

"We need to pick up and head back to the Keep now," Jan said, his eyes sweeping over Dalyan's bare feet and shins.

"I can't," Dalyan protested. "I gave my word I would stay. What's happened?"

"One of Eldana's brothers just arrived," Jan said. "He says a couple of days after we left, *you* showed up at the Keep, Dalyan. Two of you. One had been shot, and the infirmarians aren't sure whether he'll live."

Dalyan could feel the frustration at the edge of Jan's control. His breath went short, panic making his heart race. "It was *me*?"

The door behind him opened. Amal now held a throw clutched around her. "What was you?"

"Someone who looks like Dalyan has turned up at the keep," Jan told her. "Two of them, one injured. The infirmarians aren't sure the injured man will live. We should get back there to talk to him."

"Looks like?" Amal repeated. "How much?"

"Exactly like, Grandfather says." Jan glanced down at his feet, scowling.

Amal grabbed Dalyan's arm. "Do you have any idea what this is about?"

"No," he said, mind too shocked to come up with any valid explanation. "If there were others like me made, I didn't know about it."

Jan shook his head. "Grandfather's note says one is younger. Not even a twenty. And he doesn't speak Anvarrid, or he's too fevered to recognize it." He handed a folded paper to Amal. "He doesn't have a device in his head, though, so they took him into the Fortress. The other is . . . much older, and is demanding access to the Fortress."

"I promise I have no idea who he is," Dalyan repeated. "I never saw any others like me." His breath came short. He swallowed and tried to calm himself, recognizing panic when he felt it.

So much for being unique.

Amal's hand touched his back. "I believe you."

She turned back to her brother. "Gather everyone into the sitting room as quickly as you can. We'll decide what to do and get going this morning."

"I can't leave," Dalyan repeated.

"I know," Amal whispered, pain leaking around her. "I know. We're going to have to leave you behind." She set a hand on Dalyan's arm and drew him back into the bedroom.

Dalyan sat down on the edge of the bed and rubbed his hands down his face. "Hel's tits," he whispered, borrowing Freja's favored curse.

"This," Amal said softly as she knelt before him, "is exactly what we were warning the other Oathbreakers about. We wanted them to understand that it could happen."

"Why send him to Horn?" Dalyan said. "They would have to know people would recognize him. They knew I was there, so they had to know."

Amal's lips pursed as she considered that. "True. All the more important for me to get back there and talk to them. Jan and I know more about you than anyone else, so we're the best judges of these new men's intentions."

Because one or both of them might actually be spies. "One doesn't speak Anvarrid," he said. "By now the Oath-breakers are trying out some Salonen on him, I expect."

Amal clutched the blanket tighter around her, eyes brimming with tears now. "Dalyan, I won't leave you alone, but I have to go. I can't be here while they question you. I . . ."

She was afraid for him. She worried he would say the wrong thing and end up arrested or even executed. Or even worse, that he would betray the Horn in some way. And he couldn't promise her that none of those things would happen. "I'll be fine," he promised with no guarantee at all. "Everything will be fine."

She began to cry, tears slipping silently down her face. "I hate abandoning you."

"You aren't. Even if you're a province away, I'll know you're thinking of me." He rose and helped her up. He kissed her cheek, and then urged her toward her wardrobe. "Now get dressed, and I'll help you pack. If you want to avoid the Daujom's questions, you all need to be gone before Anna arrives."

Amal nodded quickly and tossed off the blanket to dress for a day of travel, jaw firming in determination. She wiped the tears from her eyes. "I want you back at the Keep as soon as you can get there. Do you hear me?"

"I hear you," he said. "Be safe. Don't push too hard. And be careful around the other versions of me. Don't think that they're me. Don't make that mistake. I don't lie to you, but I know how I could."

She had trousers on by then, but stopped dressing. She came back to stand before him. "Make no mistake, Dalyan. There is no other you. I am not going to be fooled by a similar face."

She kissed him, hard, and then stepped back.

Dalyan hoped she was right.

THE END

If you enjoyed Original, please help other readers enjoy it too.

Review it. Reviews help other readers find the books they love with the themes and characters they're excited about. Let other readers know what you thought of the book by leaving an honest review. It doesn't have to be fancy, just honest. It can be one sentence long! It's a little known fact that for every review a unicorn is saved from destruction.

Recommend it. Help others find the book by recommending it to friends, reading groups, and message boards. If you're a member of Goodreads or another social media site designed especially for book lovers that is a great place to make recommendations (in groups you might be a member of, or voting for this book on the various lists it's on).

Join J. Kathleen Cheney's Newsletter!

Get updates on future publications, free fiction offers, and goodies! Your privacy is important; your email won't be sold or exchanged with any other email lists. Scan the code with your smartphone to sign up:

EXCERPT FROM OVERSEER

CHAPTER 1

THE LITTLE BIRDLIKE woman watched Dalyan through narrowed eyes. Despite being dressed like a servant, Anna Lucas could crush him under the heel of her unadorned slipper if she wished. "Start at the very beginning," she told him. "Leave out nothing."

There were two scribes in the room, both coolly impersonal. One had the look of Lucas Family, middle aged with blonde hair worn in multiple braids and a black uniform not unlike his own but with different trim markings. A series of swirls across her chest identified her as a chaplain, but an additional design on her left cuff said she was part of the Daujom—the king's private investigative body. She was probably a sensitive, here to judge his emotional responses in addition to his words. The other scribe was a young man of mixed blood, perhaps Larossan like Anna, but his height and leanness suggested he was at least part Anvarrid. Like Anna, he wore clothing that suggested a servant, a plain tunic and black trousers. Neither of the scribes looked at Dalyan.

"The very first thing I remember," Dalyan began, "was waking alone in a room with gray walls and gray ceiling. No windows. I was restrained, cuffed to the bed. I couldn't hear anything or anyone, and I didn't know where I was or who I was."

"Were you warm or cold?" Anna asked.

"Chilly," he said. "I was naked and there were no blankets."

The last member of the team interrogating him sat in the corner, merely listening. Rachel Lucas was the niece of the king and an Oathbreaker. She wore a black Family uniform similar to Dalyan's own, with the stair-step trim of an engineer across her chest. She was part Anvarrid, part Family, and was there to hear what he said about the Cince and the facility in which he'd lived. Like Anna, she had the king's ear, so Dalyan made a special effort not to think ill thoughts at anyone.

"How did you feel when you woke?" Anna asked him.

Leave out nothing, she'd said. "I was fairly uncomfortable," he answered, flushing. This was going to be humiliating. "I needed to . . . urinate."

Her head tilted, dark eyes amused. "But you knew you shouldn't pee your bed?"

"I knew that," he admitted. "I knew *information.* I knew waking like that wasn't normal. I knew the restraints weren't normal. I yelled, and after a few minutes, a man came into the room."

"What sort of man?"

Eight years had passed since that day, but he could still remember it clearly. "Medium height, fair skin, light brown hair, perhaps thirty, slight tilt to his eyes."

"So not a Cince?" Anna said.

"No. I later learned that the guards were from a people called the Kostakov—one of the Cince's subjugated races that serve as their military—but I didn't know who they were at the time, and I knew nothing of the Cince. The guards never spoke to me. He unstrapped my hands and feet, gave me a robe, and pointed out the chamber pot in the corner of the room. Then he left, locking the door behind him."

Anna's brows raised at the words *chamber pot*, but she didn't pursue that. "You were a prisoner?"

He'd tried hard not to think of it that way. Later, his masters would tell him that he was there to be reeducated, that he'd lost all his memories due to a mysterious plague. But his room had been a cell, and he had, for over six years, been a prisoner. "Yes."

"Did your room have bars? How did he hear you yell?"

"No bars. A solid door. I couldn't see out. I don't know how he heard me."

"What language did you yell in?"

Dalyan licked his lips. "I honestly don't know. I have to assume it was Salonen, although . . . I couldn't seem to speak that when my first instructor came to the room."

"Tell me about your first instructor, then."

Dalyan sorted through the sketches he'd made of the twelve instructors who'd taken up six years of his life. He presented her with the correct one, the image of a lean and dark man with angry eyes and narrow lips. "This man. He taught me language, starting with the items of clothing he brought me, the walls, the bed. He never spoke to me in any other language than Anvarrid, and never told me his name. I was Dalyan to him, and he was Instructor to me. I thought that was his name at first, but quickly figured out it was a title instead."

"Learning a language by immersion," she mused. "An excellent method."

It went on like that for hours, in painful detail, Anna digging up memories that Dalyan wished long forgotten. How many guards, how many instructors, how did he manage to pick the lock of his cell. At this rate, he would be stuck here in Noikinos for weeks.

Amal ordered the coach to halt near a wheat field before they reached their second stop. She tumbled out with Jan's help and leaned over the edge of the road before she threw up her hastily eaten lunch into the ditch among the weeds. When she was done, her brother wiped her chin with a handkerchief and handed her a flask of water. Once she'd cleared her mouth, he dragged her into a reassuring hug, pushing his desire for her not to worry at her.

Pregnancy rarely made her physically ill. It had happened only a handful of times when she carried Sander, but she was eight years older now . . . and she was worried. About what was happening to Dalyan back at the Noikinos estate, and what awaited them when they reached Horn Keep. "Let me just walk for a few minutes," she said.

They were pressing the horses, hoping to compact an eight-day trip into six. It could be done, especially since the moon was nearly full and the traveling coaches were four passengers lighter. Mikks, Nohr, and Sofie had stayed behind with Dalyan in Noikinos. They meant to guard Dalyan with the same caution with which they usually guarded her. More than that, they were there so he wouldn't be alone.

It had been a simple decision for Eldana and Magnus to return with Amal, since Magnus was the First of the Twenty-Sevens and therefore responsible for the whole yeargroup. Jan and Freja had headed back with her as well. Jan was her primary guard, tasked with keeping her safe, and Freja was an infirmarian, and wanted to get back to tend the Horn's new injured arrival.

There were two newcomers, one for Freja to tackle in the infirmary, and one for Amal to handle in the Keep above.

Grandfather Johan hadn't been willing to commit much to paper for fear of it being lost, but Eldana's brother Bjorn, who'd ridden like a madman all the way to Noikinos alone, told them more.

The two newcomers had appeared near the glacier where the Horn had an encampment, and thus were picked up by the Horn military personnel stationed there almost immediately. As if their simply appearing on the plain near the glacier hadn't been enough proof, both of them looked enough like Dalyan that there was no mistaking their origin. They were created by the Cince from the same pattern as Dalyan, although according to Bjorn, both were fairer in coloration—blondish hair and hazel eyes. Dalyan's coloring had been altered to make him look more Anvarrid, giving him brown hair and dark blue eyes with a hint of violet in them. The two newcomers had his tall, lean build, though, his facial features, and even that flat spot on the bridge of his nose.

But the younger of the duo had been shot in the stomach before they'd appeared on that plain. He apparently looked Bjorn's age, or even younger. And he was incoherent, not from a fever but because the language he spoke wasn't Anvarrid. But fever had set in almost immediately, even before they'd managed to make the partial day's journey to the Keep, so the elders had taken the young man—after ascertaining that he had no threatening device in his head—down into Horn Fortress for the infirmarians to treat.

The older man had proven the real problem, though. He spoke Anvarrid, and immediately began ordering them around as if he was lord of the province. He called himself Aulis, and said he needed to get inside the Fortress. The elders were not amused.

The horses were getting restive, and Amal knew they needed to keep moving. The more time they lost on the road, the greater chance that these newcomers could cause trouble . . . or summon the Cince.

Freja had climbed out of the carriage and joined Amal in walking up and down the side of the road. The fairest one of them, Freja possessed the pale skin and almost white hair commonly associated with the Six Families, but her dark eyes hinted that there was some Anvarrid blood in there somewhere. Not all that unusual for the Horn Family. "How are you holding up?" she asked.

Amal took a deep breath and focused on calming her nerves before glancing down at Freja. "I'll be fine."

Freja smirked. "I don't know what you mean by fine, just don't throw up in the carriage."

Freja preferred acerbic humor to coddling. Amal turned and headed back to the carriage, waving to the second carriage as she went so they would know they were ready to start moving again. Jan pulled Amal back up inside, and then Freja. He settled with Freja on the rear-facing bench and regarded Amal with characteristic brotherly concern. "You're not putting yourself at risk, are you? Or the baby?"

"She'll be fine," Freja said, laying her hand over his. "Women have been having children for a long time. A little sick won't stop her."

He turned his gaze on his wife, as if unsure whether she was wholly serious. Freja had miscarried before when she caught a terrible influenza six years past.

"This is not the same, Jan," Freja snapped. "I throw up all the time when I'm pregnant. You know that. So stop worrying, both of you. You're making my head ache."

Freja was the strongest sensitive of the group, so it was possible that their worry *was* wearing at her nerves in the tight confines of the coach.

Amal was needed as Lady Horn back at Horn Keep, *and* as Amal the Oathbreaker back in Noikinos, and yet would be stuck on the road for days, unable to do anything to help in either place. As the vehicle resumed its clunking down the road, Amal leaned back against the leather bench, closed her eyes, and fought for calm as her now-empty stomach roiled and twisted.

Amal hated being helpless.

CAST OF CHARACTERS

THE TWENTY-SEVENS (named)

Amal Horn—House Lord for the Anvarrid House of Horn, Master of Horn Province (Master being a non-gender specific term), engineer, Oath-breaker

Jan Horn—Amal's half-brother, son of the previous Lord Horn, Amal's Primary Guard and Chaplain

Freja Horn—Jan's wife, Guard and Infirmarian, Second of the Twenty-Sevens

Mikks Horn—(Mikkel) Guard and Sentry

Nohr Horn—Guard and Sentry

Eldana Horn—Guard and Carer (Livestock)

Magnus Horn—Guard and Sentry, First of the Twenty-Sevens

Juliane—Sentry and Carer (Children)

Philip—Juliane's Husband, Sentry and Carer (Children)

Sofie—Sentry and Quarterguard

Anton—Sentry and Quarterguard (now deceased)

Children of the Twenty-sevens (named)

Hedda (9)—Freja's daughter by Mikks

Sander (8)—Amal's son by Anton
Arthur and August (8)—Eldana's twins by Magnus
Astrid (7)—Freja's daughter by Jan (but she's in the
        8s because she's precocious)
Sara (6)—Freja's daughter by Jan
Johan (3)—Freja's son by Jan

Horn Elders (named)

Grandfather—(Johan Horn) Jan's Family Grand-
        father
Signe—Senior Engineer
Elin—Head Infirmarian
Vibeka—Head of the Guards
Victor—Head Quartermaster
Malthe—Head Fightmaster
Sebastian—Head Legal Counsel

Other members of the Horn Family

Gyda—Amal's secretary
Villads—oldest of the engineers
Theo—Oathbreaker (Villads' son)
Sidana—Eldana's mother, in charge of Livestock
Milas—Sidana's husband
Berend and Bjorn—Eldana's younger brothers
        (twins—19)
Nils—young sentry

In Noikinos

Enala Hansine—Horn butler at Noikinos estate
Rachel Lucas—Lucas Oathbreaker and niece of the
        king
King Khaderion—House of Valaren
Amdirian—the king's consort
Jason Lucas—the king's bodyguard

Anna Lucas—senior member of the Daujom
Vigdis Lee—member of the Lee Oathbreakers
Willem Jannsen—member of the Jannsen Oath-
    breakers

In Evaryanos
Oradion—Amal's lawyer and distant cousin
Idan—Oradion's son and secretary
Indaris Coatine—manager of the Horn estate
Iladin Coatine—Indaris' brother

House of Horn
Samedrion—Amal and Jan's elder brother (deceased)
Manedrion—Amal and Samedrion's father (deceased)

In Horn Town
Mrs. Farzan—shoemaker

Cities, Towns, and Locations
The Horn—seat of Horn Province, including the town
    of Horn
Melyrep Station—town in Horn Province (near glacier)
Farden—small town at the foot of the mountains in
    Horn Province
Calanos—town in Horn Province
Evaryanos—city in southern Horn Province, a busi-
    ness center for the province.
Evaryenist—Horn estate outside Evaryanos
Noikinos—capital of Larossa, seat of Lucas Province

Some Notes on the Horn Family

The Military

A Guard is a member of the military charged with protecting a specific person. Guards are generally part of a team, with one being the Primary and coordinator of that team.

A Quarterguard is a member of the military charged with protecting the quarters or residential areas of the Anvarrid House, and are required by treaty to be sensitives.

A Sentry—the bulk of the military—is a member of the military charged with protecting *a place,* such as the Keep itself, or the Fortress. Sentries are further divided into Rifles and Hand-to-Hand to indicate where they would usually stand duty. (Rifles on the rooftops, for instance, but Hand-to-Hand guarding doorways.)

Fightmasters—train the military to fight

Battlemaster—coordinates the defense of the Keep

Engineers

Engineers are charged primarily with maintaining the Fortress.

Oathbreakers are engineers who speak with the Fortress in a forbidden language and can access the Fortress' memories.

Infirmarians

Infirmarians run the infirmary. It's worth knowing that many of them must speak some of the Horn Language in order to interface with the Fortress' instructions. Despite that, they aren't considered Oathbreakers since they only have access to a limited set of commands.

Carers

Carers is the broad category of nonmilitary personnel who support the Family: Quartermasters (which includes Laundry and Mess), Chaplains, and all manner of caregivers: Children, Elderly, Livestock, among others.

About the Author

J. KATHLEEN CHENEY taught mathematics ranging from 7th grade to Calculus, but gave it all up for a chance to write stories. Her novella "Iron Shoes" was a 2010 Nebula Award Finalist. Her novel, *The Golden City* was a Finalist for the 2014 Locus Awards (Best First Novel). *Dreaming Death* (Feb 2016) is the first in a new series, the PALACE OF DREAMS Novels.

Social Media Links:
Facebook
    https://www.facebook.com/CheneyJKathleen
Twitter:
    @jkcheney
Tumblr:
    http://jkathleencheney.tumblr.com/
Website:
    www.jkathleencheney.com

ALSO BY J. KATHLEEN CHENEY

The Golden City Series
The Golden City
The Seat of Magic
The Shores of Spain
The Seer's Choice
After the War

Other Works
Dreaming Death: A Palace of Dreams Novel
Iron Shoes: Tales from Hawk's Folly Farm
The Dragon's Child: Six Short Stories
Whatever Else

And the Books of The Horn:
(From the world of *Dreaming Death*)
Oathbreaker, Original, and *Overseer*

An EQP Book

E-QUALITY PRESS
http://EQPBooks.com/

CPSIA information can be obtained
at www.ICGtesting.com
Printed in the USA
LVOW03s1754060917
547738LV00001B/50/P